THE MURDERS BEGAN
A NICOLE LONG LEGAL THRILLER
BOOK 3

AIME AUSTIN

THE MURDERS BEGAN

The Murders Began

This edition published by
EbooksWow an imprint of Moore Digital Media
P.O. Box 480400
Los Angeles, CA 90048

Cover Designer: Wicked Good Book Covers
The Murders Began/Aime Austin. — 1st ed.

eISBN: 978-1-64414-094-9
ISBN: 978-1-64414-095-6

THE NICOLE LONG SERIES

ALSO BY AIME AUSTIN

The Casey Cort Series of Legal Thrillers

"When you have eliminated all which is impossible, then whatever remains, however improbable, must be the truth."

~SIR ARTHUR CONAN DOYLE

ONE
ANNA MORETTI POPE
MAY 9, 1953

"Doctor Hicks," the man in the pale blue suit announced as he strode in to the office. He patted me on the shoulder with an ink-smudged hand, then cast an eye toward Rainey. She'd run to the floor-to-ceiling window and had been staring out since we'd come into the empty room twenty minutes earlier. "What brings you and your daughter in today?" Hicks asked. "I don't see a referral in the chart."

My right hand had been extended waiting for an introduction. Instead of letting it flop about like a dying fish, I pulled it back, put it behind my back, straightened my spine.

Dr. Henry Hicks was a pediatric psychiatrist at the Cleveland Clinic. I hadn't gotten any kind of referral to his office. Over the last few months, when my husband, Frank, was on the beat, I'd made a lot of phone calls that had gone nowhere.

Fortunately, a couple of kind nurses thought *this* doctor

would be able to help. So I'd made an appointment, then driven all the way over to the clinic with my daughter. From the parking lot, through the lobby, and up to this fifth floor smelling of disinfectant, I'd tried to take deep breaths to push down the panic that he too would dismiss me out of hand.

When no one, especially Rainey, was looking, I'd shaken out a Miltown and swallowed it dry. Except for a cigarette and few tablespoons of oatmeal Rainey hadn't finished, I hadn't eaten since last night. In the minutes between taking the pill and meeting Dr. Hicks, I could feel my pulse coming down.

"I went to the library, did some reading," I offered to the doctor's skeptical face. "I think you can help Rainey."

"Hi, Rainey, is it?" He walked to the window. Gently turned her around. He tried to meet her eyes. My daughter looked everywhere but at him. "I'm Doctor Hicks. How are you?"

"Fine. Kind of tired. Mommy made me get up early and take a bath and wear these clothes. I'm hot." Rainey started pulling at the long-sleeved shirt under her bibbed overalls. I'd tried to get her into a skirt, but that had been a losing battle. In a carbon copy of my daughter's body language, Dr. Hicks looked out the window.

"It *is* warm outside. Supposed to be in the nineties this weekend. The hospital won't turn off the heat quite yet, though. Cleveland could give us another snowstorm before summer." Then Dr. Hicks turned to my daughter, knelt down to her level. "Rainey. I have a wonderful nurse outside. She's got some toys and a puzzle you'd like. Can you walk out the door and say hi to her?"

"What if I don't like her toys?" she asked, her face the picture of mutiny.

"She has a Mister Potato Head." Dr. Hicks tried to make it sound like the best toy ever.

"That's stupid." Rainey stamped her foot. She wasn't having it.

"Rainey! Can you please go with the nurse." I could hear that my voice was too loud for this all-gray office with its fancy flocked fabric wallpaper. Said nurse had opened the door and come in. There were a series of buttons and lights on Hicks' desk and I had to hope that was how he'd summoned her, and that she hadn't come in to put me in a straightjacket.

"Okay, Mommy," Rainey said, then turned a smiling face to the doctor. When she passed me, she hissed, "You'll be sorry."

After the door closed, I turned to Dr. Hicks. "Did you hear that?"

"What?" He cocked his head to the side like a dog trying to pick up a sound miles away.

"Rainey. She just told me I'd be sorry."

"Is that the kind of thing you hear her say often?" He asked like I had voices in my head. I'm not sure why everyone thought girls were made of sugar and spice and everything nice. My daughter had something else going on inside, more like snips and snails.

"Even when she doesn't say it out loud," I elaborated,

"her face turns into something horrible." I'd tried to get a picture of Rainey's sly face with the Brownie. But when I'd gotten the pictures back from the drugstore, the ugly face was gone and replaced with a sly smile.

"Tell me about your family," Dr. Hicks sat in an upholstered armchair, then picked up a clipboard with the intake form I'd filled out half an hour ago. Gestured to a couch. I took the cue and sat, making sure my own Sunday church skirt was tucked under my thighs.

"There's only one child, Rainey." I ticked on my extended index finger. He scribbled a note with his left hand.

"Are you planning another?"

"She's a handful enough right now."

"What does your husband do?"

"He's an officer with the Cleveland Police Department."

"Got a great job, then." Dr. Hicks wrote some more, then slid his pen behind his ear. Put the notepad down in the crease of the seat. "Sounds like a lovely family you have. What brings you all the way over to this side of town?"

"I'm concerned about Rainey."

"Concerned, how?"

"She's...her behavior isn't quite right. I come from a big family. I'm the fourth of six kids, two older sisters, one older brother, and then two younger brothers. I practically raised the last two. They're boys' boys. They ran around, broke everything that was breakable, kicked everything that was kickable, but they were just...normal, you know. I don't want to say it out loud, but I have to, I think."

I took a long, deep breath while I gathered up the bits of

resolve I'd been banking between the weeks I'd made this appointment and now. Let some air out of my mouth. Forged ahead.

"Rainey…" Despite gathering up courage, I still found it hard to get out what I needed to say. Finally, I blurted something I'd concluded after the last five years. "She's not normal. Something's wrong. I think you could talk to her and tell me what it is, maybe."

"How is she different than the other children you've observed?"

I paused to really think about his question. With other doctors, like her pediatrician, I'd minced words. The worst example came to mind, and I shared it.

"She tried to jump out of her bedroom window. It's on the second floor."

"Tried, how?" Dr. Hicks reached for a thick blue pad, but not his pen.

"I was talking to her about making her bed, or moving her toys, or something like that and she was just standing in the middle of the room. It was like she'd tuned me out. Wasn't listening to anything I said. She was rubbing the windowsill. I told her to stop flicking at the paint otherwise it would peel. She asked if she could fly. I told her no, birds fly, people don't. Then as bold as you please, she pushed at the screen, lifted her little leg over and said she was sure *she* could fly."

"What did you do?"

"Grabbed her back, obviously. Spanked her bottom. Told her she'd die if she did that."

"Anything else?" His eyes were hooded. I wasn't quite sure what he was asking. I tried to explain the scope of her behavior, but the Miltown had slowed my thinking.

"She doesn't throw tantrums."

"Isn't that a good thing?" Dr. Hicks lifted his wool-clad shoulders in a small shrug. "I've met dozens of mothers who'd like a tantrum-free life."

"When she's angry or frustrated, she's icy. Won't look at me in the eye. Won't talk to me. She can keep it up for days." What toddler perfected the silent treatment? My parents never allowed it in our house. They said it was the meanest thing to do to another person.

"How old is she again?" He glanced at the door where Rainey's laugh was coming through from the other side.

"Almost three and a half."

"Kids grow out of these kinds of things. They have no sense of danger. They don't know how to handle their emotions. That's all part of growing up. You said that you're not working on a second baby. How are *you* doing?"

Here was the tightrope I was always trying to balance upon. Perfect motherhood was impossible to achieve. By asking for help, I was obviously failing at my God-given job.

"I keep house, of course. I make breakfast and dinner for Frank, lunch for Rainey. Sometimes my sisters come by with their kids or I go over to theirs."

"What do you do to relax?"

"My doctor gave me some pills," I admitted. I snapped open my purse, tilted it toward him so he could see the brown bottles. "These are if I'm wound up. He gave me others if I'm tired."

Dr. Hicks stood up to take in the prescription labels. Shook his head, finally picked up his pen. Scribbled something on the pad.

"Those are strong drugs."

"Everyone's taking them." My doctor had offered one. My sisters had suggested I ask for the other.

"That may well be. Let me say that one of the side effects is that they can alter your perception. I heard what you're saying, but I don't think it's too far outside normal early childhood behavior. Maybe you focus a little too much on her. If I were you, I'd get cracking on a second child. Have a big family like the one you came from. With attention elsewhere, I promise you, she'll shape up."

TWO
ANNA
FEBRUARY 28, 1954

"Why am I here?" I asked my husband. Frank Pope's face wasn't the mask of sympathy it should have been. I was in a white bed in a white room that was as quiet as a church on Sunday. What was scarier than my husband's face, was the fact that I didn't fully remember how I'd gotten here.

"You've had a nervous breakdown, Anna. You wouldn't stop ranting about Rainey killing Francis Junior. Not until the paramedics sedated you."

The minute the words left his mouth, it all came flooding back to me. How I'd found out I was pregnant a couple of days after meeting Dr. Hicks. Frank had been overjoyed. I'd been scared to death that I'd birth another child like Rainey. Scared there was something wrong in my genes. Scared that my daughter would do something horrible....

"She did." I shook my head because I knew he'd never believe me; not because I didn't believe it. "Our daughter put her hand over her little brother's mouth until he stopped breathing."

"Frankie died because of *you*, Anna. His breathing was depressed because of the pills you took while you were pregnant and continued to take while you were feeding him. The doctors said he had an addiction to barbiturates. An addiction! No baby should be born on drugs."

"They were prescribed, Frank." My voice was weak with guilt, with resignation. "I did what the doctor said."

"You were supposed to stop taking the pills when you found out you were pregnant."

"I tried. I really did." I'd woken up every morning vowing not to swallow another pill. Rainey would do something, and by lunchtime I was in the bathroom with a Miltown and a Dixie cup. "I didn't think they'd hurt the baby."

"But they did."

"Aren't you sad?" I asked because I couldn't stop the tears that were dripping from my lashes or coursing down my cheeks. "I'm very sad."

I saw the briefest flash of grief on my husband's face, but it was gone before I could really register it. Maybe Rainey had gotten her coldness from him. Maybe I wasn't the broken one.

"That's why you're here. To get better."

"When am I coming home?" I looked around. Nothing about this bland place could make anyone happy. "Exactly how long have I been here?"

"Four weeks."

His answer took my breath away. I'd have figured one,

two days at the most. A month was a whole different kind of thing.

"That long?"

Frank had been standing near the bed. He stood and walked toward the door. He was quiet for a long moment. I had a weird premonition that he was going to leave and never return. Tried to shake my head, clear it. The drugs they gave me in here were so strong that I had nightmares and hallucinations. Today was the clearest that I could remember.

"You can talk to the doctors about all this sadness and when you can leave. I'm here to talk to you about something else."

"Is Rainey okay?" I tried not to panic. Too much emotion and a nurse or orderly would be here in a heartbeat to strap me to the bed. Using my calm voice, I said, "You should take her to a psychiatrist. She's not right. You have to know—"

"This isn't why I came here, Anna."

"Okay, Frank. What is it that you have to say."

"I filed for divorce." His voice had gone even colder. He wasn't here to comfort me. Frank was here to get away from me—forever.

"What?" I looked around feeling like a spooked horse. Nothing was making sense.

"What you've been saying about our daughter, about the death of our son. I looked into it, Anna. Really did." I'd seen his cop voice and demeanor only once. He'd been all business at the Cuyahoga County fair when a drunk man tried to grope me. Patrolman Pope was in full force right now. I didn't like the look or sound of it. "None of it is supported by facts," he was saying when I took in the actual words he was speaking.

"I'm not lying," I insisted, probably sounding like the guys he rounded up on the street.

"No one is saying that you're lying." My husband's voice was whisper soft. I could barely hear him from across the expanse of squeaky clean linoleum. "It's probably the drugs plus the stress of little Frankie that has you seeing things that aren't there. That's what Dot says."

"I'm not seeing bogeymen." I *was* seeing them. But I was pretty sure I could separate dreams from reality.

"You're making our four-year-old daughter out to be."

"Does she ever look you in the eye, Frank? She talks about death all the time."

He shook his head in a way that made me realize we were more than feet apart, there were miles between us.

"These are phases. Kids have them. All of them are little crazy people. We teach them how to be adults. We don't give up when they act weird or act out."

"So you admit that she's weird."

"Not any weirder than any other kid, Anna."

"Are you serious about divorce?"

"I left the papers with your doctors. We're already divorced."

"What?" I was losing the plot. "How could you do that? I never got any papers. I never went to court."

"Your doctors accepted them because you weren't competent. The judge granted it on Friday."

"Oh my gosh. Frank. I can't believe you've done this." My brain scrambled to gain purchase. "Can I see Rainey?" I might not like her right now, but I did love my daughter. Truly.

"Not now. The doctors don't think it's a good idea that she see you here."

"When can I see her? Are you taking my daughter away too?"

"You don't love her, Anna. That's what this all comes down to. I think she'd be better off without you in her life."

"Who's Dot?" I already knew that she was my replacement. He'd married me only months after breaking it off with another girl. Back then I'd thought I was the lucky one. I waited with hope that Frank would give me a different answer.

"Some friends introduced me to Dorothy when you were committed. She's been helping out with Rainey while you've been in here."

"You've already gone and replaced me?" The question was rhetorical. "You think that you'll have your perfect little family." I pressed the button next to the bed. A nurse in a flawlessly pressed uniform and crisply starched hat appeared in an instant. "I'm tired. Can you get me a pill? I think I need to rest."

"You can't have that without the doctor's approval."

I started screaming. It might make me look crazy, but they thought I was crazy already. With Frank's timeline help, scraps of memory were coming back. Screaming led to instant sedation. I just wanted something to take me away from this world. There wasn't any reason to be here right now. I had nothing to save. My little baby boy and my family were gone.

"Mr. Pope. You'll have to leave now," the doctor said when he came in. My husband...ex-husband walked out without so much as a backward glance.

THREE
LOREN LOGAN
SEPTEMBER 13, 2009

"Victim's name?" I hated coming onto a crime scene cold, but it happened when dispatch cut me off after giving me the address.

The uniform picked up a clipboard, skimmed it. "Don't remember." He threw his thumb over his shoulder. "Go see Parker back there. She's the one that made the call."

Making an effort to keep my eyeballs facing forward, and not visibly rolling to the back of my head at the actions of this obvious rookie took everything I had. This one needed going back to cadet training.

I walked into the apartment. It was pretty nice. Not your usual crime scene location. After my promotion to homicide, I was spending nearly as much time in alleys and drug houses as I'd done when I'd been on the beat.

With a place this pulled together, I had to wonder if I was walking into an episode of *Law & Order*. Those detectives spent more time in penthouses than rich people.

Tasteful paint and nice furniture didn't mean I was oblivious to my surroundings. In fact, I walked slower than normal as I admired the inside of the condo. Once I walked in, I realized I was in one of the new Schilling Square developments on the ten thousand block of Detroit Avenue. The neighborhood had once been the west side's illegal drug marketplace hub. But some shrewd developers had the wild idea to turn the area around with hundred-grand condos. Gentrification had more or less worked. Homeowners had taken on the criminals head-on.

I took a closer look. This was one of the 1925-era townhouses. When I'd been looking for a place for myself a few years back, I'd seen a different unit on the block, but had hated the directions the renovations had taken.

The aesthetic problems with Shilling Square remained. The renovation was an architectural crime scene. All the period details had been removed on the inside of the eighty-year-old building. It had been papered over with drywall, the ceiling pocked with too many recessed lights. Pergo instead of wood.

"Parker," I called when I finally came upon the lieutenant.

"Scene's in the bedroom. Victim is a guy named Malcolm Pointer."

"What do you know?" While I liked to develop my own theories, some background often gave me a jumpstart.

"The vic was on a date with the owner. She got some kind of call and went out. She said she was gone only about twenty minutes or so. When she came back, her date was dead. Has the worst date story ever." Parker stated the obvious.

"For sure." I could feel my eyes going wide. I'd dated a bit after my divorce. Didn't want to think about my bachelor life turning out like Malcolm Pointer's. "Point me."

"Bedroom on the right."

Careful not to disturb the ever-growing group of techs, I tiptoed to the bedroom. Slipped gloves from my pocket and onto my hands. I pushed gently at the door and took a look around.

Swallowed.

After these first months in homicide, I still wasn't quite used to the sight of violent death. Looked like Pointer had been shot in the heart. His arms and legs had been tied to the metal bedposts with ribbons. He had a silk mask over his eyes. The windows were closed, though some kind of balcony door wasn't quite on the latch.

While Pointer was obviously a man, this was a woman's bedroom. The iron head and foot boards had decorative curlicues. The bedspread under the man and his blood was covered in tiny wildflowers. A corner chair had some kind of lavender fur throw. The dresser and side tables had just the right combination of cute knickknacks and clutter. No man ever got a house this homey.

I'd come back to this room. Do a detailed look. First I wanted to talk to the girlfriend before she thought better of confiding in a cop. I made my way back to Parker.

"Where's his date?"

"Dining room."

I didn't waste any time making my way to the skinny room that looked like an architectural afterthought.

"You the owner?" I asked in my softest voice possible.

A woman, whose head had been in her hands until then, looked up at me. Nodded.

She looked familiar. Couldn't place her. Tentatively held out my hand.

"Loren Logan," I said. "I'm a detective who will be investigating the death of Malcolm Pointer."

Before the woman could say anything, my partner bustled in noisily. Whenever he was late, which was... *always*...Neil Walsh made his presence known so that no one ever remembered his arrival time.

"How's it going here?" Walsh asked the room in a booming voice.

I walked up to him and shuttled him to an unoccupied corner. Debriefed him. Tried to gauge whether or not he was interested. If this were a run-of-the-mill death, I'd happily hand it over to my partner. That kind of crime with an easy question and answer is what my nearly retired partner thrived at.

The true whodunits, rare as hen's teeth, were the kind of thing I lived for. It was the reason I'd transferred over to homicide. It was the closest I think I got to genuine policing. The real work tonight was to get Walsh out of my hair and away from this murder.

"Is this the kind of case that needs a veteran like me?" Walsh asked while nodding to technicians he'd likely known for years.

This felt like a trick question. Watching the techs gave me a minute to figure out the answer that would get me the result I wanted.

"Could you organize a canvas?"

Walsh nodded vigorously, then strode away, letting me know I'd made the right choice. Naturally outgoing and gregarious, if not detail oriented, my partner loved facetime and I needed to get on with talking to the resident and most likely suspect before she thought better of it and asserted her constitutional rights.

I poked my head back into the bedroom making sure that the photographer wasn't missing a beat, then headed back to the dining room. The woman hadn't moved from her seat, though someone had the presence of mind to bring her some kind of hot tea. She sipped from the mug, the teabag tag dangling over the side. When her eyes met mine this time, her tears had dried.

"Sorry about that. That was my partner, Neil Walsh, you'll get to meet him sometime soon, I—"

"Tall Irish guy in a tan sport coat?" With my slight nod of confirmation, she said, "Nice guy. He got me this tea with warm milk." She held up what looked like a handcrafted mug. "Said his mum made tea whenever something went sideways."

I took out the small writing pad I'd started to keep in my pocket. It was so cliché, but I found note-taking to be critical to keeping track of all the threads. It was far less intrusive than using a handheld recorder I'd have to transcribe later.

"I didn't get your name." I clicked my pen.

"Tia Wetzel."

I schooled my face so it was free of outward emotion. It was something I'd learned early on in this job. Didn't do cops any favors when we were caught on video as dispassionate onlookers to violence, but when questioning it was a key skill.

"Were you born in Cleveland? How old are you?"

"Born and raised in Akron. Moved here in ninety-seven. Just turned forty-three last month. I actually met Malcolm at my birthday party. Thought my life had finally turned around." She put down the tea, waved an arm at the beehive of activity. "Happy birthday to me."

FOUR
SEASON 2, EPISODE 1:
SEASON PREVIEW

Welcome to season two of *The Murders Began*. This is your host, Blake Hardin Tatum. When I started the blog and this podcast last year, I didn't have a plan.

I'd been recently laid off from *the Plain Dealer*, and was trying to figure out how I was going to fill my time without chasing down the ever-dwindling number of journalism jobs. As a woman of a certain age, I didn't really have the luxury of selling my house and hopping around from one city to another for the sake of a career. That's a young woman's game.

Even though I couldn't be employed at the newspaper, I didn't want to stop investigating crimes or stop telling stories.

I didn't have any bigger goal than to tell the story of the prosecution of alleged pedophile priest, Monsignor Gregory Quinn. Alleged because as you may remember, Quinn was convicted, not of a sex crime, but of the murder of a witness to his alleged crimes.

Anyway, what I wanted from this podcast was for my readers and listeners to get a more intimate and in-depth experience mirroring what I know; what it's like to follow a crime story from beginning to end. Not only know what happens in court, but hear interviews from the victims, families, and luckily enough last season, the defendant himself.

I really didn't think more than a few episodes ahead, then that case took a huge turn. Quinn was a bigger mastermind than most priests out there. He committed his alleged abuses outside of Cuyahoga County, the state of Ohio, and the United States. He carefully manipulated parents to sign permission slips, and boys to do what he wanted. He did something most criminals don't think of, he insulated himself from prosecution. He'd almost committed the perfect crimes, and almost got away with it.

The podcast took off, becoming one of the most popular crime podcasts of the year once the witnesses to

Quinn's crimes started dying off during the investigation.

This year, we're doing something different. I want to pursue what happens to people on the fringes of the criminal justice system.

The United States has the highest incarceration rate in the world. At the end of 2008, one in one hundred ninety-eight Americans were in either state or federal prison for a total of 1,610,446 according to the U.S. Department of Justice.

That's only half the story, or thirty-one percent of the story. At the end of last year there were 5,099,086 people under community control sanctions, probation, and parole. That's one in forty-five Americans.

I won't go into a debate here about how high that total number is or how that sets America apart from the rest of the civilized world. What I want to talk about is what it's like being under control of the authorities.

I also want to talk about women in the system. Last year, 105,300 women were incarcerated, and 828,804 were on parole or probation.

For many reasons, physiological and sociological, I'm not going to delve into here, men perpetrate the majority of the crimes in this country. Often women are in prison as an ancillary to these men's crimes. Prostitutes who work for pimps, women who mule drugs for their male bosses, and some who get caught up for merely being associated with a man's criminal behavior like living in the apartment where he packages drugs, or unknowingly driving a getaway car.

I want to promise you now, this isn't going to be some liberal rant against the criminal justice system. You can make your own decisions about crime, punishment, and rehabilitation. There is no limit to articles, studies, and white papers on the topic that could keep you reading for the next fifty years.

Instead, I'm going to do what I do best: tell stories. In the next episode, I'm going to talk about Cynthia Wetzel. She has a compelling story that doesn't yet have a resolution. Maybe during this season, we can see her finally leave the criminal justice system she's been fighting so hard to be free of.

FIVE
NICOLE LONG
SEPTEMBER 21, 2009

"You caught a lucky break," my boss, the Cuyahoga County prosecutor, Lori Pope, said at the exact same time a thick file was tossed onto my desk. She'd never been one for pleasantries. I'd stopped any attempts at being more than civil years ago.

"Lucky?" I parroted.

"Tia Wetzel is on the wrong side of the law...again. Once a criminal, always a criminal."

The name sounded familiar, but I couldn't place it. So many defendants had come across my desk over the years. Even the bounce-backs didn't always register until I read the files.

"What's the charge this time?" I asked as if I recalled every detail of the earlier case. I didn't share the photographic memory my boss seemed to have.

"Murder."

"Seriously?" That was a shocker. There was usually some

office buzz when someone was killed in the county. Prosecutors were always hungry for a murder conviction. It was great for a résumé or running for political office.

Curious, I pulled the file toward me. Flipped to the part where the defendant's rap sheet would be. Wetzel was forty-three, old for the criminal game. I wondered if it was an abuse case. Where men had been terrorizing their female partners for years, mid-forties was about when the battered women hit their limit and sometimes struck back.

Skimmed my nail down. Then it all came back to me, where I'd encountered Wetzel. My first serious case, one I tried to put out of my mind. Not put out, *block out*. I'd been lit during the case. Had been having bad flashbacks around that time after a visit to Louisiana celebrating one of my nieces' accomplishments. Wetzel had been dropped on my plate right after I'd moved from juvenile cases to felonies.

It was supposed to be an easy case, one to get my feet wet. A straightforward probation violation. Wetzel was under community control after pleading to a drug charge. She'd gotten probation and drug testing instead of jail time. The rest followed the usual timeline: traffic stop, cops search her house, they find more drugs, and this time with my help, the judge sentenced her to time in Marysville. It should have been routine.

The rub was that Wetzel's lawyer claimed the drugs were planted by the traffic stop officers after they'd allegedly assaulted her. Her attorney hadn't had enough proof of any wrongdoing to make a complaint or open an internal investigation. Pope had been pushing me to get my first stat, so I'd done everything in my power to" make sure Wetzel went to jail.

I looked for something more in the non-official file Pope had brought. Flipped the pages. There was nothing. Wetzel had been the model of rehabilitation that Americans loved. She'd done her time, then left the system.

Looked like she worked at a real estate brokerage. With a felony conviction, she was disqualified from being a licensed agent, so probably some kind of administrative job, was my guess.

"What's the gist of the case?" I asked Pope. My boss had made herself comfortable, which meant she had more to say. Lori Pope was never upfront. As though she were a law school professor, she was into her own version of the Socratic method where assistant prosecuting attorneys were subjected to an oral exam before any information could be relayed or an important case assigned.

"Well...did you know that Vernon Dinwiddie was just in my office a few weeks ago, giving me the heads-up that he was possibly filing a civil rights case against both the Cleveland Police Department and our office over the Wetzel matter?"

"Civil rights? Her case was resolved ten, eleven years ago." I looked at her record again. It was a fourth-degree felony that she served time for. She did only twelve months in prison. The judge could have given her eighteen.

Wetzel could have sealed this, essentially wiping this whole thing from her record. Then she could have become a full-fledged real estate agent or gotten bonded or whatever.

Filing a civil rights claim made no sense. It was the equivalent to opening a can of wiggly worms, with the little buggers going everywhere and no one but lawyers being happy in the end.

"You didn't answer my original question," I said, mad at myself for getting distracted by whatever bait she was throwing out.

"She strung up a guy on their date."

"What? Hung him?" After my last big case with a murder by defenestration, nothing should surprise me.

"Not exactly," Pope said.

With nothing more forthcoming from my boss, I turned to the front of the file bracing myself for a makeshift noose and bloated face. Instead I found a naked man, splayed, his wrists and ankles bound to the bed's railings with silk ties.

If it weren't for the bullet hole in his heart and blood-soaked sheets under him, I'd have guessed sex gone wrong. Breath play was a varsity-level kink that too many rookies practiced. This wasn't a choking mistake.

A gunshot was a deliberate act.

SIX

LOREN

"This is just like before," Tia Wetzel said. "I'm going to be smarter about it this time. It will end differently." The way she scooted back her chair was a metaphor for her relative freedom.

I'd called her in for questioning, not only because she hadn't answered a single question on the night of the murder, but because logic and proximity made her the prime suspect.

She was being much more savvy. Those who'd weathered the criminal justice system learned quickly. This time Wetzel had brought a lawyer. A famous one at that. Everyone in the state of Ohio within broadcast range of a radio or television knew of Vernon Dinwiddie. If there was a high-profile case in the black community, he was there front and center. I'd never seen him sitting alongside a white westsider, but there was a first time for everything.

"It's your right to have an attorney," I acknowledged. "It's also my job to investigate homicides. So let's get to it."

Secretly I had to agree that Tia Wetzel was making a good choice. What I hadn't said out loud was that she got on my radar after Cincinnati law students had poked around from the Ohio Innocence Project some months ago. That hadn't gone anywhere, that I knew of, probably because she was free from confinement if not from a felony conviction record.

Now, here she was some eleven years after that first conviction, facing the same system she'd said had done her wrong. Wetzel couldn't know that while I wasn't on her side exactly, I was different than some cops I knew because I was on the side of truth. Not to pat myself on the back, but I'm not sure she'd have gotten fair treatment from Walsh or anyone else in the department.

I opened the murder book. Instead of my usual move of sliding the photos over to the suspect to spur feelings of guilt, I played it straight.

"Do you remember meeting me on the thirteenth of September?"

"I can't see how I'd forget." Wetzel's tone was dry.

"Can you tell me, in your own words, what happened that night?"

"When do you want me to start?" She shrugged, resigned to reliving what had to be one of the most horrible moments in her life.

"Let's go back before that night. How did you meet Malcom Pointer?"

Wetzel ducked her head in what looked like embarrassment. Then she lifted her head. Her eyes met mine, steady. "I met him in a bar a few weeks ago."

I was a divorced man in Cleveland. I knew how it worked. If no one was willing to set you up, there were two choices, sketchy online dating via AOL personals or bars. This new assignment, and a certain squeamishness, had kept me too busy from either recently. The idea that I could run into a potential suspect might keep me celibate forever.

"What bar?" I asked.

"It's this new place near the West Side Market—"

"Market Avenue Wine Bar?" I interrupted her answer with a question.

"You've been?"

"Once. Pretty good tapas." I'd gone ostensibly to try the small plates. The reality was that I was interested in staying away from the same places and same people. The food and wine had been good, the female company, not so much.

"I went there after work with a couple of the agents to celebrate my birthday," Wetzel continued. "It was a Monday. They left after one drink. I stayed. Malcolm came over, introduced himself, bought me a glass of Australian Shiraz and we got to talking."

"What date was that?"

"August tenth."

I made a note to add that to the timeline I was building.

"Did you see him again after that?"

"At the Cleveland Air Show on Labor Day weekend."

"Any other times?"

"Not until I invited him over for dinner on the thirteenth."

"What time did he come?"

"Around six thirty, I think. Maybe a little later. He was surprised at the address, had driven around a bit convinced there was some 'other' Detroit."

"How'd you end up there?" At her confused glance toward Dinwiddie, I clarified that I meant her townhouse location.

"You mean a street that used to be an open market for prostitutes and drugs?"

I dipped my head.

"My office had the listing. It was an opportunity to buy something in good condition at a lower price than I'd get someplace else. Plus there was this whole 'revitalize the neighborhood' sales pitch from the developers. Malcolm had never been over this way because of the reputation, so I think he was a little thrown off. Plus he said in some cities there are some places that would always be no-go zones, even with gentrification."

"Got it. When I first talked to you, you said that you'd gotten a call."

There was silence for a long beat. I didn't think I'd stepped on a trigger, so I looked between Wetzel and her attorney.

Finally Dinwiddie spoke. "There wasn't a question there. I don't want anyone to put words into her mouth."

It was a good callout of police technique. I was getting pretty used to putting all levels of bait out there and seeing what got bit. From testifying, I knew that lawyers in court had far greater limitations for good reason. I decided, for the moment at least, to adhere to Dinwiddie's rules.

"Did you receive a call after Malcolm arrived?"

"Yes."

"How? Cell phone? Landline?"

"I didn't get a landline after I moved. With all the taxes and fees, Ohio Bell costs nearly as much as a cell phone nowadays."

"Who called your cell?"

"It came up unknown or maybe something else? But I answered before I thought about it."

Wasn't unreasonable. The only people I knew who paid attention to caller ID were my daughter when waiting for a boy to call, drug dealers, and women with stalkers.

"Who was it?"

"I don't know."

"What did they say?"

"That I'd left my credit card at a stall at the West Side Market."

"Weren't they closed?" The murder had been on a Sunday. Cleveland had loosened its blue laws up a bit. When I moved here, nothing was open on the same day when churches were. Times had changed, but many businesses were still open only half day or less.

"The guy said that he'd stayed after to clean up, but wouldn't be there too much longer. I have some stuff on autopay now and didn't want to have to cancel the card, get a new number, change out bills and all that."

All three of us nodded. In the name of fraud, banks would change your card numbers in a heartbeat, but were no help with the economic carnage left behind.

"What did you do then?"

"I explained to Malcolm what happened. It's like a ten-minute drive, so maybe twenty minutes tops? We didn't want to end the date, so I said I'd go."

"Is there a reason he didn't go with you?" I'm not sure I'd trust a date in my place alone. But my job made me more suspicious than most.

"I had food in the oven. He wouldn't be able to pick up my credit card because I might have to show ID, but he could get food out of the oven."

I could practically recreate the frantic conversation in my own head. It all seemed plausible and reasonable, so far.

"What was dinner?"

"Baked ziti."

"What happened when you got to the market?"

"It was closed. I was a little anxious, so I ran around the building, but I couldn't find any open door." Wetzel waved her arms. "Then I looked at my phone and realized it was an unknown number and I couldn't call it back. Then I checked my wallet and realized my card was still there."

"You didn't think to check before?" I asked. This is where the story started to get hinky. Her brief statement to Parker on the night of the murder came out as if she'd been framed. I could see, though, how any jury would think it was creating a false alibi.

"I didn't think. I panicked."

"Did you drive back home right away?"

"Yeah. I was pissed that I might have messed up my date. I really liked the guy. Was trying to impress him. What if he forgot to take the food out? What if it was cold?"

"When you came back, what did you do?"

"I noticed that music was playing from my speakers. That was nice. Aimee Mann. I ran to the stove first. There wasn't smoke or anything beeping, but I wanted to make sure. I'd gone to the West Side Market earlier that morning for the ingredients. I'd put a lot of work into it."

"Where was Malcolm?"

"After I found the ziti with a towel over it, and knew dinner was safe, I started looking for him. I called his name a few times. My guess was that he was on the rooftop deck. I'd kind of mentioned having some after-dinner drinks up there to see the views. I ran up two flights, but he wasn't there. Then I came down going from room to room...then I found him."

"Where was he?" I was writing quickly now, trying to get every detail as she told it. Her attorney had objected to me making a recording. Unless I was willing to arrest and detain her, I wasn't in control. And if I'd read her rights, no doubt she'd have exercised the right to remain silent. With only the information from the crime scene and her brief interview that night, I'd have had very little to go on. Me scribbling on a pad was the tradeoff.

"There was so much blood," Wetzel whispered.

Dinwiddie covered her hand with his. Probably a signal

they'd worked out to keep her from talking too much. Loose lips turned suspects into defendants.

"He was in my bedroom," she said once she'd composed herself.

"Was he alive?"

"I don't think so. It doesn't seem like it was possible. I didn't check. I couldn't go in there. I ran out and dialed nine one one."

"Did you kill Malcolm Pointer?"

"No." Wetzel's answer was firm, confident, oozing truth. "I wanted to date him, not end his life."

"When you walked in here, you said it was just like last time. What did you mean?"

"This isn't the first time I was framed."

SEVEN
BLAKE HARDIN TATUM
OCTOBER 4, 2009

I kept my wits about me as I stood on the front steps of Tia Wetzel's townhome. Neighborhood revitalization plans were an interesting idea, but it didn't mean that all the criminals had suddenly closed up shop. It being Sunday meant that not too many people were out walking around. Wary, I waited.

It was only a minute before the door opened. I'm not sure what I'd expected but the woman in front of me wasn't it. She was striking looking with glossy black hair in a very layered pixie cut. She had a bunch of tiny hoops along the rim of her right ear and a single tiny hoop in her left.

"Blake Hardin Tatum," I said, introducing myself. "I think I can help you."

"Help me?" She stepped back about half a foot.

Had I made the wrong bid? I tried to imagine it from her perspective. A random black woman wandering up to her doorstep. I spoke quickly to try to smooth over the awkward moment.

"I used to be a reporter at the *Plain Dealer*. I'm now doing a blog and podcast on cases I didn't have the time or backing to investigate before I got laid off from the paper."

"Podcast?" She gave a small shrug of unfamiliarity at the new medium. "My lawyer told me not to talk to anyone about anything pending before courts here in Cleveland."

"I get that. I do. But there's something else I think you should know." I paused as I tried to gauge her receptiveness. "Loren Logan sent me."

Her eyes went wide as she tried to digest the idea that a cop and a reporter were somehow working together.

"Come in." She backed up again, but this time waved me toward her. I went into her side of the semidetached building. It was better than I expected. Better than the renovation the previous owners had done on my two-family house. Everything in Wetzel's place was new, brightly lit, shiny. Maybe I needed to slap a coat of paint on my apartment, instead of treating it like temporary digs.

"Nice place," I complimented.

"Cheap place. I'm a canary in a coal mine. Might die."

I couldn't help my laugh. After a moment, she joined me. Ice broken, I followed her from the tiny vestibule and into the bright, spacious eat-in kitchen. I tried not to be jealous. It was like the house I owned, but had rented out when I'd been laid off and couldn't cover the mortgage anymore.

After I took off my raincoat, I gently laid it on the granite counter. Then I put my bag on one of the leather chairs surrounding the small table. I held up empty hands toward Wetzel flagging that I'd come in peace.

She was standing on the kitchen side of the counter nursing a glass of wine. She'd been in the middle of dinner prep. A knife lay next to smashed garlic. Plump, pink chicken breasts glistened under the recessed lights. Wetzel lifted the knife, then lowered it as she turned to me. I knew that I needed to plead my case quickly and well, otherwise she'd push me back out into the rain in a heartbeat.

"First, let me say this entire conversation is off the record," I started. "I want to explain why I'm here. After that, I'm going to leave the decision as to whether you talk to me in your hands, okay." I held up my hands again. "I'm not recording anything. I'm not taking notes."

I could see her doing the math in her head. She picked up the knife, went back to food prep. It was a half-minute before she spoke. Finally she said, "Okay, then go ahead."

"Up until the end of last year, I worked at the *Plain Dealer*. Lost my crime-reporting job in the last round of layoffs." In the last ten months, I'd made peace with the new story I had to tell people. Didn't mean I'd tossed out my *Plain Dealer* press pass just yet. That was tucked safely in my bag in case I needed it. When Wetzel didn't respond negatively to my layoff, I continued. "Rather than chase down another job and probably have to sell my house and move, I decided to go another route."

"What's that?"

"Newspapers may be dying, but blogs and podcasts are

growing. People still want information. They get it differently now. Therefore—"

"How do you know Loren Logan?" Wetzel interrupted as if she'd just caught up.

"I met him while I covered my last story."

"What was that?"

"The prosecution of Monsignor Gregory Quinn." I didn't say more. She'd have to have been in a hermetically sealed chamber not to have heard about the infamous case.

"The pedophile priest?" She opened a cabinet and took out spices.

"I think murderer is more accurate." The lengths Quinn had gone to hide his crimes—even if Logan was right and he hadn't committed the second murder—were legendary.

"My mom really wanted me to go to Catholic school. They couldn't afford it." Wetzel shook various seasonings on the chicken. "I'm starting to be grateful for growing up without."

We were quiet for a moment. She turned on a high BTU burner on her shiny stainless steel range, then slid a cast-iron skillet over it. After a few minutes she poured in a healthy glug of olive oil. The garlic sizzled, then the breasts followed. She browned both sides, tossed in shallots, then more seasoning, lemon wedges and broth. She turned the fire way down, then came back to the counter so she was facing me across the gray granite.

The smells coming from the stove had my mouth watering. I wanted to say that Malcolm Pointer had probably missed out on a great meal. Fortunately, I thought better of it. I needed to get down to it so I could let her enjoy her gourmet dinner, and I could get home to whatever frozen diet meal waited.

"What I'm going to say is strictly off the record, between us. I'd even ask you to not share with your lawyer."

"What?"

"Loren Logan is the real deal."

"What do you mean?"

"A cop you can trust." The minute those words left my mouth, I wanted to stuff them back in and swallow them. I'd never trusted the police. I was a black woman in America. Any random encounter with the cops could kill me dead.

These were men and women I had enough brains to stay away from. When I'd been with the paper, I'd asked my questions, then scurried away. Talking with Logan was one of the longest conversations I'd ever had with someone with a badge.

"And you trust...him?" Wetzel asked as if she could hear my thoughts.

"Look, I've got no love lost for the police. There are enough stories in this city of brutality and mistreatment to fill an entire set of encyclopedias. What I've always wished for, though, is a cop who got it. Who didn't think the system was fair. I think Logan could be that person."

"Think? Could be?"

"*Know* as well as I could know. He's the one who suggested speaking with you. Before your...friend was murdered, he'd come to me suggesting that we look into your other case. There were rumors that you were saying that being sentenced for a probation violation had violated your constitutional rights. Loren believes that you're not the only one. Before the latest...development, he was doing an off-the-books investigation trying to get to the source of the possible corruption."

"Damn. There might be others. I hadn't thought about it that way. That's fucked up." The reporter in me knew she was softening as she thought out loud. "Okay," she said softly.

"He's one of those 'change from within' believers." I was talking after the close, but in this case, I couldn't help it. I wanted her to be sure. Even if I wasn't at the state's biggest newspaper, that didn't mean going public wouldn't make her life more difficult.

"Do you think he can make a change?"

"Probably not in the whole Cleveland Police Department. But why not let him try in your case."

"What are you proposing?"

"I want to feature your story this season on the podcast. I'd record what was going on with you simultaneous to it happening. I think I'd broadcast it a few months after everything gets resolved. Or maybe not. The audience likes the idea of them being there in the trenches with you." I shrugged. "We could discuss that part, the timing."

Wetzel went to the fridge and took out some heavy whipping cream. She poured a generous amount into the pan, stirred, then turned off the fire. From the oven she pulled out some kind of casserole. Put that on the stove covered in a towel. She wiped her hands on another towel as she came back across the kitchen and leaned toward me. I continued with my pitch.

"Loren thinks." I paused, reframed it away from a man's opinion. "More importantly *I think* that having another pair of investigative eyes on your case couldn't hurt, and even could maybe help. But second, shining a light on darkness could make it easier to find the culprit...the man or woman who murdered Malcolm."

"Do you think I could help, me doing your blog or podcast?"

"Honestly? Even if we don't find the smoking gun, as they say, I don't think it could hurt."

EIGHT
BLAKE
OCTOBER 4, 2009

"Let's start at the beginning. How in the heck did you get in trouble the first time?"

I took my last bite of the chicken, paired it with the last of the cauliflower casserole. The food had been as good as it had smelled. I could bake pretty good, but hadn't cooked like this in years. My ex, Woody, had done the cooking for all the years we'd been together. I'd lost a lot of weight—in more ways than one—in the ten months he'd been gone.

Wetzel took my plate and hers, put them in the shiny stainless steel dishwasher. She came back at the table, poured a little more white wine into our glasses, then sat and made herself comfortable.

"Bad dating choices."

"Wait, what?" I had to think back to the question I'd asked. I shook my head because it still didn't make sense even after thinking about it for a moment.

"I was thirty. I'd dated the same guy from high school until I was twenty-nine. Of course my sixteen-year-old self thought we'd be together forever. From high school sweethearts to retired and holding hands on twin rocking chairs on a front porch in Akron."

"But that didn't happen?" I could see that she wanted to tell a whole story, that we were going way back in time. I poured myself a little more wine and got comfortable in her kitchen chair.

"Well, he got his happily ever after. My best friend and him had been seeing each other in secret. They broke it to me one day because she was pregnant."

"Ooof. I'm sorry. That sounds hard." I had to wonder if it would have been easier if my ex-fiancé, Woody, had dumped me for someone else rather than because I lost my job and the gravy train dried up. I shook my head.

Didn't matter, did it?

Betrayal was betrayal.

"They got married at city hall. From what I hear, they're still together."

"You were born in Akron?" I asked to steer her off of sad memory lane.

"My dad was a lifer at Goodyear. He just retired this spring. I left after the breakup. It was too small a town for all three of us."

"Why Cleveland?"

"Big city, but still near my parents. I'd considered Chicago, but I got a job here first, then got an apartment. I was out at the clubs, on the rebound. That's when I met

Felipe Carter. He was a black guy with great conversation. Articulate." Wetzel's face held regret at her words. "You know what I mean, right? It's just that he had some dangerous, kind of thuggish friends, but he himself was pretty laid back. I fell for him. Let him move into my place right away. I hadn't ever lived on my own. Didn't take to it."

Pulling up in a moving van on the second date was the reddest of red flags. Woody had been a hobosexual guy like that. I kept all that to myself.

"Where had he been living?"

"With an ex. I think they were still sleeping together. He offered to move in as a way to put distance between the two of them."

Despite trying, I couldn't keep my eyebrows down.

"Yeah, it was stupid." Her shrug was exaggerated. "But I'd just gotten out of a relationship where I was sharing a man, so it seemed like the perfect solution and a way to start our lives together."

"Then what happened?"

"Felipe was kind of at the top of a drug-dealing business. Like he didn't sell drugs on the street anymore. He bought large quantities from some cartel guy, then distributed it to some guys who then had other guys sell on the street."

"Did you know all this when he moved in?"

"Of course not. He said he brokered in car parts. Gave him an excuse to sometimes carry lots of cash and drive around all day."

It was...pretty believable. Any of us with an older car had

probably experienced that wait for parts. Obviously there was a middleman, though no one I knew had ever met one.

"Did you have reason not to trust him?"

"Look," Wetzel started, her face turning a little red with embarrassment. "I spent too much time checking his pager when he was in the shower. But every number I ever called was a man." She paused. Squinted. "You know that was part of the evidence against me. He'd never made a call from the house. Only used payphones. But I did. Used the landline when I was checking up on him. Put me straight in the crosshairs."

Another reason snooping wasn't a good idea.

"Where were you working back then?" I was trying to get a fuller picture of their life together.

"Retail. Was an assistant manager. Selling jewelry and doing ear piercings at the mall. He'd taken over paying the bills, so I worked part-time and made some new friends who I'd go bowling with and stuff."

Sounded easy, if not long-term ideal.

"How did you get arrested?"

"One day I'd closed the store. It was sleeting and it was taking me forever to get home. When I pulled into the street where my building was, there were lights and sirens everywhere. There were lots of apartments, so I didn't think too much about it. I wanted to get home and dry, more than I wanted to be nosy. Finally, I found a parking space and tried to run in so I didn't get more icy rain down my back. When I got to the apartment, the door was busted open." Wetzel's hands flew up in demonstration. "Like it was splintered around the hinges. Lots of cops were in the hall."

"Did they tell you what was going on?"

"Not at first. They kept asking who was on the lease. I said it was me, then asked them had anything happened to Felipe. I'd worried about him being robbed if someone noticed he was carrying a lot of money. He'd told me a story that the guy who'd had the job before him had been robbed at gunpoint. Pistol-whipped."

Her boyfriend had probably told her that story as insurance to cover if something happened to him during a drug deal. I had to wonder if all of us women were so gullible in the face of some guy telling us he loved us. I hated that we were all suckers in our own way. I scribbled some notes to focus myself, then asked my next question.

"Then what happened?"

"They led me inside. Felipe was on the floor facedown with his hands cuffed behind his back. On my dining room table was a pile of what I later found out was heroin and cocaine. A gun. Stack of cash."

"Did you ask the police at that point what in the hell was going on?" It was something white people could do with little fear of reprisal.

"He didn't answer. Just put me in handcuffs. Took me down to the cop car. I thought maybe it was for my own safety."

"Until?"

"Until he started the car and drove to the station. Said he was taking me in for questioning. I still thought I was somehow helping them out." Wetzel shook her head at her own naivete. That explained why she was all lawyered up now.

"Which department?"

"Cleveland Heights. But there had been Cleveland police there as well."

That suggested the bust was the result of some kind of interdepartmental sting operation. Every so often the city police put together a task force with suburban cops. No doubt a buy-bust of midlevel dealers. Newspaper readers never got tired of full-color photos of the guns, money, drugs, and porn these takedowns yielded.

"When did they read you your rights?"

"After they put me in a room for questioning. I hadn't done anything wrong, so I signed the Miranda paper, and answered all their questions. Felipe had betrayed me, in a different way than my ex, but still he'd lied. I didn't think it was my job to protect him."

Or vice versa.

"Was that when you learned about his drug dealing?"

"They explained the whole operation. They were being kind and understanding. They made it out like I was helping the investigation by answering questions."

"Did you feel any loyalty to Felipe?"

"At that point, no. It felt like a me-versus-him situation. I knew his friends weren't all on the up-and-up, but had thought he was legit."

Wetzel had been willing to overlook a not-quite-ex, a beeping pager, and sketchy friends. Summit County wasn't

Cleveland, but they had the internet too. Could she really have been that clueless? If she was, then she'd gotten railroaded by cops who didn't believe her.

"So you signed a Miranda waiver and answered their questions. Did you in any way protect yourself in this situation??"

"Hindsight is twenty-twenty." Wetzel shook her head emphatically causing her curtain of hair to swish around her face. "Would I be as stupid now? No. It's why I went into the meeting with Logan with Vernon Dinwiddie."

"When did you realize you were in trouble?"

"After I answered all their questions, I asked if I could go home. They said no. At first I thought it was because it was a crime scene, so I was like can I call my parents to get me. They said I'd probably not want to waste my phone call that way. They put the handcuffs back on and said I was charged with possession and intent to distribute, because of those damn phone calls."

"Did you get a lawyer then?"

Wetzel tilted her head to the side and lifted a single shoulder in affirmation.

"It was too little too late. My parents got a lawyer from Akron, from some lawyer assistance program that was a job benefit. Anyway, this guy said he probably could have gotten me off if I hadn't talked to the police.

"Pleading guilty with no jail time was the next best thing. I figured I'd do probation easy. I already had a job and a place to live. Then, he said because it was a low-level felony, I could get it expunged. It would take three years after I finished community control, but I could keep working retail. I'd started taking real estate classes. Figured I'd work on my next career in the meantime. When it was all over, I could get my license."

On the one hand, I could see how she thought the plan was reasonable. On the other hand, that's how so many people got trapped in the various systems. They'd give up their kids to foster care thinking it was temporary, or take probation, thinking it was an easy way out. Maybe it worked for some people, but not most.

"It didn't work out that way." It was a statement not a question.

"Not in the least bit. I got violated and went to prison for twelve months."

"Violated?" Was she talking about being arrested for a parole violation or sexual assault? I waited. Sipped my wine. She gazed past me out the front window. Her eyes went soft as if everything in her world was out of focus. After a moment, she looked me in the eye.

"In the two different ways that you're probably imagining," she answered. "They took my body, *then*...they took my freedom."

NINE
NICOLE
OCTOBER 8, 2009

"So where are we? Are we ready to go to the grand jury?" I asked the detective. I was way more polite than my boss. I'd let detective Loren Logan sit before I'd started in with the questions.

"She has an alibi." Logan put his police file on the table. Pushed up the sleeves on his sweater. He had to be hot. The building heat was on even though it was warm outside. Myself, I was sweating like a woman coming up on menopause.

"Is it confirmed?" I asked as I pulled my blouse away from my body to keep it from sticking.

"From Wetzel, sure," he said.

I'd only worked with Logan once before. He was a little more taciturn than before. Didn't have time to dig around as to why. I leaned forward to get something out of him about the case.

"The main suspect?" I probed. "We're now taking their word?"

If innocence and guilt were up to the defendants of the world, the prisons would be empty. As far as I could tell, we weren't at the truth serum stage of human evolution. *In vino veritas* wasn't yet court approved.

"Her attorney was present during questioning," Logan offered.

"Do you believe her?" I asked. I'd seen more than one detective's head turned by a pretty face. Lizzy Borden had ridden the demure train to acquittal after all.

"I'm not in the trust business," Logan said, monotone. "I'm in the verify business."

I pulled my pad toward me. Turned to a clean page. Somehow this "should be easy" murder trial was going to be a lot of work. Seemed to be my lot in life. I wasn't at all looking forward to this like I once would have when I was young and didn't know any better.

Pope would be breathing down my neck. My boss had some kind of hard-on for Wetzel. My cop was going all wishy-washy. Looked like Logan thought the defendant was innocent. They were never innocent. Not guilty, sure. But something had gone on there with Wetzel and the guy. Smoke and fire and all that.

My guess was that she'd either faked the phone call or had someone call her. Wetzel had tied the victim up, then she'd shot him through the heart. I hadn't pinpointed a why, but I didn't have to prove motive. Just means and opportunity. Sprinkle a little DNA, expert forensic testimony, and previous felony conviction on top and the twelve in the box would pronounce her guilty as sin.

"Who's the carrier?" I asked, pen poised, ready to entertain Logan's trust but verify theory.

Logan flipped open the file, though I suspected he knew the answer without cribbing.

"AT&T. She's got an iPhone."

"Damn." I pulled at my blouse again. Silk was hot even though it looked cool. Then I sighed. Apple's security was nearly as hard to crack as Blackberry. "That's going to be some work. Let's get started on the warrant." I'd put together an airtight request. The judge would sign it, no problem.

Then it would disappear into the carrier's legal department while they determined if this somehow fit into the narrow band of cases where they'd give up the phone location information.

Logan shrugged in sympathy. "We're in that weird place where the law hasn't kept up with technology. I think—"

I didn't get to hear what Logan thought because there was a knock, and before I could speak, my door swung open. I'd expected Pope. She had an uncanny knack for forgetting social niceties, and showing up when I wasn't prepared for whatever interrogation she'd planned.

When I looked up, I was surprised to see Cleveland Heights police detective Darlene Webb. Don't think I'd seen her in nearly two years. Not since we'd flamed out on the Juliana Clarke murder case.

Webb must have worked on her appearance, because for once she didn't look like a child playing dress-up. Her suit quality was upgraded, and she'd gotten a real haircut somewhere outside of a discount salon or her bathroom mirror.

"Can I come in?" Webb asked, though she was already moving toward my desk. Then she was standing, shifting from one foot to another. More of a party than I was expecting.

"Darlene Webb," I introduced. Pointed toward the man sitting across from me. "Do you know Loren Logan?"

They shook hands warily. Not a lot of blue brotherhood vibes flowing. Maybe it was the different departments. City versus suburbs and all that.

"Nice to meet you," Logan said. Webb nodded.

"I'm working on a warrant with Detective Logan." I looked at Webb and waved toward the door. "Can you wait outside for thirty minutes or so?"

When Webb didn't move, I looked at her more closely. Our eyes met.

"Ja Roach was murdered," she blurted out. I dropped my pen. Forgot about Logan and digital privacy and probable cause for the long minute it took me to process what she'd said. When they both looked at me, I realized I'd been silent for a long time. Maybe too long. I wanted to point out that I was sober this morning. But saying that would reveal how often I wasn't. Shifting my weight forward in my chair goosed my brain into action.

"What? When?" I asked a second question before Webb could answer the first.

"Saturday night."

"As in October third?" I inquired as I counted back from today's date.

"Yes."

"Who is Ja Roach?" Logan asked.

"Drug addict," Webb said.

"Confidential informant," I clarified.

"So he's dead, huh? Did someone he inform on kill him?" Logan asked.

"Don't think so." The detective shook her head. Her hair wasn't messy when she steadied. Fell right back into a neat bob. "He wasn't really active," Webb said to me and Logan.

"Do you have a suspect?" I asked. I assumed she needed a more complicated search warrant than the lower-level prosecutors could do. Or even maybe another cell records request. In some ways, the Fourth Amendment law was getting more difficult to navigate with more spheres of privacy popping up the founding fathers hadn't anticipated. I made a mental note to propose a continuing-ed class for the rank-and-file attorneys.

"That's kind of why I'm here," Webb said.

Logan looked between Webb and me. I think the expression on his face could have been described as incredulous. "You think the prosecutor here can help you figure out who the suspect is?"

"Roach worked with the prosecutors for years," Webb said. "It's not unrealistic to think someone he informed on figured out the source of the information. Anyways, I believe he was a pet of Pope."

"A pet?" Logan didn't hide his confusion. I didn't point out that his inexperience was showing. Maybe Walsh would take him aside and give him a rundown on county politics someday soon. There were ever-shifting hierarchical relationships that one needed to navigate in order to succeed.

"He worked for Pope in Lakewood, Cleveland, and maybe even Cleveland Heights," Webb explained. "I will try to get access to records and any detectives he worked with. But if you already have that info, then I could shortcut the investigation and get closer to possible murder suspects."

What went unsaid, but was understood by everyone in my office was that an inverse relationship exists between time and likelihood of solving a murder.

"Have you talked to Tyisha Cooley?" I asked. A lot of bodies had dropped around her. Irrationally, I feared for the safety of a woman I'd unsuccessfully prosecuted for murder.

"You think she's a suspect?" This time it was Webb whose face was a mask of confusion.

"Not exactly." I had no facts to back up my hunch that the former defendant may be in possible danger. "Can you contact her PO, though?"

"I guess." Webb shrugged. I hoped it meant she was taking a mental note to do what I'd asked.

"How was he killed? I didn't see anything on the news or in the papers." I tried not to read too much news, otherwise I got depressed by the state of the economy or whatever war was brewing. But I did keep an eye on the local crime section of the papers to see what trends there were or what was coming down the pike.

"Shot."

"In Cleveland Heights? I thought he lived in Lakewood. Had that apartment forever." When Webb and I had checked his RAP sheet during the Cooley case, he'd been the most stable drug addict I'd ever come across. He'd never moved.

Webb shrugged, again. She'd never been particularly talkative. Finally, she filled in some details.

"Abandoned house up near East Cleveland. He still lived at that same loft in Lakewood. But maybe it was easier to score drugs over on the other side of town. Maybe he was visiting someone. Who knows?"

It wasn't unheard of. Some people liked to get high together. It was kind of a social occasion. Or it was a way for the ones who couldn't afford to score drugs to barter whatever they could for a hit.

"Ballistics?" I asked because eventually we'd need to pin down a suspect. Every so often a gun could give us a suspect.

"It's a three fifty-seven Magnum."

"The murder weapon of the moment," Logan said.

"Your case too?" Webb asked.

"Guy shot through the heart with a Model 19."

"Old police gun, wasn't it?" Webb asked.

"Think so. Lots of old-timers still use it as their personal weapon. Walsh...my partner, close to retirement, uses it as his concealed weapon."

Police regulations allowed every officer to carry a concealed personal weapon in addition to their department-issued Glock. As if one gun weren't enough.

"So, you'll get me what you have?" Webb asked me.

"Call me after you've checked on Cooley," I said not promising anything. The fact that Ja Roach had worked closely with Pope over so many years meant I'd have to think out my next steps very carefully.

Our computer database access was logged. I don't think anyone in county IT or Pope ever monitored what we did. But that didn't mean they couldn't. Like the proverbial guy who watched the "wrong" kinds of videos at work, it wasn't an issue until it was.

"I'll let you get back to your warrant," Webb said. To Logan, "Good luck with yours. Hopefully you're closer to a suspect than I am."

Webb strode out with the same confidence she'd come in with.

"Pope's pets?" Logan asked. He furrowed his brow. I didn't think he was playing at naivete.

I was quiet for a moment. Weighing the need for discretion. Couldn't think of a reason to keep my mouth shut or how sharing information could come back to haunt me.

"Between you and me, Pope has a cadre of people who do her favors. Informants. Her favorite cops. Snitches. Probably has one in this office." I thumped my chest, held up my hands, empty palms facing the detective. "It's not me."

"Cops?" A wrinkle puckered between his brows. "Quid pro quo?"

That last question I didn't acknowledge. Instead I said, "Obviously it's not you. Otherwise you'd know it."

"Here's what I have for the warrant." Logan pulled his notes closer, ending the discussion of my boss' manipulation of those in her orbit to suit her purposes, mixing political and prosecutorial expediency in a way the no legislator had ever intended and therefore didn't quite outlaw.

"Let's get to work." I sighed. "Maybe I'll get at least one guilty verdict this year."

TEN
SEASON 2, EPISODE 2:
ABROGATION OF RIGHTS

H ello and welcome to *The Murders Began*, I'm your host, Blake Hardin Tatum. Today you and I will start the first steps on the journey on a new case. The matter of Cinthia Wetzel. She likes to be called "Tia."

I use the word "matter" deliberately. This isn't a straightforward criminal prosecution by any means with one victim and one perpetrator, a jury trial, and a verdict. It's something far more intricate.

I'm sure most of you have heard of the Innocence

Project. Twenty-seven years ago. Founded by a couple of lawyers at Benjamin N. Cardozo School of Law at Yeshiva University. Attorneys Barry Scheck and Peter Neufeld found that DNA had come far enough to pave the way to exonerate wrongly imprisoned people. Seventy Innocence Project clones have sprung up all across the United States. Over three hundred people have been exonerated in the twenty years since the project started. Deserving men and women have gotten a get-out-of-jail-free card.

While that was great for some, and I don't want to downplay how great it is to be released after a quarter century in prison for a crime one didn't commit, there is more to be done.

What is there for those not in jail or they can't take advantage of recently unearthed exculpatory evidence or ever-advancing genetic testing?

I don't know the answer, but hopefully we'll get there during this season of *The Murders Began*.

Now, let me tell you about Tia Wetzel.

About twelve years ago Tia moved to Cleveland from Akron. She met and moved in, quickly, with a man named Felipe Carter. Unbeknownst to her, her boyfriend, Felipe, sold illegal drugs, specifically heroin and cocaine in its various forms. The couple's apartment was a distribution center of the alphabet soup of drugs.

Carter told her he brokered car parts which explained him getting calls and pages at all times of day, and why he sometimes carried around large amounts of cash. But she was working retail, so she was gone lots of hours, called before she came home. It was easy for him to do this right under her proverbial nose, as it were.

Unfortunately as Felipe's live-in girlfriend, Tia took some of the blame for possession when cops raided their apartment. Tia's boyfriend got a few years in prison, and she got probation, which meant her prison sentence was suspended. But being under community control sanctions is not the same as freedom.

For eighteen months, Tia's constitutional rights were being curtailed. She was subjected to regular meetings with a probation officer, she had to report all work, including any side gigs or hustles. Tia also had to report any travel outside Cuyahoga County. This included going to visit her parents in Akron for family gatherings. Her Cleveland home could be searched at any time, day or night, without a warrant, without notice.

On November fifteenth, nineteen ninety-eight, Tia woke up to three probation officers at her front door, armed, guns pointed. They searched her apartment while she stood there in her pajamas, handcuffed, not permitted to move.

The officers found nothing, so she was able to go about her day. That day was a Sunday. Eventually, after she couldn't shake off the traumatic feelings of her home being invaded, being detained, and then subjected to a pat down, she went to the gym. After an hour on the treadmill, Tia felt better. Her equilibrium restored.

After her workout, Tia stopped at the supermarket on the way home to stock up on groceries for the workweek.

Before she could get back to her apartment, she was pulled over by two police officers who said she failed to signal before making a right turn. Most people would get off with a warning or at worst some kind of ticket.

This is where things take a departure from normal procedure.

Long story short, after this traffic stop, Tia Wetzel went to prison.

Tia has one story. The police have a story that's entirely different. I'll tell you both, starting with the Cleveland police on the next episode of *The Murders Began* with me, your host, Blake Hardin Tatum.

ELEVEN
LOGAN
OCTOBER 16, 2009

"We meet again," Lieutenant Parker said. She was standing under the porch overhang that ran along the right side of the narrow house. Rain dripped from the debris-filled gutters in front of her like a curtain.

Careful of the muddy terrain, that was either a driveway or a yard, I stepped up alongside the uniformed cop.

"I hope it's not a spike in suspicious deaths," I said. "Not itching to take the 'murder capital' title from Baltimore."

"I hear Detroit recalculated and edged them out in a last-minute steal." Parker allowed a small smile at the humor and horror of the statistics.

"At least it's not Cleveland. Not yet. What's tonight's deal?" I asked as I pulled out my small notebook and ball-point pen.

Parker lifted the clipboard so the bottom rested on her

hip bone. She looked at the incident report she'd started to complete.

"It's bad." Parker shook her head. "Really bad."

In the quickly waning light at dusk, I took a glance around the little wood-framed house that looked if not idyllic, at least peaceful.

The neighbor on the right had a big pile of construction debris in the yard that looked like it had been there through too many rainstorms. The house was only about two feet from the small alley that fronted it. There was no grass to speak of, just clover sprouting through cracked asphalt.

Across the street were garages for much bigger houses one block away. Like other neighborhoods in Cleveland, vacant lots, and empty buildings weren't more than a hop, skip, and jump away.

I shook my head. No matter what was on the outside, the inside was likely to be a horror show. I'd signed up for this, to be the barrier between civility and inhumanity.

"What do you mean by bad?" I probed. I read something that said that we can't unsee things. What we observe can stay embedded in our brains forever. I liked to give the first officers who arrived to the scene a moment or many to process. To do what they needed to do to cope with the more gruesome parts of the job. But I'd been here at least ten minutes by now and had to get on with my part of things.

"Murder-suicide." Parker's sigh was heavy. "The dad took out the mom and kids, then killed himself."

My "Oh shit" came out without a filter. "No one alive inside?"

"There was a cat." Parker pointed toward the backyard overgrown with tall trees and bushes. "Ran out when the patrol officers opened the door."

"Victims?"

"Liberdad Saldaño, Placidoand Quirita Fernández-Saldaño." From the surnames, I knew she'd given me mother and children.

"And the dad?"

"Ermano Fernández."

"Walsh been by?" I asked while I copied the names from her clipboard. Between darkness looming and the rain, Parker needed to use her flashlight so I could see her notes. In answer to my question, she shook her head.

"Not yet. Not tonight. He likes to have a full weekend. If you need him, I can have someone call the Zone Car." My erstwhile partner was likely taking up a barstool at the cop bar not too far from where we stood. I kept my relief from my face.

"I'm good for now. When are the techs coming?"

"Soon? They're at some pileup. Trying to get as much evidence as they can before the rain washes it away."

That everything here would be safe from the elements and easily preserved went without staying. I stuck a hand into my raincoat pocket, put the pad and pen back, got out the vapor rub and smeared some of the greasy concoction on the stubble where a mustache would start if I didn't shave this weekend.

After I huffed in a deep breath, I took three large strides and pushed open the unlocked front door. It was as if I'd walked into a house frozen in time. A toy stroller stood in the hallway with a baby doll in the seat as if some child were going to push it outside in any moment. Five Matchbox cars were in a pileup, a little firetruck and ambulance coming to the rescue.

Careful not to disturb anything, gingerly I stepped inside. The TV was on in the living room. I put on a glove and hit mute on the remote. I wouldn't be able to think with some Disney Channel sitcom's laugh track blaring in the background.

A recent remodel had made what was probably a rabbit warren of rooms into a generic gray-and-white vinyl plank-floored open plan. The kitchen had a half-eaten pizza on the counter. An open two-liter bottle of cola was near the fridge. The cranapple juice was capped. I took in the rest of the first floor and saw two doors that were slightly ajar. One was a closet full of brightly colored kids coats and boots. Another was a half bath with muddy footprints on the floor.

The only other feature in the big open room was a carpeted staircase. I put on paper booties and took one step at a time until I saw him. The father was prone in the hallway, with blood and brain matter all over the wall. A gun lay a few feet away. Took my gaze away from the body and to the upstairs layout. One door had a crayon rainbow taped on it. The girl lay there on a twin bed, looking like she'd fallen into an exhausted nap. A single gunshot was barely visible in the space between her ear and hairline. Probably a .357-caliber revolver.

If she weren't pale, or had blood-soaked sheets under

her. I could have convinced myself that she was sleeping. I knew she would never wake up. The room with the blue wooden letters screwed to the door that spelled out Placido was next. I had to close my eyes seconds after I saw the boy crumpled on the floor near the door. He'd obviously seen what was coming, tried to run past his father because he was shot at close range, powder burns marred the green cartoon dinosaur on his white t-shirt.

The wife was probably in the bedroom. He'd have to have started with her otherwise she'd have been in one of the kids' rooms. I looked around the door and she was there, tiny bloodless hole in the middle of her forehead. Her eyes were still open looking startled.

Despite the carnage, the case would be cut and dry. To close it, the question I'd need to answer was motive. My guess was that I'd find gambling debt or embezzlement or a history of domestic violence—some reason the husband thought death was the only solution to his problems, his shame.

I backed out of the master bedroom and was on my way downstairs when something weird caught my eye. It was the husband's left hand. I did the cop crouch and looked a little closer. The pinky side of his hand was covered in blue ink. The kind of smudge lefties always seemed to have. I shifted my gaze to make sure what I saw the first time was what I'd thought. The gun was a few inches from his right hand. There were ambidextrous people in the world, but I'd bet my overtime pay that the percentage was probably miniscule.

Down the stairs and out the front door I went. The rain outside was preferable to the blood inside. I remembered when my daughter was the age of that little girl in there. Clementine was well past that age now, safely away at college, but this scene haunted me nonetheless.

After I turned up my collar against the rain, I pulled out my phone. Dialed my daughter.

"Daddy, why aren't you out on a date?" my daughter asked before saying hello.

"Who said I'm not?"

"If you're calling me from a date, then you have a bigger problem."

"How are you?" I asked. Switched gears. "Do you like Wilberforce better now that you're a sophomore?" She'd been at the small college for about six weeks into her second year.

"This feels like a Sunday conversation, Daddy." The nineteen-year-old was right. Since the divorce from her mother, we talked either in person or on the phone on Sunday. It was how I caught up with the life she lived without me.

"I just wanted to tell you I love you," I said, my voice hoarse with emotion.

"Yeah...I'll be right there." My daughter must have turned her head from the phone because her words were a bit muffled and not meant for me. "Sorry. I have to go," she said directly into the phone. "We're driving to Dayton. I have to get to the city, so I don't have to party with the same three people in town."

"Drive safely in the rain," I admonished.

"We'll be good. Love you."

Clementine had hung up before I could say my own good-bye. It was exactly what I needed. Once the techs and coroner rolled up, I was ready to go back in.

TWELVE
NICOLE
OCTOBER 19, 2009

"Is that what we need for the Wetzel indictment?" I asked. I made a "give me" gesture with my hand. Loren Logan had showed up to my office without an appointment. He'd knocked, then come in before I could offer an invitation. Yankees really had no etiquette.

Logan had a folder with him. Tucked under his arm. He made no move to hand it over. Manners were going the way of the dodo in this city. I didn't admonish him because I needed for us to work well together.

"Still waiting on the stuff from the cellular warrant." He stayed standing, shifted his weight from one foot to another.

"We can indict her." I shrugged. "If she comes with a valid alibi, we can dismiss later."

"She'd lose her job or her bond money," Logan protested. It was the exact opposite of what I expected from a cop. They were usually the first to want to lock someone up and ask questions later. He continued, "The woman just bought a house. I'm not thinking she's a flight risk. Plus, there's no statute of limitations on murder."

I had to pull my eyebrows down from my hairline, and be grateful for him taking work off my desk, if not Pope off my back. Once Wetzel was indicted, we'd be working against the speedy trial clock.

"Fine. Pope isn't breathing down my neck on this one right now. But she will be soon enough. You may get a grand jury subpoena before the records come in."

"I'll be prepared for that." Logan nodded. He was savvy enough to get the subtext.

"If you don't have new evidence against Wetzel, then why are you here? I don't have any other cases assigned to you." Some cops, early in our acquaintance, mistook my office for a kaffeeklatsch. I usually made an effort to disabuse them of that notion as quickly as possible. If they wanted to socialize and gossip, I wasn't their girl.

"Maybe you should." Logan's resolve didn't waver. Could be there was something to his visit.

"Shut the door and tell me what you want."

The detective did as he was told. Sat down on one of the chairs across from my desk, but he still didn't let go of the folder.

"My partner and my boss want me to close a case. A murder-suicide." The implication being, of course, that he thought it wasn't an open-and-shut case. That he needed someone to intervene and tell the cops that the case needed to be investigated further. If he wanted me to do that, it would be a big ask. Both cops and prosecutors were used to independence and autonomy. Ironic for hierarchical organizations.

"Tell me the facts," I said with some emphasis on the last word.

"It looks like a father lost his shit. Shot his kids and his wife, then himself."

Cleveland wasn't some idyllic small town with rare bouts of violence. That said, the case he was talking about had made the news with the family unidentified. I imagined it was going to take the cops more than a couple of days to find and notify the next of kin, since the usual nearest relations were all killed.

"Saw that on the news. It's sad, but a murder-suicide is the very definition of an open-and-closed case. Kind of like when a guy goes on a shooting rampage and then he commits suicide by cop. It's not a whodunit."

Logan was shaking his head before I'd gotten to the end of my sentence.

"There's no motive," he stated. "The husband-slash-father wasn't in debt. Not more than a mortgage and a small car loan. Everything was being paid on time. He didn't go postal. He wasn't going to be fired or anything even close to that. His bosses liked him."

"Where did he work?"

"Strohmeyer. Maintenance. Earned thirty-two dollars an hour. So pretty much the same as me."

It was only ten thousand less than what I earned. If I didn't care so much about putting bad guys behind bars, I'd find another more lucrative job. Maybe one day in the future. Until then, I had more justice to mete out.

"You're saying this guy who'd killed four people in the span of an hour probably wasn't hurting for money." I paused, shrugged. "The other motive is usually poor mental health," I explained.

"No evidence of that I can find."

"Men don't seek out services." I softened my tone. "You know that. Your own department can't get officers, some with serious issues, to take help unless it's mandated. Every mass shooter has mental health issues. Some diagnosed. Most not."

"No motive is only half of it," Logan said as he batted away my rationales.

"What's the other half?"

"He was left-handed."

"So is ten percent of the world population." I had knowledge of a slew of human idiosyncrasies. Fourteen and a half percent of men were over six feet. Twenty-seven percent of the U.S. population had blue eyes. Needed this internal database to knock down lazy defense arguments.

Loren finally put down the folder. Opened it slowly. Slid three photographs across the table. I lifted them, had a quick glance at the carnage, then put them back down.

"What am I looking at?"

"That first one. It's the perpetrator on the ground after he was shot. The gun is on the carpet near his right hand. That second is the lab image of the gunshot residue result. You can see it's his right hand. That third picture is of his left hand. See the ink smudges. He was writing something and it left blue ink.

"His coworkers tell me that they have to log certain maintenance activities for state and county inspectors and such since they make consumable products. It's up on a clipboard, mounted on a wall. So he can't lift his hand like he probably would if he was trying to be neat."

"A lot of left-handed people use their right hands. For scissors. For lots of rarely used items because it's easier than making the adjustment."

It was another fact I'd learned along the way. There were a lot of things about human behavior that weren't absolutes. Like race. Some of us looked white, while we were black.

"For a gun. For premeditated murder, then suicide?" Logan looked skeptical. "Have you seen a lefty shoot with his right hand?"

"Not that I've come across," I admitted. "Even with all the years I've been here, I wouldn't say I've seen everything. But all this talk about which hand writes or shoots begs a much bigger question. You have a suspect? Because if your guy didn't do it, then who did?"

"That's why I came to you."

I threw up my hands in the air like the police were standing with guns drawn.

"*I* didn't do it."

"I know that." Loren allowed a small smile. "I think the answer may be somewhere in your files, though."

I turned toward my computer. Shook the mouse to wake

it up. "Well, start talking. You're here. I'm here. Let's see if there's anything to it."

"Do you know anything about Maximo Rea? Known associates?"

I paused before typing anything in. "Rea is the murderer?"

I started typing the name into the list of former defendants. Before I could hit "return," Logan spoke.

"Our perpetrator, the father...he killed this Rea guy in ninety-seven."

"What do you mean killed? How is he not in jail? You were just saying he had a good-paying job, a house, a wife, and some kids?"

"The story as best I can tell is that this Maximo and our guy Fernández got into it over a woman. Ermano Fernández, that's the father. He punched Rea. The victim's head hit the bar in just the wrong way and he died in the hospital a few days later."

"One-punch homicide," I acknowledged. "Involuntary manslaughter if he was charged. But that's totally discretionary. If he was a good guy, Rea a bad guy, and maybe the other guy started it, I could see how he got to go home. Okay, I'll bite." I took my hands from the keyboard, put them back on the desk. "If we start with the premise that there are no coincidences, then what's the tie? You think after twenty years someone from this Rea's family came back for revenge?"

"Rea had a kid. Turned twenty this year. Just got out of a stint at Marysville for dealing heroin."

"Stop. This is getting in the weeds. Give me a second."

I turned back to the computer. Opened the prosecutor's database of cases. Fortunately, we'd been computerized since the mid-seventies. I put in Maximo Rea. His name was uncommon enough that there was only one result.

Rather than scrolling, I hit the print button. Went out to the central printer and picked up the laser-warm pages and brought them back to my office. I shut the door and sat down on my side of the desk. The first page was an indictment of Ermano Fernández for involuntary manslaughter. Okay, so he didn't get to go home, at least right away. I flipped past all the motions and filings until I got to the deposition.

"Dismissed." That was somewhat unusual. Not filing was discretion. Dismissal of charges without conviction was something entirely different. I scanned for a different check-marked box. "With prejudice," I said looking at the hastily handwritten "x."

It meant that something had happened after the jury was empaneled. That was even rarer. Once we sat a jury, jeopardy attached and the defendant could not be tried for the same offense. As prosecutors, we tried really hard to make sure that didn't happen. I flipped back to page one, got out a pen, so I could follow along. It wasn't until page four that I stopped and looked up at Logan.

"What?" he said.

"This was a Pope case. Her first murder case, in fact. She lost it because the only witness left town for months."

"Who was the witness?"

"Liberdad Saldaño." My eyes snapped up. Liberdad had

been flagged, internally. Pope wanted the book thrown at this woman should she turn up in the system. I'd only found out when we'd followed her instruction on a woman with a similar name. Elizabeth Saldana had escaped, almost unscathed when Pope realized her mistake of identity.

"The mom?" Logan looked agitated.

"Whose mom? Wait. What?" I hadn't had a drink this morning, I was saving it all for nighttime these days. Suddenly, though, I wanted one more than anything. To steady me. Clear my brain. Put me in the right state of mind for all this stuff coming at me. I'd prepared for a chill morning of reading email and clearing out last week's paper-work. Reflexively my hand reached for the drawer where I still kept Maker's Mark in brown vanilla extract bottles. Before I could pull the handle, I fisted my hand. Put it back on the desk. Logan was talking.

"That's Ermano's wife," he said. "They're Cuban, so they use Spanish naming conventions," Logan explained. Before he could say more, I held up my hand, hoping it wasn't shaking from withdrawal...or panic.

"You have to go."

"What?" Now he looked confused. I wasn't at all. Clarity was dawning on me moment by moment. The detective was too damned good at his job. Something was hinky and I had an idea what it might be. For both our sakes, it was better if we pretended this had never happened.

"Go. Now." Frantically, I wiped my prints from the pictures with the edge of my blouse. Slid them back across the table and waited until he tucked them back into the brown kraft folder. "We never had this conversation."

"What about this case?" Logan looked earnest. I suddenly missed his partner. Walsh would have shoved any misgivings into some compartment in his mind, taken me for a drink, and we'd never have spoken of it again. Logan needed some advice. I decided it was my duty to give it to him.

"If I were you—"

"If you were me—"

"I'd walk away. Far, far away."

THIRTEEN
SEASON 2, EPISODE 3:
REASONABLE GROUNDS

This is *The Murders Began*, and I'm your host, Blake Hardin Tatum.

During every election cycle, the talking heads go on about the importance of electing the "right" president, or the "right" senators because our choices will shape the highest court in the nation. While that can be true, most people couldn't even tell you the names of the nine justices, much less what cases were decided during the last October-to-June session.

I was just as ignorant as most until I did a little

research. I can tell you that two of the cases included interpretations of arbitration clauses. Another was a dispute between the state of New Jersey and the state of Delaware. Many were criminal, but addressed issues at the margins. Most cases are not landmarks like *Miranda*.

Let me tell you about one case that makes a difference in Tia Wetzel's life:

In nineteen eighty-seven, the U.S. Supreme Court in a five–four decision, with Scalia writing for the majority, ruled in *Griffin versus Wisconsin* that probationers and parolees did not have the same Fourth Amendment constitutional right to be free of a police search as would a citizen who isn't under community control sanctions. That the right to search extends beyond the home, to the probationer's car and their person.

Now back to Tia Wetzel.

According to the report they filed several days after the traffic stop by detectives Rocco Nicola and Thomas O'Callaghan, Tia was driving somewhat erratically along Mayfield Road on November fifteenth at about five in the afternoon.

Though it was a Sunday afternoon with very little in the way of cars on the road, they wrote and highlighted that they worried both about the safety of the public as well as the safety of the driver. When they got closer to observe her, they said her taillight was also out. The Cleveland Heights detectives turned on their lights and sirens and pulled her over.

While they ran Tia's plates and then her driver's

license, they learned that she was on probation for drug possession with intent to distribute. They put two and two together and their suspicion about her being high may have been confirmed.

They decided to exercise their authority to search her. They didn't find anything on her body or in the car she was driving, so they put her in the back of the squad car and drove to Tia Wetzel's apartment.

Nicola and O'Callaghan wrote in their report and later testified that they left her in the back of the car, searched the apartment and found drugs. That finding put her in violation of her probation. Ultimately, after a contentious hearing, the judge sent her to Marysville for a year.

As you might have expected, Tia Wetzel tells an entirely different story. According to her, it had taken her some hours to shake out the jitters from the six a.m. probation entry and search. She ate some eggs and toast, then watched a DVD from Netflix. When that was done, she went to the gym, then the grocery store.

Wetzel says that she was driving home under the speed limit, and definitely not under the influence when a cop car pulled off a side street with lights and sirens, like they do in speed traps. Realizing it was her they were after, she went onto the shoulder immediately, realizing of course that she was on probation and needed to obey every law and command of any peace officer.

Wetzel said they knew who she was, and never asked for her license or registration, and started searching the car right away. When they didn't find anything, they told her she had to abandon her car because they were going to search her house. She pleaded to be able to take the car because she could afford neither the hundreds in tow fees nor the spoiled groceries.

Nicola and O'Callaghan didn't agree to let her drive, so they put her in the back of the squad car and took her to her apartment on Ridgefield Road. The detectives took her to the front door, had her unlock it, then handcuffed her once they got inside. Which was the same procedure that probation officers had used early that morning.

The rationale for this handcuffing, which is a policy across departments, is to limit possible violence or the confiscation of contraband from the probationer.

Then, according to her, they took her to the bedroom and took turns assaulting her. When she protested and said something about reporting them, they produced drugs, said she was going to jail now. That no one would believe someone like her.

There's what they say, what she says, and the truth. Whichever story you believe, that was in the past. Tia finished out her sentence. She paid her debt, and is a free woman. She finished college and got a job at a real estate brokerage. Bought her own townhouse, and had started dating. This story, even if the middle is in controversy, has all the hallmarks of happily ever after. The kind of story we all wish for out of the criminal justice system, but rarely get.

On September thirteenth, Tia Wetzel invited

Malcolm Pointer to a home-cooked dinner of baked ziti. It would have been their third date. She ran out when she got a phone call, and when she came home, he had been shot dead in her house.

Now, the Cuyahoga County prosecutor is investigating her for murder. Tia Wetzel maintains she was framed, again, because she'd hired an attorney who had just asked the same prosecutor's office to look into how the revocation of her probation all those years ago had been a violation of her civil rights for which she deserved compensation. Because she'd finally had the courage to think about prosecuting Nicola and O'Callaghan for her alleged sexual assault. But this case, this murder will be first and foremost in the minds of the prosecutor's office, in the minds of the public who are ready to call for justice on a recent gruesome premeditated death.

The statute of limitations for rape in Ohio is twenty years. Premeditated murder carries a possible sentence of life without parole or death.

This has been *The Murders Began* with your host, Blake Hardin Tatum. Tune in for the next episode where I'll talk about this case taking an unexpected left turn.

FOURTEEN
LOGAN
OCTOBER 31, 2009

"You said you'd call next time," Blake said. Her tone was stern, but a smile played around her lips. She was sitting on the front porch in one of those old-fashioned straight-backed wood chairs with the basketweave seats that I always found uncomfortable. My ass was inevitably cradled in one when I needed to question a witness or suspect in their home. A pain in the coccyx kept me on my toes.

"Your light was on." I pointed toward the globe dome speckled with dead insects. "You are on the porch."

"My downstairs neighbors aren't fans of the doorbell. Makes their dog crazy. So they took him to a friend's house somewhere out in Hudson. Left me as the only one to hand out candy to these kids. I figured it was my civic duty."

A witch and a vampire wandered up. After they announced themselves, Blake pulled a couple of orange and purple packages from a giant plastic pumpkin and put them into the kids' pillowcases. Seemingly satisfied with their booty, they ran down the walkway toward waiting parents under golf umbrellas.

I looked into the pumpkin.

"Popcorn balls. Really?" I joshed. "You're *that* neighbor."

"I can't justify giving out bunches of candy. Cavities. Diabetes. We had so many stories in the paper on the evils of sugar."

"You think the kids eat these?" I picked one up. Tossed it from one hand to another. Tatum plucked it out of midair mid toss, put it back in the pumpkin.

"Maybe their parents enjoy them. I don't know. At least I can sleep easily."

"My daughter wasn't a fan of the candy either." I could feel myself smile. I had no idea when she was born that she would own my heart. "She mostly liked dressing up and running around past dark with her friends."

"You have a daughter?" Tatum asked the question as if I'd said I kept dragons in my basement.

"Clementine. She's nineteen."

"You have a kid that old?" She gave more popcorn balls to an Elmo and three princesses in a row.

"I started working at eighteen. Thought I was an adult when I got married at twenty-one and had a baby at twenty-four."

"You still married?" Her glance at my left hand wasn't too subtle. I wanted to tell her that a band around your finger did not lock you in your house at night.

"Not anymore." I shrugged because I had the same story as dozens of cops. Marriage and being on the job weren't that compatible. "Got divorced around the same time I transferred to homicide."

Two miniature football players came up. Took the last of the popcorn balls. It was nearing nine. The street was as empty as a normal night.

"Going to call it," Tatum said. She pushed herself up, then stood with the empty plastic pumpkin pail swinging from her hand. "Did you come to relive your young fatherhood, or are you here for a reason?"

"Can we talk upstairs?" It was a presumptuous question, but I really needed someone to bounce all this off of. Someone I could trust to keep what I knew under wraps, at least for a little while.

"C'mon." She beckoned me, then flipped off the porch light. "It's Saturday night. The little kids will be watching scary movies and the teens are going to be partying. They don't need candy collection as an excuse to get out on a weekend."

"I'm gun-free," I said as I held up my hands. The last time I'd come by, she'd only let me in as long as I didn't have a weapon on me.

I followed her up the stairs for the second time trying to ignore the sway of her hips. Wetzel's case had put the nail in the coffin of online dating for me. Not that I thought I was going to be a murder victim, but the random nature of the dating prospects had lost its allure in light of a bullet through the heart of a guy coming over for ziti.

Like the last time I was here, we ended up in the kitchen. I didn't see any lemon poppyseed bread. Knew it was impolite to ask her to feed me when I'd turned up without an invite. I took one of the popcorn balls from the counter. It was kind of salty, sweet, and *dry* all at the same time. I coughed up a few kernels that had gone down the wrong way.

"Thirsty?" Tatum took what looked like a pitcher of Arnold Palmer from the fridge. I nodded and she produced a second glass, added ice, and filled it. I took a long drink. The sweet tart beverage hit the spot where the popcorn ball hadn't.

"Did you talk to Tia Wetzel?"

"She made me dinner." My eyebrows must have gone up. "Okay, maybe I crashed her kitchen on a Sunday night. She made a really good lemon garlic butter chicken."

"I guess I'm not the only one eating, uninvited."

"Maybe you're up next." I tried to push down the little bubble of happiness I felt at the thought of Tatum barging into my home. I was going to have to do something to combat the loneliness creeping up on me. After I got to the bottom of these cases, I promised myself I'd think more about who I wanted to spend my time with during these empty-nest years and beyond.

"Was she willing to talk?" I asked after I finished the remaining popcorn balls and two tall glasses of tea-and-lemonade mix.

Tatum nodded. "She told me the whole story of what

happened to her all those years back. The boyfriend, the assault by the cops after—"

"Assault? Sexual?" I interrupted her because this was news.

"I thought you knew." Tatum squinted at me. "You were the one who told me about the possible civil rights claim. What did you think it was?"

I felt stupid, naïve. I'd assumed the best even when I knew better.

"Not having due process during her probation hearing. Maybe an accusation of planting evidence."

"That wasn't it." Tatum tilted her head, held up her hands.

"Or at least that wasn't all of it."

"Who were the cops?"

Without a word Tatum walked out of the kitchen. I heard her shuffling through the huge stack of papers that I'd seen covering the dining room table. She came back with a notebook. She opened the spiral-bound book, licked her fingers, and went through about ten pages before putting a brown lacquered nail on a line.

"Rocco Nicola. Tommy...probably Thomas O'Callaghan. Cleveland Heights."

"Are they still with the department?"

"I checked and the answer is yes. They were younger then. Rookies, most likely. Veterans now. I don't know any more information though."

I took out my own notebook and jotted down their

names, then flipped through the pages I'd dedicated to Wetzel.

"Have you heard of Ja Roach?"

"Sounds familiar." She squinted for a moment as her eyes went out of focus. "Murder victim. It was in the paper a few weeks ago. Why?"

"The Saldaño/Fernández murder-suicide of the whole family?"

"There weren't any names published about that. The one on the near west side?" She shrugged.

"What about Tyisha Cooley?"

"Nothing on that one. Who is she?"

"She was indicted for the murder of Pope's sister."

"Oh, I kind of remember now. Another reporter worked on that one. I was working on a story down in Akron. Do you remember that basketball star accused of felony domestic violence?" Tatum put her notebook down on the table, folded her hands into her lap. "I thought we were working on Tia Wetzel. My sole focus has been on that. The original charge, the probation violation, her assault accusations, and a potential murder charge. That's a lot. What's all this other stuff?"

I tried to figure out what I was asking her. It was all still jumbled in my own head, but I was the kind of person who needed to talk things out sometimes to figure them out. My erstwhile partner wasn't the one I wanted to hash this out with. Not while I didn't know what I had. Rather than try to gussy it up, I put it plainly.

"Something in my gut tells me these are related. Cooley. Wetzel. Roach. Saldaño/Fernández."

Tatum didn't immediately dismiss my nascent theory. It was the reason I was talking to her. Reporters usually had suspicious minds. She took a beat, held up her hand and bent her fingers one by one as she spoke.

"A murder victim. A murder defendant. A murdered family. A woman accused of murder. The only thing in common is death. Unfortunately, it's something all animals share."

She was right, but there was more to it. I tried to articulate it.

"What they have in common is Pope," I said.

"County prosecutor, Lorraine Pope?" She spread her hands wide. "Every case in the last however many years she's been in the prosecutor's office has her in common. Are you saying she's corrupt? Politicians? They all are."

"I—"

"Look, I don't want you to think I'm crazy," Tatum interrupted. "I'm not one of those conspiracy theorists who thinks every president gets a freebie murder. But I'm no Pollyanna either. I know that there are probably honest prosecutors or totally above-board cops. But I've met too many people who've been on the wrong side of the law, unfairly accused, or overcharged. If they're white or rich or hopefully both, they can pay enough for an attorney to get them out of it. But if they're poor or brown or unfortunately both, then the odds are not in their favor. So I get that Pope may be what you'd call corrupt. That's just business as usual."

"Wow. Okay." I hadn't expected that speech. She was so neutral and objective in her reporting. The truth was that she didn't really trust any of us. While I understood where she was coming from, it didn't mean her words didn't make me a little bit depressed. Sad that she didn't see much justice in the justice system.

"I'm sorry. Look. I'm a black woman in Cleveland. I'm over forty. I don't have a filter. Not in my own house. But I'll shut up now. What is your theory on Pope?"

I wanted to high-five this no-filter journalist. But that would have been weird. Instead I drained my third and what I promised myself would be my last glass of the Arnold Palmer, then started.

"There's something about Pope that doesn't sit right with me."

Tatum nodded. "I gathered as much the last time you came by."

"Look," I started. Spread my hands wide. "There are prosecutors who are a little bit slimy. There are the true believers. Then there are the ones who really need to be defense attorneys or are on the edge of burnout, but either way do a half-assed job. She is none of those. Or maybe it's that she's the first two, but alternating. She doesn't even have a clear agenda. She's not anti-gang, or a buy-bust advocate, or into vice prosecutions. Usually one of those gets someone elected and they lean heavily on that."

"You don't like her...lack of agenda?"

"If she doesn't have an agenda, then the cases start to

feel personal. Like she's using the job for a reason I can't figure out."

"I hear what you're saying." Tatum's mask of confusion smoothed into something bland and inoffensive.

"You think I'm crazy?"

"We're all a little crazy. Some of the nuttiest tips I got at the paper turned out to be the best stories. All that said, you seem to be working something out in your head. And that's all good. But what do you want from me? You are the police. You have all the power and a gun besides."

At that moment, all the things I wanted hit me like a ball of fire. I kind of wanted to kiss Blake, wanted her to want to kiss me back. I really wanted a better partner than Walsh. I needed to untie the knots in my head that were like tangled yarn. I was only likely to get the last, if I was lucky. The first two, I needed to push out of my mind as one was nearly as unlikely as the other.

"I want your help. You can go places and ask questions I can't. Some people don't trust police. Others don't trust the press. These aren't usually the same people."

"Interesting theory...but..."

I wanted to blurt out that I wanted to investigate Pope. I wanted to tell her that Nicole Long's reaction to my questions about Saldaño both put the fear of God into me, but also solidified that I was probably on the right track. But it sounded crazy to my own ears. Not to mention career suicide. I'd already lost my marriage, I didn't want to lose my job as well.

"Can you be my second set of eyes and ears? I know I'm

not being specific, but I have a hunch that there's a bigger thing going on here. You have curiosity and resourcefulness and I need someone like that. We worked well together on Quinn." I snapped my fingers. "Danica Lozano. Five is a pattern. No matter what the deal is, I think we can crack something open here. You get a story and I get—"

"What *do* you get?"

"Justice."

FIFTEEN
BLAKE
NOVEMBER 6, 2009

"**D**o you need help with that?" I turned away from the back of my car toward the familiar voice of Cleveland police detective Loren Logan as he walked up my driveway.

"What does it look like?" I asked Logan who'd turned up —again—without so much as a heads-up or a phone call. I wanted to be mad at him. Instead I was intrigued enough that I'd bought this dry-erase board that I couldn't get out of my car. I didn't even want to think how I planned to get it up the tight turn in the narrow stairs to my apartment.

The guys at the office supply store had been very helpful in getting the six-foot-by-four-foot box into my Jeep after I'd taken three tries to try to wedge it in on my own. Now, I couldn't get the dammed thing out even if logic dictated that it should be easy.

A year ago, I'd have brough my ex, Woody, who would have gotten it in and out on the first try. Though what I saved in paying for him to live with me rent-free, more than covered the cost of the expensive board.

Logan pushed up the sleeves of his flannel, then tilted the box in just the right way that it slid out of my truck without so much as a ding in the cardboard. I didn't mention that I'd been standing there almost twenty minutes. I'd been only seconds away from getting an X-ACTO knife and taking it apart outside.

"You want this upstairs?" Logan stood with his arm around the box.

"Um, yes."

Without my help, the detective managed to heft the box up the narrow stairs, past the bend, and after I unlocked it, through my front door.

"Where do you want it?"

"Dining room," I said slightly embarrassed.

My dining room looked like a little worse for wear. After seeing Tia Wetzel's place, I'd gone to the hardware store, twice. The first time, I paid twenty dollars for one of those paint fans with about a million colors in it. The next week, I went to Lee Hardware and got three pints of sample paint.

The red square looked like every other dining room on Zillow. Gray was the new beige. Brown was the old beige. Any of them probably would have made the place look better than the off-white walls the previous tenants had left dingy and stained. None of them was going to help me figure out which end was up in Loren Logan's rogue investigation which is why I'd lugged home a whiteboard instead of more paint.

I went to my kitchen and got the box cutter. Carefully, I undid the plastic ties, popped out the big staples, then lifted the top like a pizza box. Inside was the brand-new dry-erase board. Logan helped me lift it out. Underneath was the stand that would keep it upright, and a bunch of hardware.

"Why don't I take this box out for you. Give you room to put it together. Where do you want it?"

"Just prop it up next to the garbage. I'll break it down and put it in the recycle bin later."

"Got it."

The assembly instructions were pretty straightforward. Pop in the casters. There were six screws attaching the board to the frame. I was able to do it all without tools. Now assembled in my dining room, it hid my attempts at paint color swatching. I pulled a plastic shopping bag from my purse. Cracked open the blister pack of sixteen markers, and chose a blue. I consulted my notes and wrote five names on the board:

Danica Lozano

Tia Wetzel

Ja Roach

Tyisha Cooley

Liberdad Saldaño

I'd already looked at these names so many times since Logan had been here on Halloween that I could write them from memory. Whenever I thought about all these people without nearly anything in common, it felt like going on a wild goose chase. Murder was not a common enough denominator.

"It looks like a TV squad room," Logan said when he came back. I looked up and realized that the shadows had grown long. I stood and turned on the overhead light to dial down the creep factor.

"All I need are some pictures of dead people at murder scenes or fake driver's license photos that look more like headshots."

I noticed he was carrying more stuff than he'd left with. How long had he been gone and I'd been in my own head? Woody claimed he was always "in the flow," when I needed him. However, when I zeroed in on my job, he claimed I was working too hard. Purging my ex's voice from my head, I turned to Logan. "Where'd you go?"

He held up a bag and a cardboard box. "I hope you like pizza. If you don't, there's antipasto salad in here."

"Can you stack some of that stuff on one side of the table. I'll get some place settings."

I came back from the kitchen, hands full. Logan took the placemats and set them down. I finish setting the table. He served us each some salad and a slice of pizza.

"Extra cheese?" I asked pointing to the loaded pie.

"I hope you don't mind." Logan's smile was unexpectedly shy.

"I love extra cheese," I assured him.

We ate in silence for a few minutes. I pointed to his breast pocket.

"What's that?"

Logan wiped his hand on a napkin. Patted the pocket.

"This? It's my phone."

"Do you know how it works?"

Logan took out the compact device, then slid the screen over revealing the keyboard.

"Sure. It's a new model. It's pretty cool. The keyboard makes it easier to text my daughter. Are you in the market?"

"No. I just wanted to know if you were familiar with the phone because you've so far never used it to call me. You just show up whenever."

My tone was serious, though I'm not sure if I cared as much as my protest suggested.

"Sorry. You're right. It's just without my daughter at home, the days kind of sometimes run together and I just want to keep up momentum."

I remembered those days at the paper. I ran from one lead to another regardless of day and time. Great for my career. Not great for my relationship.

"I get the momentum thing," I said patting his hand with mine. "Really I do. Just call next time, okay?" My fingers lingered a moment too long. I tried to pull them back without looking like I was avoiding touch.

"Does that mean there will be a next time?" Logan's voice was soft. I shifted my weight, started eating my slices in earnest.

"This little murder riddle you created isn't going to solve itself." My voice was all business. He took the hint. Sat back from the table and eyed the list.

"Do you have some ideas?"

"You see the names I have up there. The five people you're suspicious about." I wiped pizza grease from my fingertips onto a paper napkin, then pulled a blue notepad from my color-coded stack. Blue was for investigative notes. It's where I jotted down everything that came to mind before trying to organize my thoughts. In my business, so much information came at us that I'd learned early on to make note of all of it. Until it was time to write a piece, it wasn't always clear what was important and what wasn't.

"Any connections?" Logan asked. His voice was cautiously hopeful.

I shook my head.

"That's not how my brain works." I flipped through pages on my various pads. "After you left I started compiling a dossier on everyone. Birth date and place. Where they went to school. Where they've lived. Who they've married or dated. Family. Significant friends. And except for Tyisha Cooley, the circumstances of their death. Speaking of—"

I got up from the table, pulled out a marker and added two names to the list:

Wayne Cooley

Sarah Rose Pope

I answered the question in Logan's knitted brows.

"Tyisha's brother's murder was unsolved, but Sarah Pope and Ja Roach were there at the time he was shot."

"Sarah Pope is related how?"

"Lori's sister. Sarah died of a drug overdose where Tyisha Cooley and Ja Roach were present. Cooley was put on trial for her murder. She pled to a lesser charge. Justin McPhee, remember him as one of Monsignor Quinn's victims? He was Cooley's attorney. Weird coincidence? At the time McPhee was representing Cooley, he was also representing this woman named Elizabeth Saldana, known as Libby."

"The dead wife came up clean. What was Saldana charged with?"

"The same as Tyisha Cooley, giving a fatal hot shot."

We ate in silence for a few more minutes. When our plates and the containers were empty, I picked it all up, precariously balanced, then stuffed it in a trash bag. I took that bag and stuck it outside the front door. When I came back in, Logan was standing at the board, marker in hand. He hadn't written a single thing. He turned to me, phone in hand.

"I called in. The vic doesn't have an arrest in her background, but did have a bench warrant out more than ten years ago."

"Aren't those usually for not showing up to court?"

"Exactly. She didn't show up as a witness for a case."

"Nothing about drug charges?"

"Not a single thing."

"What if they're two different people?"

"Saldana. Saldaño. Libby is a nickname for Elizabeth. For Liberdad isn't a stretch."

"So what was the mistake?"

"Mistake?"

Logan held up a hand. Made another call. When he was done, he slipped the phone back in his pocket. Leaned forward in earnest.

"Neither Libby ever went to jail. The dead one wasn't ever arrested. The living one wasn't convicted."

"It's not Jane Smith, or Bob Jones, but still in a state as big as this, lots of people have the same name."

"Did you grow up here? Cleveland?" Logan asked.

"No. Pittsburgh." I shrugged with nonchalance. It was a move I'd perfected in the face of that question. Cuyahoga County wasn't always friendly to out-of-towners. "Moved here in ninety-eight when I got the job with the *Plain Dealer*."

"The first lesson I learned as a detective is that there are no coincidences. Pittsburgh was probably like this, too. Rust belt city with a dwindling population, but a political and social structure that's been there forever. I think McPhee's representation may be coincidental, but Ja Roach showing up, not so much. Two Libbys makes for too many flukes."

I shook my head. All the stuff he was spouting felt like buzzing bees in my head. I held up my hands in a "stop" motion.

"We could go around forever. Between us, we don't have the time and resources to do a deep dive here, not unless we have months. But with the Tia Wetzel case moving forward, time isn't on our side. I think we need to focus on what you talked about earlier."

"What's that?"

"The common denominator." I walked right up to the dry-erase board and picked up the blue marker from the tray I'd just screwed to the rails. "There's one person missing from this board. One person who could answer the questions we are asking, if they were willing."

"Are you thinking of talking to Nicole Long?" Logan asked.

"God no. She drinks on the job." I knew I was repeating only half-verified gossip, but for the sake of our respective careers and reputations, I felt like I had to assume it was true. "I'm going to assume, for the sake of argument, that she keeps her job by keeping her boss' secrets. It doesn't really make sense any other way."

"Jesus." Logan shook his head. "I hope she can sleep at night."

"Maybe Pope *is* the reason she drinks," I speculated. "Who knows? Everyone has their demons, and ferreting out hers is above my pay grade."

"So what's the play here?"

"We need to build a picture of Lori Pope. Where was she born? Who are her parents? Where did she go to school? What jobs did she have? Did she come into contact with any of these people outside of the courtroom? That kind of thing. If we put our heads together, I think maybe we'll get somewhere."

I took the fat side of the dry-erase marker and drew a thick line under all those names. Wrote down another with a big asterisk.

  Lorraine Pope

SIXTEEN
NICOLE
NOVEMBER 9, 2009

"I brought you something I know you'll like," Lori Pope said as she came into my office. She held two take-out coffees in molded cardboard. She plucked one with a red stirrer plug in the lid and put it on my desk.

"Thanks?" My upward intonation was faint, but I couldn't help myself. I'm sure she caught it. It's not that I wouldn't be thankful for a coworker bringing me coffee. It's that Pope was the last person to give something without strings. I just worried a little bit about what those strings were going to be.

"Have some," my boss insisted.

I plucked the little stopper from the hole it was plugging in the plastic lid. A tiny stream of steam escaped. I took a sip. It was a vanilla latte...with a kick? I took a bigger drink and swallowed. It definitely had a good ounce of whiskey added. As if it were radioactive, I plunked the cup on the table.

"I hope I got the ratio right. That is how you have your

morning coffee, right?" Her smirk almost came and went before I saw it.

Lori Pope's question was no different than anyone would ask rhetorically. I decided it didn't deserve an answer.

"What's up?" I asked instead.

"I'm here to discuss priorities with you."

"Okay." I pulled a pad toward me, clicked my pen to the ready.

"You need to get in front of the grand jury," she said.

"Which case?" I got poised to write.

"First, you need to indict Tia Wetzel."

I tried not to let any feelings show. Instead I carefully transcribed the name of a woman who was very likely not guilty of murder on to the pad in front of me, possibly sealing her fate. I was a prosecutor, not judge, jury, and executioner. I would try for a little discretion.

"She's coming in with an alibi," I pointed out in an attempt at low-key persuasion.

"Do you have that information? Her notice of alibi?"

I didn't mention that a defendant didn't have to pony up that notice until they were indicted, and even then only seven days before trial.

"Waiting on the cell phone company," was my oblique reply.

"There's no reason to wait, that I can see." Pope clicked her tongue. "My constituents need to know I mean business."

"If the alibi is solid, we could wait. Preservation of evidence is not a problem in her case. Plus, Tia Wetzel could lose her job, maybe. It could look like retaliation for her lawsuit. And if she's not the doer, then maybe this will bolster her claims of reprisal." If doing the right thing didn't work, I hoped that possible embarrassment would push my boss in the right direction.

"Don't you think I've considered all that." Pope's face held not a single ounce of consideration. "Just do it."

"Fine." I tapped my pen on the pad. "Anything else?"

"Ja Roach was murdered. He supplied my sister, if you remember."

"Of course, I do. I—"

"I checked with Cleveland Heights," Pope interrupted, "and they have no suspects."

"Cleveland Heights?" I asked though I already knew the answer. I didn't like where this was going, but she was on the warpath. When she was acting like this, I just tried to stay out of the way of her wrath.

"O'Callaghan and Nicola took a look at the file." Pope pulled the spout from her coffee, and despite the curl of steam rising from the tiny hole, she gulped down half of her hot coffee like it was cold water. She paced a small square on the carpet.

"Are they not assigned to the case?"

"No, that honor went to rookie detective...Darlene Webb. The one who botched the first Cooley prosecution."

"What do you need from me on this one, if there's no suspect?" I had an inkling, but needed her to say it out loud. I wanted to reach for my phone, but hesitated. I was starting to consider recording our conversations. My boss' actions had always skirted ethics, even when law abiding. But there was something wild in her eyes lately, that made me think she was taking unnecessary risks, if not actions that may bring her down.

Even though Ohio was a one-party consent state, I was afraid that she'd catch me somehow. Turn evidence of her wrongdoing into mine. I had no capital, political or other-wise to push back against her. If anything happened, I'd go down. Evidence of that wouldn't help me.

"I need you to meet with the detectives. Then take it in front of the grand jury."

"Indicting who?"

"Tyisha Cooley. This time, she's going down."

"What evidence do you have?"

"Don't worry about that. It'll be there. Nicola and O'Callaghan will get that to you." Seemingly calmer, Pope wrenched open the door and put one leg out. Before she could leave, she pivoted on her low heel. "Oh, and you might want to toss out that coffee. I've scheduled a random breath-alyzer for ten this morning." She looked at her dainty wrist-watch. "That's a good forty-five minutes from now."

There was nothing Pope did that fit the definition of "random."

SEVENTEEN
BLAKE
NOVEMBER 11, 2009

Every pointed look I'd gotten since I'd parked my car shared a singular meaning: *I did not belong in Parma.* I wanted to tell them that I'd be gone as quickly as I could. It was the whitest city in a county that was thirty percent black.

After one particular unwelcoming glance, it brought up the fear I sometimes had that this job would kill me. Straightening my spine, I checked my notes, then went to the apartment complex front door and pushed a button labeled Moretti.

Cuyahoga County prosecutor, Lorraine Pope's mother had been shockingly easy to find, once I knew her name. It had taken more than a little digging. A long-ago, not-digitized profile from the first time Pope had run for office had highlighted her Italian heritage which had meant giving her mother's full name. It had taken the full part of a day and an endless number of sneezes from too many hours in the dusty central public library basement, to get that information.

Once I had her name plugged into the myriad of databases on the web, I was able to find her in less than an hour. She was eighty and lived alone. When I'd called her on the phone to set a time to meet, Anna Moretti seemed to have her wits about her. Though I was surprised she didn't ask too many questions about why a reporter would want to come to visit. I hadn't seen more than that single article about her, so my kind couldn't have visited too often. Unless a person wanted to be in the spotlight, reporters tended to make people wary, but not her. It was all a bit curious. I had so many questions, some of which I hoped to be answered by the time I left here.

It took a minute to work the decades-old buzzer system, but once the intercom sounded, I yelled my name into the metal box. The glass entry door clicked and I opened it before it locked again. Looked at all the little brass numbers screwed on the apartments until I found 21C. The door opened before I could knock.

"I think you're looking for me." The voice came from a woman who looked every one of her eighty years. She was wearing the cliché of a leisure suit, the top unzipped to reveal a too large t-shirt.

"Blake Hardin Tatum." I thrust out my hand. "I'm a journalist."

"Anna Moretti." She took it. Her hand was bony, cold, dry. It was like shaking hands with a dead person. I tamped down a shiver.

"Not Pope?" I asked. Moretti had been married in an era where women had almost always taken their husband's last name.

"I changed my name years ago...after the divorce." Her headshake was slow. "Or rather it was ordered by the judge. I think Frank wanted to make sure I was never associated with his family again."

Someone walked out of the apartment next door and toward the exit as I stood awkwardly on the worn industrial carpet.

"Can I come in?"

"Where are my manners? Yes. Sure. Sorry." Moretti stepped back and let me directly into the living room. It was a tiny room with a small love seat, coffee table, and TV on a stand. From where I stood I could see directly down the narrow hall to the bathroom at the back of the apartment that reminded me of a railroad unit.

It wasn't cluttered by any stretch of the imagination. Usually when I visited old people, their space was filled with oversized furniture and too many framed family photos. Their whole lives crammed into a tiny space.

"Can I get you something to drink?" Moretti offered while standing awkwardly.

I wasn't at all thirsty, but my curiosity got the better of me.

"Sure, let me help you," I offered.

I followed her to the tiny galley kitchen. With some difficulty, Moretti pulled a two-liter bottle of Coke from the fridge and then lifted a glass from the drainboard. I took over pouring pop while I surveyed the surroundings.

A single plate and fork were in the sink. I wondered what she ate? What she did? Where she'd been all these years? In the photos of Lori Pope during election cycles, unlike her opponents surrounded by cherubic children and dutiful spouses, she was always alone. Her father and stepmother had long retired to Arizona. Her sister had died. The top prosecutor had never been married.

I took the soda in hand, and pretended to walk the wrong way down the hall. It was what I'd guessed from the front door, a bedroom on the left, and a small stacked washer/dryer in a nook next to the small bathroom.

"Sorry. Got mixed up," I said and turned around. I made a space for myself on the couch. Moretti perched on the arm.

"You said on the phone, you thought I could help you. I haven't been able to help anyone in years. Not since my favorite sister died. I was there for her as she battled cancer."

"I'm sorry for your loss."

"Life is about loss."

"There's some joy there as well, right?" I made a point to make eye contact. It usually loosened people up, that connection. "You got married, had a daughter. There had to be happiness there."

"Some. Early on. Frank, that was my husband," she explained. I held my tongue as I did in all interviews. Subjects no matter how famous or infamous didn't want to know that they'd been fully vetted before an interview, that little of what they said was new. "Frank," Moretti continued, "was kind of a typical cop, you know. Back then the guys on the job, they were never home. When he was home he was stressed out. Drank. Didn't talk to me much. Sometimes I'm jealous of women your age. You were born in a time when men talked to you. Considered your opinions. I was supposed to be happy that I had a house to clean and a baby to nurse. It wasn't enough."

"You only had one child?" I didn't think Pope had some siblings I hadn't been able to find, but women changed their names, or didn't have credit in their own names, and were absent from some databases—even now.

"I was one of six. I thought I wanted a big family. I think I just wanted something to do during the day. But I only had two."

"Two?" I was glad I'd asked. Databases couldn't yet replace oral histories.

"My son died when he was a baby." Even these many years later, I could see the pain in Moretti's eyes, hear the grief in her voice.

"Again, I'm sorry."

Moretti waved away the memory. The cavalier movement of her hand was in sharp contrast to her demeanor.

"Losses. So many losses. What is it you wanted to ask me about? Must be Lori. There's nothing else in my life that would get someone smart and pretty like you to come see this old bag of bones."

There was a lot of truth in what she said. It's what a lot of people I interviewed said. So few even had a single person to talk to or spend time with. Loneliness was an American epidemic that I couldn't heal, a huge problem that I wasn't trying to eradicate. Maybe I'd write about it one day. Until then, solving the mystery of these as yet unlinked deaths was paramount.

"Can you tell me what it was like when you were raising Lori?"

"I'm not sure how much I can help you. She was born in nineteen forty-nine. Three days before Christmas. Baby boomer, I guess, though Frank wasn't in the war. He was sixteen when the Japanese bombed Pearl Harbor. My brother Giuseppe, he went to Germany, Poland. Never got to Italy like he wanted. Wasn't the same when he came back."

Living history in our greatest generation was one thing, but I needed to pull her back from a long and winding walk down memory lane.

"Why did you get divorced?"

"Because Frank wanted it. Got a new girl and was over me."

"Did *you* want it?" I asked. Just because one spouse had the right to divorce another, didn't mean it was easy.

"I was a guest of the Cleveland State Hospital." At my slight frown, she explained. "It was a mental institution. Back when they had those. I had a breakdown after the baby died. Plus I was taking pills back then. Prescribed, mind you. Mommy's little helpers everyone called them. Uppers. Downers. Frank blamed me for the baby's death."

"For SIDS?"

"They didn't have that back then. It was called crib death."

"What about visitation, then, with Lorraine?"

"He got full custody of Rainey. He got remarried. He had another daughter. I tried to see her, Rainey, but none of them wanted me in their lives."

"Rainey?"

"It was my nickname for Lorraine. Lori is her politician name, I guess."

"So you didn't see her. Haven't seen her for fifty years?"

"It's not like that. I...after I got out of the hospital, I didn't have anything to live for. I was staying with my parents. Then with my sister. I was the crazy, spinster aunt in the attic, when I wasn't out on the street. But I was also a drug addict."

Which explained how she looked. I couldn't help glancing at her arm, exposed by the loose t-shirt she was wearing. She'd zipped off her jacket at some point. The thick scars inside of her elbow confirmed the truth of what she was saying.

"How do you think your...absence affected Lor...Rainey?"

"I think she didn't care. The other times she...found me, she made sure to hammer that point home."

"Sometimes victims of trauma act that way. They always care deeply. At least that's what some of the experts I've interviewed have said."

"No. I'm telling you, my daughter, Rainey, didn't care."

I wanted to say, "how could you say that," but I was in the business of questions, not judgments.

"What makes you say that?" I asked. It was my go-to

question when something someone said didn't make sense to me.

"She's a sociopath, or maybe a psychopath. I could never make up my mind as to which."

I felt like the cliché of a therapist or a parrot, but plowed on nonetheless.

"What makes you think that?"

"She doesn't care about anything except power and control. Someone on *Sally Jessy Raphael* once called it the dark triad of pleasure, power, and profit."

That was pop psychology in a nutshell, reducing pathos to alliteration.

"When did you start thinking this?"

"When she was two? Three? I took her to the leading child psychiatrist at Cleveland Clinic. He said I was the problem. That if I had a second baby, then maybe I would be sufficiently occupied."

Mental health had come a long way. Sexism, not so much.

"You still believe it, though?"

"She killed my baby. No one in their right mind could do that without remorse. And believe me, she has none."

EIGHTEEN
LOGAN
NOVEMBER 13, 2009

"How did you get my number? My address?" Darlene Webb was standing outside of her apartment building's front door, hands spanning her waist. Classic cop stance. The plaid flannel shirt she wore over a turtleneck and jeans did little to hide the shoulder holster and weapon at her side.

Ambush may be the right word for what I was doing to her. I'd parked, gotten to her building, then called her from the sidewalk announcing my presence on her literal doorstep. She had hung up and come outside to meet or confront me, I still didn't know which.

"I came bearing gifts," I said while lifting a single shoulder in a shrug that I hoped was the opposite of intimidating.

"What?" Her question communicated her bewilderment.

I pulled a small paper bag from my jacket pocket. Thrust

it out toward her. Reluctantly Webb removed a hand from her hip and accepted it.

"Great wrapping," she said, sarcasm in full effect, as she opened the bag. Looked inside as if something was going to jump out and bite her. When she realized it wasn't alive, she took out the coaster I'd purchased at a novelty shop in a neighborhood full of them.

"Camp Crystal Lake?" she read. As she looked down at the cabin sketch and the tiny drops of fake blood, I could clock the exact moment when she got the joke.

"A little Friday the Thirteenth humor," I said in reference to the gift *and* today's date.

"You're lucky that I like camp movies." Webb allowed a very small smile.

"Camp...or *camp*?"

"Cheesy horror. My babysitter let me watch on Fridays when my mom and dad were working. She'd let me watch *Halloween* and even *Alien*."

"It's getting cold," I said. The balmy Indian summer daytime temps were quickly giving way to freezing nights. "Can we talk somewhere other than the steps?"

Webb looked me up and down as if assessing my capacity for violence. She had the same skeptical look that Blake Tatum had the first time I'd showed up to her place. After years on the force, I got it, police were sometimes considered armed and dangerous even to our own. I tried not to take it personally.

"C'mon in," she said, then turned toward the building. I assumed it was an invitation to follow to her apartment. She opened the living room door and I stepped in behind her. I was both surprised and charmed to find that the entire living room area was dressed up in autumn decorations including cornucopia of dried gourds, and fairy lights twinkling through a string of multicolored leaves along the molding.

"This is interesting," I said taking that in as well as the exposed brick wall of her living room and the outsized fireplace in her kitchen all of which I could see from the door.

"It's cheap," she said defensively. I wanted to backpedal and tell her my "interesting" was a compliment, not Midwestern passive aggression. "The rest of the folks here are medical students, so it's quiet. New building owners. Hoping they install some outlets." She gestured toward the wires snaking along the brick wall. "Extension cords shouldn't be my best friends."

"Can I sit?" I asked in response to her disjointed monologue. She nodded and I parked my butt in a wood-and-leather Ikea chair.

"Would you like something to drink?" she asked as if I were...almost...a welcome guest. "I have a coaster."

I felt myself relax a little at her small attempt at humor.

"What are the options?"

Webb walked over toward the open-plan kitchen. I wanted to ask if the fireplace was functional, but didn't think she'd want to talk architecture with her impromptu guest. I knew I should be grateful for the beverage offer. She opened the fridge, and bent her head to assess the contents.

"Club soda. Water. Fruit punch soda," she announced.

"Faygo pop?" I inquired. She answered by pulling the

colorful plastic bottle from the fridge. "I haven't had that in years. Bring it on."

She brought over a glass of bright red pop, placing it and the coaster on the small brass-and-glass table at my elbow. I took a big sip and it was like a walk down memory lane. Every organ in my nearly forty-three-year-old body would probably protest later, but for now, it was good.

"Why are you here?" Webb was done with small talk.

"Everyone seems to ask that question," I muttered under my breath.

"What?"

"Nothing." I hunched forward, steepled my forearms and fingers, elbows on my thighs. "You know I'm investigating Tia Wetzel, right?"

Webb's head shook almost before I could finish my question.

"I'm not familiar with the case." Webb's voice was carefully neutral. She'd go far in policing. Even farther if she was promoted up the command chain. "Is that why you were in Long's office?" she asked.

"Wetzel is a murder suspect. I was working with Long to get a warrant for cell phone records."

"Oh. Okay." She was still standing, hovering between the kitchen and living room. "I'm not even sure we should be talking about this."

I couldn't decide if Webb was in full "cop" mode or just bad at the kind of camaraderie cops usually shared. My own agenda still hazy in my mind, I decided to plow ahead anyway.

"You said something about a guy named Ja Roach being killed."

Webb nodded, but didn't speak.

"I think your case may be related to mine."

"How?" Her hands were back on her narrow hips.

"Who do you think murdered Sarah Pope?" Detectives often had a theory of a case that didn't one hundred percent jibe with the prosecutor's.

"Tyisha Cooley was indicted for that crime." Her answer made me think I wasn't wrong about Cooley's prosecution going against the grain.

"You didn't answer the question," I blurted. This dance with her was exhausting. I was getting an inkling as to why the interaction she'd had with Long was so terse and awkward.

"What are you getting at here?" When I didn't answer, she stood there for a long time coolly appraising me. "Do you know anything about me?"

"I only looked up your phone number and address. I didn't do any asking around if that's what you mean." What I didn't say was that she was a woman in a man's field and I knew the answers to questions about her would inevitably be tinged with sexism. There were still a lot of men on the force who thought women shouldn't be there. I wanted to meet her myself, make my own judgment.

"I used to be Cleveland police."

I smoothed my face against the surprise.

"Why did you switch?" Most cops did not go from big-city action to suburban boredom unless there was a good reason. She had neither of the two usual ones, having kids, or being close to retirement.

"It wasn't quite voluntary. Do you remember a guy named Troy Duncan?"

I wracked my brain, but couldn't exactly put a finger on it. "It sounds familiar—"

Webb didn't wait for me to puzzle it out. Instead, she made a swift motion with her arm cutting me off.

"Let me shortcut it for you. He was African American. My then partner, Marc Baldwin, shot him in an alley behind a restaurant in the Flats. Baldwin thought he was a gang-banger with a gun. Turns out Duncan was a chef with a knife roll."

I held up my hands when the memory of the civil unrest that followed came to me. "I remember now. What happened to Baldwin?"

"He put up a fuss about losing his job. I think he kept his pension. I had to stop following the case...for my own sanity. I didn't have anyone going to bat for me and I got screwed over by the city. This job was my consolation prize."

"I'm sorry it turned out that way." I was empathetic. Despite how it looked to the public, in the wake of the shooting of an unarmed man, someone somewhere often got sacrificed, and not always the person who deserved it.

"I broke the code, but I wasn't going to take the fall for something I didn't think was right. What I'm saying is that I'm not a cat. I don't have any more lives to give. The vibe I'm getting from you is that you want something I probably can't give you."

"Vibe?"

"You're here on a Friday. You came bearing gifts."

"I—"

"Tell you what. You get one free pass. We'll have this one conversation where you get to push whatever off your chest. Maybe I tell you if you're barking up the wrong tree. Then you go back to your job, and I go back to mine."

"Webb—"

"One chance. Don't waste it. Go."

One chance.

I considered my words. Whether to go in slowly, try to lead Webb down a Socratic path where she'd eventually jump to the conclusion I'd made, or get to it. I had a sense she was serious that I'd only get one bite at this apple. I decided to put it all on the table, go for broke.

"I think Lori Pope is a cold-blooded murderer. I believe that she's responsible for that guy Roach, for Cooley, and probably for more."

"You think *the* Cuyahoga County prosecutor is out putting needles in someone's veins and shooting people?"

"Maybe. Maybe not her. Maybe she's got cops on the take to do it for her."

"Are you accusing *me* of murder?" Webb took a defensive posture, stepping back while never breaking eye contact as if I were some drug-addled criminal.

"No. No. Sorry. I didn't mean to imply anything like that. It's just that Pope has all of us chasing our tails. Indicting the wrong people. Investigating the wrong people. Throwing suspicion on the wrong people."

"There's corruption at every level." Webb slow blinked.

"Why do people keep saying that?" Corruption was one thing. Straight up violent criminal behavior was a wholly different category.

"Because...it's true. We all do the best with the resources we have. Sometimes we get it wrong. Police get laser focused, then get it wrong. Prosecutors pile on, and then get it wrong. It's not a perfect system. It's the one we have."

I hated that butt-covering speech. Every cop and every prosecutor and every judge gave it. I wanted them to get it right, to not need to give the speech at all.

"It's way less than perfect. I get up every morning and fight against that. I try to be the change that I think the department needs. But that doesn't mean that I can sit back and allow a murderer to go free. Especially when it's someone who pulls all the strings like a puppet master."

"Fine. I hear what you're saying. Do you have any proof?"

Hunting Lori Pope was like trying to find snipe.

"That's where you come in," I said. "I need eyes and ears on the ground over here. I can't go it alone. If I say any of this to my partner or my boss, they'll crucify me."

"And what? You'll end up in Cleveland Heights or any of the other small suburbs surrounding the city."

As if inner-ring suburb was equivalent to exile. That was not my worst fear.

"No, not that. A murderer could go free. I need to stop it. *We* need to stop it."

I tried to look in her eyes to gauge her empathy. I wasn't

encouraged. Webb closed her eyes. Looked away. Shook her head slowly, but emphatically.

"I already gave one for the team," she said taking my glass to the sink, rinsing it slowly. Then she deliberately made long strides to the apartment door. Webb opened it wide. She stood there until I got the hint, stood, and walked toward the exit. Finally, she spoke again once I was in the hallway.

"Count me out."

The click of the door in my face brought the point home.

NINETEEN
NICOLE
NOVEMBER 14, 2009

"I didn't think you ate anything more than air," Valerie Dodds said while walking into my office. I didn't think I'd heard a knock. Maybe she thought that because it was Saturday, normal workplace habits could be relaxed. Maybe I should have closed my door all the way. I shuddered at the thought of being hotboxed in a haze of fast-food odors.

"Oh, I didn't think anyone was here," I said trying to chew and swallow the food already in my mouth, *and* keep it down.

After Pope's little stunt of giving me a drink followed immediately by ordering a breathalyzer, I was going cold turkey. I mean I'd had a drink immediately after the breath test. But I knew my continued drinking was unsustainable. Pope would catch me sooner or later. I wouldn't get a warning the next time.

These first forty-eight hours were killing me, though.

Sitting at home would have me adding bourbon to my coffee. I'd decided to go to work where there wasn't a hot and cold running supply of liquor. I'd stopped at a drive-through because my sudden carb craving came over me like a fog. Seeing her look askance at my food, I flipped the Styrofoam container closed flashing the golden arches.

"McDonald's food passing your lips seems well out of character," Dodds added.

It *was* out of character. I think I hadn't eaten at the fast-food joint since I'd gotten some fries at a drive-through with friends after an alcohol-infused prom. My mother had brought me up to live on air or as close to it as I could manage with indulgences to be saved for when men were around.

"Came in to do some work and got hungry along the way is all," I said as I pushed aside the Styrofoam container with the remains of the Big Breakfast I'd ordered from my car. There's no way Dodds would understand that filling up with carbs was the only thing standing between me and a drink.

Dodds' head tilted like a curious cat.

"Are you okay?"

I was until...I wasn't. Up in a flash, I started running down the hall toward the bathroom. I took off the blue spiral band at my wrist and jiggled the key in the lock all the while trying to swallow down the breakfast that was about to come back up. No matter how many times I twisted the brass, it wouldn't catch.

Dodds was somehow behind me. She snatched the key from my hand and got the door to open. Before I could thank her, I ran in to a stall, not bothering to shut it behind me. In a moment the hotcakes and sausage and bacon and hash-browns were all over the toilet and seat and floor. Dodds handed me a damp paper towel, then took my hair out of my hand, held the long strands away from contamination.

With the damp paper towels, I wiped my mouth and the seat as best I could before I stood. The automatic toilet flush echoed.

Dodds let go of my hair and I went to the sink. Used about a dozen more towels to clean myself off. Rinsed my mouth several times so it didn't taste like bile and bacon.

"You need to go home," Dodds said.

My hand shook. I took one with the other to hold it still.

"I have work to do," I said. "Grand jury this week."

Dodds' head moved slowly from side to side.

"We control the grand jury, not the other way around. You're coming with me." She put her hand on my back and steered me from the lavatory and back into my office.

"Pack up your stuff," she ordered while pointing to my open bag and the files spilled out on my desk.

"Seriously?"

"I'm taking you home."

"Why?" It wasn't my real question, but it was the only one I was comfortable asking.

"We have to flee the scene of the crime." Dodds' voice was conspiratorial. "If the janitors see us here, they'll be talking about us until the end of time. I don't want anyone assuming I was the drunk one."

Disappointment sagged my shoulders. For one long

minute, I'd thought she was going to take me up on my offer from a year ago to be friends, or at least to be something more than colleagues. In the end, she was like everyone else —protecting herself.

I let her pack up my stuff. Put my bag on one shoulder, the one she'd brought she picked up from my chair and added it to her other shoulder.

"I'm not drunk," I insisted because for once it was the truth. "I can—"

"Hungover, then. You overdid the carb cure."

"Actually, I'm clean, for real."

"You expect me to believe that?"

"Two days clean, then." At this moment, I was the most honest I'd ever been. "This is what withdrawal looks like."

"Shit. Seriously?" Dodds looked around with furtive glances. Her voice was a whisper. "Let's get out of here. I know it's the weekend, but these walls have ears."

Out of options, I followed her to the parking lot. She walked right past my 3 Series BMW to a white Honda Accord.

"What about my car?" My luxury car was still a bit of an anomaly in Cleveland. Made a lot of different people feel some type of way. I liked to keep a close eye on it.

"No cop who ever wants or needs a favor is going to allow a tow of a prosecutor's car from the Justice Center parking lot. They have our make, model, and plates. Get in."

Valerie Dodds drove west toward Lakewood like it was a job. Cars held her rapt attention. She signaled. She followed laws I didn't even know existed. Eventually, I directed her to one of my two parking spots under the building, then took the elevator from its depths all the way to my floor.

"You live on the thirteenth floor?" she asked after I pushed the number.

"Good thing I'm not superstitious," I said. I didn't tell her that I'd already been so unlucky in life that a little thing like triskaidekaphobia wasn't going to trip me up.

"Did you get a discount?" Her smirk was near enough to a smile that my cold heart melted a little bit. I was struck with a strong pang of longing. That little bit of warmth from a woman reminded me of my first days at Mount Holyoke, when we first-years stopped circling each other like feral cats and established trust.

All those other girls became each other's best friends. Back then, I wasn't yet in a place where I could trust anyone after everyone I'd ever loved had betrayed me. I wish something had been different all those years ago, could be different now. With all the warmth I could muster, I answered her question. Maybe these little confidences could put us on the path to friendship.

"I didn't negotiate a phobia discount. But the prices in Cleveland weren't too bad." I lived in one of two thirty-story apartment towers near the water, so it wasn't exactly cheap real estate, but it wasn't a brick suburban with a white picket fence that seemed to be the norm around here either. I didn't have a problem with a key this time. My door swung open after the lock turned smoothly.

It took Dodds a full thirty seconds to pick her jaw up from the floor

"I knew you were rich, but I didn't expect this. Though I probably should have. Underestimating people is a huge problem that I have. Overestimating too." She shook her head, then walked across the room to the wall of windows in my living room. "You have Lake Erie views for days."

"I have to sit down," I said as I dropped my bags on the floor, then myself onto the couch. My head was spinning, my stomach was roiling, and my heart was beating like I'd run a race.

"Where are they?" Dodds' voice had turned serious in an instant.

"Where are what?" I looked around as if bogeymen were going to jump from the built-in shelves under the windows.

"The bottles." Dodds' voice was dead serious. No awe at my view. No humor at our narrow escape from my bathroom shenanigans. No smile for superstition. I looked around, confused.

"I don't understa—"

"Look, I don't have the energy for bullshit. So just point me."

I got it then.

The jig was up.

Really up.

Holding my hair and giving me a ride had come with a price. The bill was about to come due.

"Cabinet over the microwave." I sighed, waited for her to go to the kitchen. Her stare was glacial. "Freezer," I added.

I couldn't watch good booze go to waste. I went to one of the built-in storage cabinets under the plate glass windows and got a hand-knit blanket I'd picked up at some artist festival on the east side.

Wrapped the chunky wool around me and looked at the "great view" that had sold me on this condo. I heard Dodds banging around the kitchen. There weren't any sounds of liquid pouring down the sink, so she was doing something else entirely.

Cooking.

She was using the pots and pans for their intended purpose.

In about ten minutes, my house smelled like my family's lifelong housekeeper—and biological mother—Aubrey was there. In another ten minutes, Dodds came into the room with a tray in hand. She slid it on the coffee table. A steaming bowl of grits stared at me with a soft-boiled egg, split with golden yolk exposed, on top. Next to it was what looked like a mug of herbal tea.

"I don't have anything red like this in my kitchen," I said looking down at the liquid in the cup.

"Rooibos tea. Supposed to be good for you. I carry bags in my purse. Drink it. This will be better for you than that fast-food crap."

Blinking away tears, I bent my head down and ate the hominy grits that tasted like Metairie. I even choked down the tea that tasted like boiled tree bark.

"You're really good at this," I complimented Dodds.

"What? Taking care of drinkers. Yes, I am. It's one thing I really wish I wasn't good at."

"Sorry."

"For what? Drinking too much? That's all on you. Nothing to apologize to me for. Probably a lot of other people though."

Dodds wasn't exactly shooting daggers at me, but the warmth from earlier had all but disappeared. If there was one thing I didn't want to have to think about...it was all those other people who'd been disappointed.

"For having to clean up after me. I feel bad for whoever's on Monday morning bathroom cleanup at the Justice Center."

She shrugged with the nonchalance of the privileged.

"I'm gonna guess this isn't their first rodeo either."

"Who did you have to manage?" I asked. It was a pretty personal question for a coworker, and my subordinate, but I thought we'd long passed pretending the superficial was our relationship.

"Mike Betancourt." I nearly dropped the bowl and spoon in my hand at the mention of the former prosecutor I'd hoped to make my boyfriend.

"You told me he didn't want to date me because *I* drank too much." She'd said to me as much a year and a half ago when I'd accused her of breaking the girl code.

"It triggered him. You triggered him. He thought you'd push him out of sobriety."

"You never mentioned he was an addict," I said as I had to sort and recharacterize all the memories I'd cast in one light.

"It wasn't my secret to tell, I guess."

"Why now?"

"You asked. This time, it's *my* story to tell."

"So did he start drinking again?" I tried to imagine the in-control lawyer I knew, losing control to a substance. My brain couldn't quite put the puzzle pieces together. He'd seemed like the kind of person without a single demon that needed alcohol to keep it at bay.

Dodds nodded. "He was always looking for some better situation. Something that didn't make him stressed or anxious. In the *legal* profession of all places. When he didn't find it in Cleveland or in D.C., he got solace from a bottle. I didn't wait around for him to fix himself or figure it out."

I guess that was the *other* half of the story. She'd said that Pope had recruited her here for optics, to have a high-ranking black face on the team. I'd never shared my background with Pope, so she'd never considered that a reason for keeping me around. Sadly, I couldn't see any upside to telling most people about my true heritage. Now I wondered if I could have used that to my advantage. That was the problem with decisions. They couldn't be unmade.

"So why are you here?" I was feeling better, so my question was sharp, pointed. "You were very clear that we're not friends."

"I'm not here to be your friend. That black-girl code you were spouting on about. Consider this your onetime pass. Even if your demise would help my career, I'm not that interested in you flaming out publicly. Suddenly the papers might find out you're a member of the tribe, as it were, and I'd spend the rest of my time here trying to make excuses."

"I'm not sure you can save me. I think my demise is inevitable."

It was the first time I'd uttered the truth out loud. What I really believed. I'd always assumed one day my fuckup would be too big, and I'd get fired. It was then, I guessed, I'd have to get my life in order. Until that happened, I'd kind of planned to cruise along hoping I'd have an epiphany.

"Look, Alcoholics Anonymous isn't for everyone." She pointed toward that million-dollar view I had never really enjoyed. "You look like you could afford some serious rehab, therapy, all that stuff to get your demons sorted."

"I thought my job would do that." My demons were bad men who did bad things. I'd always thought putting bad men who did bad things behind bars *was* sorting the demons.

"There's nothing external that can fix anyone's life. Except for money. That helps...a lot. But beyond money? It's an inside job," Dodds said. She was starting to sound like the magical black character who appeared in movies to drop some knowledge before the hero got back to figuring out stuff. That wasn't going to work here.

I needed her to understand why I was spiraling. I didn't have time for all this philosophical stuff. I got up, got myself a glass of water from the fridge dispenser, drank it down, then came back to the couch. She was sitting across from me, perched on a side chair I'd never used.

"Lori Pope wants me to indict Tyisha Cooley," I said to Dodds. She and I had been on the receiving end of the first directive to prosecute Cooley for the murder of the top prosecutor's sister. We'd been unsuccessful. I'm not sure I'd ever believed Cooley was guilty. Pope had insisted on prosecuting her based on the letter of the law, but not the spirit, and certainly not the policy of noninterference with drug overdoses Cuyahoga County's various law enforcement departments had adopted.

"For what this time?" Dodds asked. Outside of the office, her mask off, my colleague did nothing to hide her skepticism.

"The murder of Ja Roach."

"Did she do it?"

"Probably not," I said. I took a long pause. "Pope wants me to prosecute this other woman...Tia Wetzel for murder also."

"Did Wetzel do it?" Dodds asked again. I think it was telling that probable guilt was under scrutiny. The base assumption of our job was that we only went after the guilty.

"She has an alibi, Wetzel," I clarified. "Not bulletproof, but almost rock solid."

Dodds looked at the lake. Only the movement of her closed, pursed lips let me know she was debating the dilemma.

"You could leave it to the grand jury." Her shrug was half-hearted.

I gathered my hair and twisted it up into a bun. Snapped a crap scrunchie around it in response. "A good prosecutor can indict almost anyone," I said.

"Except for cops accused of police brutality, apparently."

I didn't want to touch that one with a ten-foot pole.

There was some truth to what she said, but we weren't talking about peace officers here. I tried to think of how to get through to her through the cotton wool in my own head slowing down my brain.

"When you were down there in D.C.," I started, "you worked as a public defender. You have to know that the promise of justice is a false one." Surprised at what had come out of my mouth, I backpedaled. "I'm not saying that we haven't put some bad guys away. I'm saying what we all know that the 'system' has biases that can be exploited by unscrupulous actors."

"What's going on for real?" Dodds leaned forward, her elbows on her knees. She squinted at me as if trying to bring something into focus. "It's like Pope is a record stuck on repeat."

"I think Pope had these people killed in revenge." My very short sobriety had weakened my filter.

Dodds went wide-eyed.

"Are you still drunk?"

I shook my head very slowly, very deliberately.

"I think the detectives on Roach and Wetzel are onto her. There's one from Cleveland Heights that I think has been suspicious for a couple of years." I left out the fact that I'd been the one to arouse Darlene Webb's suspicions. "One in Cleveland who's sniffing around." There was something about Loren Logan that wasn't easily swayed. Most detectives were happy to have a suspect and a ready-made case. He seemed to live for ambiguity.

"This is your evidence of Pope's master plan?"

"She killed Sister Danica Lozano." It was the first time I'd told that truth out loud. Admitted that we'd prosecuted a man guilty of many crimes, but innocent of that one.

"What the fuck? Did you add something to that rooibos? You sound batshit crazy."

"I think I need to tell you some things," I said. Then I explained the complicated history of Lori Pope. How I'd come upon her at the Lozano murder scene. All the things my boss had said implicating herself.

Dodds put her hands over her ears like a toddler.

"I didn't want to know any of this. You're telling me I quit my job defending the most vulnerable in one of the most prestigious offices in this country to come to corruption central. That I'm going to now be tied to a woman who's going to bring us all down or die trying. I need to get home and update my résumé."

Dodds actually stood up. Put on her red jacket, picked up her bag.

"You're actually going to leave?"

"Sooner rather than later."

"You just said in your grand exit speech that you had a job defending the most vulnerable. You should stay and help me do that."

She looked at me like I'd really gone over the edge. The thing is, I was feeling saner and clearer than I had in many, many years.

"Help you do what?" Dodds asked as she fiddled with the car keys in her pocket.

"We can't let Lori victimize more people." I heard passion

in my voice for the first time in a long time. "We could be the change from the inside. We could keep the wrong people out of jail."

"Then what?" Dodds asked. I could see she needed an endgame. She wasn't interested in setting herself on fire to keep anyone else warm. I didn't have a plan...yet. I just knew I could no longer be a spectator to injustice.

"Then maybe we could put Pope where she needs to be."

TWENTY
SEASON 2, EPISODE 4:
GRAND JURY

A ham sandwich. That's the joke. Lawyers claim that it's so easy for a prosecutor to influence a grand jury, that a savvy one could get those citizen volunteers to indict lunch. Some statistics conclude that less than one half of one percent of defendants escape grand jury indictment. The exception is the indictment of law enforcement officers, but that's a different podcast.

This is *The Murders Began*, with me your host, Blake Hardin Tatum.

In Cuyahoga County, Ohio, for which Cleveland is the county seat, at any time, there are four grand juries serving, each with fourteen members, one of whom is the foreman.

When most of us think about jury duty, we think of being called for a civil or criminal trial. The twelve in the box, so to speak. That's actually called a petit jury—the opposite of grand, I suppose. I wasn't paying that much attention in American Government.

It was ninth grade, I had a crush on a cute boy. The three branches of government didn't seem all that interesting compared to the curls at the back of his neck.

Anyway, let me tell you what I've learned as a journalist. These fourteen fine folks serve two days a week for four months. Local, state, and even federal law enforcement can bring a case. The prosecutor assigned to the grand jury calls the witnesses, presents evidence, and instructs the jurors on the law.

Then the jurors decide, based on the witnesses, police, and prosecutors, whether there's probable cause that the defendant committed the crime.

Probable cause is a legal standard that's far less than guilty beyond a reasonable doubt. It just has to be more likely than not that someone committed a felony.

If they vote to indict, they deliver a signed true bill which goes to the county clerk's office and to the defendant of course. Then a prosecution begins. Imprisonment for a felony can stretch from a year, to life in prison without parole, to...death.

The reason you probably haven't heard much about the grand jury is because unlike a majority of other court proceedings in this city, this county, even this country, they are done in secret.

The theory being that witnesses would be reluctant to come forward if this testimony and deliberation were made public.

The Fifth Amendment of our constitution provided for grand juries and nearly all of the U.S. states, including Ohio, use them.

This was not meant to be a civics lesson. I hope there was someone cute in front of you to keep you focused during the boring parts. Let's get back to our case for this season.

On November 24, 2009, Tia Wetzel was indicted for the aggravated murder of Malcolm Pointer, the man she'd made ziti for on their third date. She faces fifteen to life if convicted.

When I started this season, I planned to follow Wetzel as she sought out justice for what she claimed happened to her all those years ago: sexual assault and malicious prosecution.

As people sometimes say: plot twist. Any civil judge worth his or her salt will postpone her other matters pending the resolution of this one.

After more than twenty years as a reporter, I have a very strong belief that there are no coincidences. So my question is, did Wetzel commit murder as the ultimate act of self-sabotage or has she been framed a second time?

I'm on the hunt to get those answers. Tune in to the next episode of *The Murders Began* to follow me on this journey to unravel all of this and get to the truth.

TWENTY-ONE
BLAKE
DECEMBER 10, 2009

I'd shown up to Justin McPhee's office unannounced. Somehow Loren Logan had wrapped me up in his belief that we could get justice if we somehow got everyone with a stake in it on our side. He'd seen the police detective from Cleveland Heights, Darlene Webb. I'd agreed to approach the defense attorney.

The old building was so warm there was condensation on all the windows that weren't cracked open to let in cold air.

"I know this is unusual..." I started as I took off my coat so I didn't pass out from a sudden hot flash.

"Highly unusual," McPhee echoed. He hadn't stood from his chair when I'd let myself in. Since he hadn't ejected me immediately, I took a seat on a chair across from him.

When I was a kid, I'd have done anything to make sure I wasn't in the spotlight. I hated when teachers called me up to the blackboard, or when I had to ask a store clerk for something. That shyness or reticence wasn't something that was allowed to last once I'd graduated with a journalism degree in hand. I'd gotten over it quickly. Probably in some ways I'd overcompensated. Nowadays I was uncompromisingly bold.

"So you're representing Tyisha Cooley." It was half statement, half question that left room for any number of responses.

"I do criminal defense work," McPhee hedged.

"You represented Libby Saldana last year."

"That's a matter of public record." This attorney certainly knew how to hold something confidential. If I ever needed a vault, he would be it. For now though, I needed his buy-in. I took out my notebook, checked my notes for today's... ambush...and pressed on.

"Those cases had a supposed hot shot in common. And yet, neither woman went to jail for that."

"Pleas to lower charges are common."

"I did some research on you, Mr. McPhee."

"I don't think—"

He half stood ready to toss me out on my ear or my ass more likely.

"Please." I held up my hands to silence him, keep him from hitting the eject button on my visit. "Let me speak my piece. I used to be a reporter with the *Plain Dealer*. Got laid off. Yada yada. I've been working on some criminal and civil cases for my blog and podcast. Last year, I reported on the Quinn case. I think I sent you an interview request. You refused." I batted away any possible explanations or excuses he might offer. "It's fine. Lots of people say no to me. Lots say yes. It evens out in the end."

I stopped talking because I was definitely having diarrhea of the mouth. Usually, I didn't act like this. Something about the scope of the problem had me on edge. We...me, Logan, Justin, all of us had jobs where we tended to keep our cards close to our vests. But a conspiracy of silence was exactly what had let Lori Pope run roughshod over rules, and law, and justice up until now.

"And you're here because..." McPhee's impatience was starting to show.

"I don't want to interview you. Not right now at least. I'm working on deep background for my current investigation."

"Who or what are you investigating?"

I was quiet for a long moment. I looked the attorney in the eye. I didn't trust many lawyers. I didn't trust too many people. My job had leeched faith out of me. At some point, I had to take a leap. Jumping was the only way to get somewhere on this case.

"Lori Pope."

McPhee's eyes widened for only a millisecond. Except for that slight movement of his lids, he kept up a poker face.

"Go on."

"I know this meeting isn't confidential. It can't be."

"Why couldn't it be?"

"Because you're going to need to share what I tell you. How you dole it out is up to you."

McPhee looked at the shelf to my left. I followed his eyes and saw a small clock between some thick hardback books.

"Okay, there was a whole lot of a preface and introduction. You're here. Let's get to it."

He got comfortable in his high-backed leather chair. I relaxed a little knowing that he'd hear me out, at least.

"There's something hinky with Lori Pope. My working hypothesis is that she's using the office to get revenge at people who've wronged her in some way. Your client Cooley is a perfect example. She thinks, rightly or wrongly, that Cooley killed her sister and is going to find some way, any way to put her in jail."

"Wrongly? How does that play out here?"

"I think she had Ja Roach killed."

I could see a flicker of something change in the lawyer. In spite of himself and probably a dozen years of skepticism, he believed me. Maybe *believed* was too strong a word, but the truth in what I was saying, spoke to him.

"Jesus fucking Christ. I'll be the first to say that prosecutors can do some shady shit. Murder? That's a new one."

"Well, your client's been indicted for the murder of Roach. If she didn't do it, then who did?"

McPhee shrugged, closed off again.

"I'm looking into that," I offered.

"You?" His skepticism was in full force. I think people always underestimated the power of the press. "You don't have a badge or a gun or an investigator's license."

"Neither do a bunch of the citizen investigators that have popped up in the last few years thanks to the Innocence

Project and the interest in true crime, yet some of them are pretty effective."

"What else is there to your theory?" He'd picked up a paper clip and was tapping it on his desk pad. His patience was running out.

"Did you know that a woman named Liberdad Saldaño was the victim of a murder-suicide a few weeks ago."

McPhee's chair hitting the wall behind him gave away his surprise.

"What was her name?"

"*Your* client was Elizabeth Saldana. You represented her last year on a case similar to Cooley's. A woman accused of giving someone a hot shot. I think your former client was a Pope target, but it was a case of mistaken identity."

"It wasn't a sudden interest in opioid deaths," McPhee said under his breath.

"Is that the excuse you got? That Lori Pope wanted to be hard on drugs despite the county commissioner and interde-partmental police policy not to arrest or prosecute overdose cases."

"That was our best guess," McPhee admitted.

"You don't think I'm crazy, then."

"I'm not qualified to give clinical diagnoses. I know that Pope can be petty, though."

It was a crack in his veneer. I wanted to put in a wedge.

"How so?"

"She low-key pushed me into testifying against Monsignor Quinn."

It was my turn to raise my own eyebrows.

"You didn't think you could say no?"

"She didn't leave a lot of room for it."

"Did you want to do it?"

"Even without her, I should have done it. I owed it to the other guys."

"Think about how you felt. Then think about how someone without your education, credentials, and experience would feel in the face of Pope."

"Even if I believe you. What do you want me to do? I'd need something more solid than conjecture to even begin to allege prosecutorial misconduct."

"Legal strategy is not my area of expertise, but I think it's in your clients' best interest to delay anything where Pope is on the other side. If I'm right, I don't see the prosecutor lasting more than a few more months," I said with way more confidence than I had. "Both are on bail, so it's not like you have three months. You have nine."

"What are you going to do while they're cooling their heels?"

"Catch a murderer."

TWENTY-TWO
LOGAN
DECEMBER 11, 2009

Blake Tatum hadn't acted the least bit surprised when I'd turned up on her doorstep at six on a Friday night. I half worried that she'd be out, on a date, having fun. Instead, she answered the door, and waved me in and offered up dinner. Setting the table was the least I could do, so while I figured out where the plates and utensils were kept, she lifted fried seafood from a huge cast-iron pot bubbling with oil.

I cleared a spot on the dining room table for the two of us, and tried not to drool over the platter of food she brought in laden with toasted baguettes, shredded lettuce, sliced tomatoes, onions, and tartar sauce. I happily assembled then dug into the hot shrimp and oyster po'boy.

"This is really good," I said right before the last bite. "I've never had it with both shrimp and oysters."

"It's called a peacemaker with the two. Had a craving." Tatum wasn't a self-conscious or delicate eater. I liked that about her. That she was exactly the same person, clear on what she wanted and who she was, in every situation.

"You made enough for two?" I gestured between our plates which had been full before we decimated the meal.

"Well, you like to come by, so I doubled the recipe." Tatum looked at me wide-eyed. Guilt at being a bad guest flooded through me.

"Really? Should I have brought something. I didn't realize I—"

Tatum's laugh broke through my confessional. She tipped back a dark brown bottle. Polished off the remainder of her spiced ale. I was still nursing mine.

"No, no. When I cook, I always make enough to freeze for later. Consider yourself lucky that you came on a cooking day and not a defrosting a single-lady-portion day."

"Very lucky, I'd say."

"It's a Louisiana special."

"I used to go down there all the time," I offered. "My ex was from New Orleans. Her family was in the city for generations before Katrina." I wasn't always so forthcoming, but something about the good food and cold beer loosened my tongue.

"Was her family affected in any way?"

"Jefferson Parish flooded." I finished my own beer then, hoping the alcohol could assuage my guilt. The memories of that time were mostly bad. "Tonya, my ex, had been glued to the television set and the phone waiting for word. I'd been no comfort because we'd just been at our final divorce hearing, right before the levees broke. Had newly signed papers in our hands when the levees broke. I was packing up to be in my new place on September first in time for school. Clementine had been horribly sad." I poked at the stray lettuce on my pate. "Most of them rebuilt," I said when I realized I'd been quiet too long. "But it took a long time. The rest went to Houston and stayed."

"Hard situation." Her voice was full of empathy. "How long have you been divorced?"

"Four years. We tried to keep it together for my daughter, but we broke up her senior year of high school."

"Sounds stressful."

"I threw myself into work. With no one to go home to, it was finally time to make the move to detective. More money. More autonomy. I could do some real police work."

Tatum stood to clear the table. I scooped up what I could and helped her scrape plates and load the ancient dishwasher.

"Speaking of," she said while washing her hands, then applying lotion from a bottle on the counter. My wife had done the exact thing after dinner cleanup. I pushed away the memories and tuned back in to Tatum. She was saying, "Can you believe they indicted Wetzel? This feels so crazy. Didn't you get the location information from AT&T?"

She handed me a bakery box to take back to the dining room, while she mucked about in the kitchen.

"I did," I said as I put the box on the table. Took a peek. Beignets. It was all things Louisiana apparently. "Turned it all over to Nicole Long. She said it wasn't a solid enough alibi."

Tatum came in with a French press full of coffee.

"Decaf," she said as she set it on the table. She went back for mugs and half-and-half. She took a seat, then gathered all the papers and documents she'd set aside for dinner. "Do you think that's true?"

"Which part?"

"The alibi? Was it believable?"

"It wasn't unimpeachable. The towers showed that Wetzel pinged at her house. Then later near the market. Then back home again maybe fifteen minutes after that."

The evidence had confirmed Wetzel's story, but wasn't beyond reasonable doubt territory. Long had been quick to point out that Wetzel could have planned the call, especially coming from an unknown number as it had. Or she'd had help. Someone, Long surmised, could have taken her phone, Tia Wetzel killed her date, then they brought the phone back.

"But she wasn't home when he was murdered?" There was hope in Tatum's question.

"The timeline isn't perfect. I'm sure Long is going to argue that it was possible that she could have done all that to create an alibi. It's also possible the time of death wasn't precise. Or Wetzel could have gone to the market and she'd had something prearranged to have someone kill Malcolm Pointer."

I sighed. Admitted, "Technical and forensic advance-ments gave us so much more information. But even all of that could be argued both ways."

"A trial of dueling experts, assuming she can afford

them," Tatum said before making notes. I nodded in resignation. "Got it. So this Wetzel case isn't going anywhere."

"Except for her to trial and possibly prison. Unless—" I shrugged.

"Unless what?"

"We find the murderer. Get evidence of means, motive, opportunity. A smoking gun."

"Seems like a *you* job more than a *me* job." Tatum pushed down the coffee filter, then filled two mugs. She opened the box and put the pastries on a blue ceramic plate. We each ate one, though I wanted two. I'd lost weight after the divorce. I missed the camaraderie of evening conversation over dessert.

"I hear what you're saying," I acknowledged. "It'll move faster if we're both poking around. I'm doing this off book. Which means I have my regular caseload as well."

I waited. I knew Tatum wanted this scoop as much as I wanted Pope, but I was an unknown factor to some degree. She sipped more coffee, sighed. With that huff of breath, I knew she was in.

"Fine. But this better pay off. I don't have my day job anymore."

"So we get help." I'd come up with an answer to any possible objection well before I'd put a toe on her doorstep because I knew in my gut she could do more for the case than any cop or prosecutor. What I'd learned over these last months was that Tatum cared about the truth and justice, even if she'd deny it to my face. It's why she'd struck out on her own rather than take a job in public relations or corporate communications.

"Help?" Tatum's face pulled into a frown. "Who are you planning to bring in on our crazy scheming? Half the time I think we're on the right track. The other half, I wish the Cleveland State Hospital were still open. Maybe we could get a rubber room together."

"Speaking of, nothing else from Pope's mom?"

"She thinks her daughter's batshit crazy. That we're probably not far off. This, of course, from a woman who's been in said institution many times over after they changed the name from the Northern Ohio Lunatic Asylum."

Tatum pulled her notebook closer, slipped on nearby reading classes. Flipped a page.

"When Anna Moretti got out of the institutional cycle, her illustrious days were spent as a drug addict. First pills, then heroin. Sure she's been clean for ten years, but I'm not thinking there are too many people who would take her seriously given what happened between twenty-five and seventy."

"Forty-five years. Geez, it's amazing she's still alive."

"Tough as nails, some of these people are. What Moretti told me is what we'd call deep background when I worked at the paper. Information that helps, but can't be quoted. So where are we, Logan? What happens if we just leave this alone? Maybe focus only on Wetzel. No Pope. No Cooley. No Roach. None of all this other stuff."

Tatum had taken off her glasses, folded the turquoise-blue frames on the notebook she'd closed.

"Then the system goes on like it always does. Some people get justice. Most people get jail. Innocent people go to prison. Can you live with that?"

I was having a hard time living with it myself. As my daughter got older and moved out into the world, I was having a very hard time leaving things the same as they'd always been. I didn't know how anyone with kids could.

"Live with the status quo? The way it's been for what feels like forever? I sleep just fine most nights."

Tatum had a point that was almost as valid as my own. The system was a behemoth that the Innocence Project and Pulitzer Prize–winning stories only nibbled around the edges of injustice.

"Look, I'm not so hopeful as to think that suddenly we're going to fix the criminal justice system," I admitted. "I think we owe it to this handful of people to not let Pope get away with any more crimes that send any more innocent people to jail."

"What if you're wrong...on Pope. I mean, where's the why? Revenge is best served cold. I get that. But who waits ten, twenty, thirty years to get back at someone? It's crazy."

"You said her mom put her in the psycho box."

"Is there some other explanation? Are you seeing bogeymen where they don't exist?"

"Occam's razor."

"Your basis is a philosophy aphorism that the most obvious explanation is usually the right one."

"And a very strong hunch. Did you do the thing you said you would?"

After I'd left, Tatum had called me with her plans to put the cases in a bigger context. It had seemed like a big project, but I assumed she had the chops.

"Review every indictment over from Pope's Cuyahoga County prosecutor's office for the last eleven months? That's almost *all* I've been doing in the last three and a half weeks."

Tatum flicked her hand toward a towering stack of papers separated by different-colored pages and thick binder clips.

"And?"

"From what I can tell, they're all straight. From the police reports filed before the indictments, the defendants either stole something, or sold drugs, or assaulted a victim, and so on from the felony menu. All the crimes and indictments are fairly close in time. Most of the ones from the beginning of the year have pled or gone to trial. A few acquittals, not strict innocence per se, but because of run-of-the-mill reasonable doubt.

"And the outliers?" I searched for a short stack, but didn't see any.

"These." Tatum gestured to the list of names she'd written on the dry-erase board when I'd been here last.

"Then it's time for the justice system to work to make our city, our county safer."

"Great speech, so what do we do next?"

We'd gotten to the hard part. I knew she probably wasn't going to like what I had to say. But I'd come at this from all angles and could see only one path forward.

"We need to do two things," I said. "One easy. The other hard."

"Start with the easy."

"Find Wetzel's date's murderer."

"Geez." She dropped her pencil, made no pretense of writing that one down. "If that's the easy part, what's the hard part?"

"We need to loop in Nicole Long."

"We fuck with her in the wrong way, then we'll be the ones hiring defense lawyers and facing jail time. In all the years I've observed her, she didn't seem stupid, maybe drunk, but not stupid. If Pope is corrupt, then Long is her right hand. Have you lost your ever-loving mind?"

"I don't think so."

"You know something I don't?"

"I think Webb is our way in."

"That Cleveland Heights detective who refused to talk to you?"

"I say we get Long, Webb, you, and me all together and make a case that we need to work to take down Pope."

"You know the saying that 'a secret isn't a secret once you tell someone'?"

"Sure."

"My momma always said that. Your plan is the equivalent of putting up a billboard on Euclid Avenue announcing that we're going up against the powers that be." She pushed back from the table. Took a long pause. "You know what? I'll just find some keys and put myself into county lockup."

"There's a different phrase my own mother used to use."

"What's that?"

"Many hands make light work."

"That's about gardening and washing dishes. Maybe folding clothes. I hate folding clothes. Should we ask Webb and Long to help me fold clothes?" Tatum's voice was laden with sarcasm, but I could hear the fear underneath. She was right that this situation could be volatile. That my plan could add a fuse to a powder keg. Blowing up. Leaving us all with collateral damage.

"No reason we can't use all the resources available to crack a case of the worst malfeasance I've ever seen," I said trying to keep my voice calm and even, hopefully convincing.

"That's a triple-word-score Scrabble word if I ever heard one."

Tatum was saying a lot of things, but she wasn't saying no.

"So are we doing this?" I probed as gently as I could, leaving her room to say no.

"Yahtzee!" Tatum threw her arms in the air.

"Different game. Either way, I think we'll come up winners with my strategy."

"Lead me to my cell, sir. I think you came equipped with handcuffs." She put her wrists together, and for the first moment in weeks, I wasn't thinking of Lori Pope.

TWENTY-THREE
NICOLE
DECEMBER 24, 2009

I checked the Post-it on my dashboard against the number on the building. I'd thought I was going to Logan's house, but this was a school. I couldn't find the institution name anywhere, but the sun was already dipping below the buildings even though it was only four in the afternoon. The dark shadows on bricks made it impossible to read any signs or metal letters affixed to the façade. Resigned to figure it out on foot, I picked a visitor space, and parked.

Someone came out before I had to figure out how to get through the front door. Even though wide corridors were empty, it took no energy to imagine it filled with students. It looked like a set from a high school drama. Logan said to come to 307, so I took all the stairs to the third floor. I walked down the hall from one classroom door to another until I landed at the right one.

I took one deep breath, then another. I did not like walking into something unknown. I especially did not like walking into a strange man's apartment. Even if I was a prosecutor and that man was a cop. Logan hadn't said why he wanted me to come, but his tone had been so urgent on the phone that I went against my better judgment because he seemed likeminded, especially after the Gregory Quinn murder case. He wanted the bad people in jail as much as I did.

All the way over here to the east side from Lakewood, I'd thought about turning around. I could be in my own apartment doing the obligatory calls to family. Gritting through sobriety. Trying to figure my own way out of Lori Pope's grip. Justice was important, but maybe self-preservation needed to come first.

I trudged through the school hallway until I found a door that matched the number I'd written down. At least this would be a distraction from all that I wanted to avoid.

"Merry Christmas," Logan greeted me when he opened the door.

"This is an actual apartment," I said when I walked in to his living room decorated with a huge gray sectional over a bright blue oriental carpet. There was even a roaring fire at one end. "A fireplace? In a school?"

"It was added, like the kitchen and bathrooms...and the loft I use for an office." He pointed above our heads. Steps on the side of the living area led to a half floor where I could see a computer and other office stuff. "The nearly hundred-year-old wood floors and windows and doors are all original. The developers also converted a church in Cleveland Heights.

There was a gorgeous unit with two-story stained glass. Got outbid on that one."

"I've only seen factories and warehouses repurposed. This is my first school. What's up with the street name?"

Logan laughed. "When I moved, no one I called with the change of address believed me."

"When I put Random Road in MapQuest, I thought it was going to throw an error, or Abbott and Costello were going to pop up on my computer and do a routine." I shrugged. There was a pause and we both laughed at the idea of a Cleveland-themed "Who's on First" improvisation. "But here I am."

"Show yourself around," Logan said. "I'll make you something to drink."

"Nonalcoholic, please." I was proud of my ask.

"Absolutely."

There was a built-in sideboard laden with food in aluminum pans. My mouth started watering when I lifted one of the foil lids to peek. Looked like Italian, which considering we were a single block from Mayfield Road, was appropriate.

"Damn, there's a lot of food in here. Who else is coming?"

"Yeah, about that." Logan looked shifty for a moment. "Just a few people."

"Is this going to be a party or is it a meeting about... work." He'd told me it was some mystery he wanted to solve. I'd thought he meant real-life crime. But now I had to wonder if he'd invited me to one of those cheesy parties where everyone plays a character in a locked room mystery. A little part of me was thrilled that someone wanted to be my friend. Especially given my reputation around the courthouse.

"A bit of both, maybe," Logan hedged.

I took his invitation to show myself around and strode down the hall while he went to the kitchen. There were a couple of bedrooms. I assumed the one with the black bedspread was Logan's. There was another that looked like a woman had been in there.

Curious.

Nope, none of my business. I heard voices. Showtime. I pulled myself together, becoming the proper southern woman I'd been raised to be, and came back through.

"It's two converted classrooms," Logan was saying to a black woman who looked vaguely familiar.

"Blake Hardin Tatum," she introduced herself. Stretched out her hand.

Without bourbon, my mind was surprisingly sharp. I let her know I clocked her.

"Reporter," I said. "You were at one of the Quinn crime scenes."

"Nice to see you again." Tatum and I shook briefly. "Wish it were better circumstances, maybe."

Was it too late to turn back? Tatum's tone gave me a weird sensation. I could walk out the door and pretend I'd never been there. My growling stomach had different ideas. It wanted a real meal and not table water crackers smeared with salmon cream cheese spread.

"I think I'm going to help myself to some of this food," I

said to the room. Took myself to the little bar area next to a dining room table for four.

Logan had pressed some button when a buzzer sounded. Three minutes later, he opened to a knock. This time Justin McPhee and Darlene Webb came in. I had to admire the detective's ability to keep a secret because I was surprised to see those two. I raised an eyebrow in greeting. Disregarded the idea that we'd be dressing up, doing fake accents, and solving a drawing room murder. So much for new friends. It was the same old people. Same old problems.

"I was in Italy a couple of years ago on Christmas Eve with my daughter," Logan was saying to McPhee and Webb as he pointed them to the food. "It was a great spread, so I wanted to share something like it tonight. Especially as we're here together instead of with friends and family."

"Did you cook?" Tatum asked.

"*No way*. I'm a stone's throw from Little Italy." He made a small flourish toward the food. "So we have for an appetizer, smoked salmon involtini, seafood risotto for a first course, eggplant parmesan for the main, sauteed mushrooms and roasted pumpkin for sides. Panettone for dessert. I have a lime-and-coconut cocktail or mocktail, driving..." Logan's eyes flicked toward me. "Let's eat before we get to it."

I took a little of everything grateful to have homestyle food. Although if I continued to eat my meals instead of drinking them, I'd have to wear something other than my signature pencil skirts to work.

The dining room only had four chairs, so we ended up gathered around the coffee table on the couch and the plush blue side chairs. It was quiet except for forks against plates. As the only southerner in the room, I felt a need to bring some civility to the party. My parents had a lot of flaws, but being bad hosts was not among them.

"Do you have a daughter?" I directed my question to Logan. "That second bedroom definitely had 'teen girl moved on' vibes."

"Clementine." He nodded. "She's a sophomore in college."

"Where?" I asked. The school a child went to either said a lot about the parents or a lot about the child. My sister went to LMU like Mommy and Daddy, that said a lot about them and their legacy. I went to Mount Holyoke which I think said a lot about me being very different from them in more ways than I'd known at the time I'd made the choice.

Logan pulled a phone from his shirt pocket, fiddled with the screen. I put out my hand getting a generic compliment ready.

"Here's a picture she texted me from a holiday party with friends. She's at Wilberforce, about three hours from here."

Tatum's brows shot up as she put her food on the table. Then she practically snatched the device from Logan's hands before he could tilt it toward me for viewing. I tried to puzzle out what the source of surprise was.

"Your daughter's...pretty," Tatum said, then she handed back the phone. There seemed to be a lot unsaid. I took the phone as it was passed. One look and it became crystal clear what was up. It jogged my memory. Wilberforce was a historically black college. One of the few north of the Mason-

Dixon Line, and maybe even the first in the country or the second. That particular fact I couldn't remember. One of the early ones at least. It had come up in some class I took on critical social thought.

I was trying to decide if it was time to say something about myself, but I hadn't yet mastered how to work it into the conversation without sounding like I was pandering or being disingenuous. I swallowed the last bite of eggplant, and stood ready to somehow reveal myself.

"My mom is black," I blurted.

Tatum's head swung around. Logan looked like he wanted to say something. When a knock came, no one seemed to care about my parents. The revelatory moment gone, I made to clean up.

Before I took my plate to the bar area or kitchen, I paused as Logan's long legs ate up all the area between the chair he'd been sitting on and the door. All of us looked as he twisted the handle. I had to imagine they felt like I did, half scared Lori Pope would be standing there flanked by officers, their guns drawn.

I took my stuff to the sink, rinsed my dishes. From the corner of my eye, it looked like a neighbor was bringing over a small gift. Logan came back in, lifted something from under the tall tree he had next to the fireplace, and gave it to the twenty-something man. They did that male hug where no one got too close, then closed the door.

By then, whether we were full or not, I think we were all done pretending this was some kind of impromptu party of people who liked each other. I helped Logan gather the rest of the plates when no one made to ask me a single thing.

"You need me to load the dishwasher?" I asked.

"I'll do it later. I think it's time we all talk."

I stacked the others' dishes on top of mine and nodded, but I didn't walk back to the main area.

"You want coffee?" Logan offered as he turned his back to the sink and crossed muscled arms across his chest.

What I wanted was a real ninety-proof drink, not a sweet mocktail or a hit of caffeine. But with Lori Pope's completely random weekly testing, I couldn't take the risk.

"I'm good. Let's do this."

TWENTY-FOUR
SEASON 2, EPISODE 5:
AN INFORMANT OR A VICTIM

This is *The Murders Began* with your host, me, Blake Hardin Tatum. During this season, we've talked a lot about Tia Wetzel. Now we're going to turn to the other crime which was indicted on the same day. I staunchly believe the accusation that Tyisha Cooley murdered Ja Roach is related to Wetzel's indictment for the murder of Malcolm Pointer.

On today's podcast, I think it's time to get to know one of the victims.

This weekend I had the opportunity to interview the

next of kin who came to identify Ja Roach. The county doesn't require the truly closest relation, but who the victim listed as an emergency contact, the person Roach wanted to be the first to know if anything happened.

That's a pretty special position. I don't have one at the moment. I broke up with my long-term boyfriend and need to replace his name with someone else's. When you think about it for a few days, or weeks, you begin to realize how important the choice is.

Shani Wilson is Roach's younger sister by about twenty months. I interviewed her at her brother's Lakewood apartment while she sorted and packed his things.

"Ms. Wilson. Thanks so much for speaking with me."

"I don't want my brother's life to be forgotten."

"What is the first thing I should know about Ja Roach?"

"That his name wasn't Ja. It was Jabari. It's Swahili for valiant. My father gave us both strong names."

"What does Shani mean?"

"A wonder, a marvel."

"That's gorgeous," I said. "How did he become Ja?"

"I don't know. I think it's something he used in his other life."

"Other life?"

"The drug life. He was an addict."

"What was he like when you were young?"

"He was a nerd. Skinny kid who liked comics and those fantasy books with dragons and shit. Oh, can I swear on here?"

I nodded. She continued, "We called them square back then."

"When did things change?"

"You mean when did he start using drugs?"

"Do you remember?"

"I was about thirteen. We were living in Hough."

"How many people were in your family?"

"There were four of us kids. My parents were Catholic. One day I came home from school band practice or maybe from playing at someone's house. I don't remember. I was just later than usual. When I walked in the back door, my father was screaming. It was so weird because he wasn't the kind of man who raised his voice."

"Had something happened?"

"My dad had walked in on Jabari with a boy."

"Walked in..."

"His room. He was the only boy and the oldest and had his own room. I know this isn't a big deal now with gay marriage laws and pride parades, but Jabari was gay."

"Your parents didn't throw him out or something?"

"No. That would have raised too many questions with the neighborhood, with the church. They said he could stay and everything could go back to normal as long as he didn't do anything perverted."

"That sounds hard."

"He was a fifteen- or sixteen-year-old boy. I'm sure he had all sorts of urges and had nowhere to go with that. A few months later I came home from school. It was so quiet, too quiet. Jabari was usually home early on Wednesdays. He played loud music. Rock and roll that drove my parents crazy. I knew I probably shouldn't go to his room. Mom had told me that boys needed a lot of privacy. I was curious, though. So I went up there. He was there with a boy. But this boy, he looked rough. You know the type."

"Describe the type for me."

"Like his hair was knotty. Kind of like those slave pictures when they had no combs or something and were working in the fields. His fingernails were dirty. His legs under his jeans were rusty. I thought they were asleep. But that didn't look right. People didn't sleep leaning up against stuff kind of cockeyed. Not unless they were those drunk guys on the street corner. Anyway, I stepped over him and shook my brother. He had some kind of needle on the floor with a tie from his Sunday church clothes. His eyes were kind of half open. He wasn't asleep, but not awake either."

"Did you know it was drugs? Did you think it was heroin?"

"All the antidrug stuff hadn't happened yet. I mean we heard of singers and comedians doing it, but the actual logistics of the whole thing was a mystery."

"So what gave you the heads-up?"

"The guy he was with. That Jabari sort of...left us mentally. He came to dinner, I mean Daddy required that. But he didn't talk. Not about *The Fellowship of the*

Ring or *Fire From Heaven*. They were kind of boring, but he was so passionate about these stories."

"He liked books?"

"Not every drug user starts out like they end up."

"What else changed?"

"His room started to get really empty. The saxophone my parents had bought him for Christmas, gone. The stereo, gone. I'm ninety percent sure that I saw his stuff in the pawn shop window. I was only a seventh grader, but even I was able to put two and two together."

"How long did he stay at home?"

"Maybe six months after that? He didn't bring a guy home, but there were rumors that he got caught out in the street with a guy who everyone knew was..."

"A known homosexual."

"He was the kind of guy who didn't hide who he was. Flamboyant, you know. He was out in a world where everyone else was locked in a closet or had moved to New York or something."

"Where'd he go? Ja...Jabari?"

"That guy's apartment, at first. But that guy wasn't about relationships, I guess. I think my brother thought he'd found love. He was wrong or naïve or maybe deluded by the drugs. He lived with some guys, but when they found out about him, they beat him up. The neighborhood was changing then, so he was holed up in some abandoned places. I didn't always know where he was."

"Were you the only one in the family talking to him?"

"I think he secretly talked to my mother sometimes.

But she couldn't say anything because Daddy couldn't know."

"Did she know you saw him?"

"No. We all operated independently. I made food and brought it for him. Told anyone who asked that I was practicing my cooking and baking for when I got married and had kids."

"People believed that?"

"From a teenaged girl, it made everyone smile. It also kept people from asking about my grades when they weren't top notch."

"Do you know when your brother met Lori Pope?"

"Not exactly. He got arrested, and I freaked out. It's the one time I broke the family rule of not talking about him. Daddy said he deserved it. Before Daddy left for work one day, Mom said she was sick."

"She wasn't?"

"No, she got me from school and talked about how we could get money together for bail and a lawyer. But when we got to the jail, he wasn't there. Then we went to wherever he was living, and he was just home. Sitting on a shitty couch."

"How did he get out?"

"He said he'd agreed to narc on some dealer."

"Were you at all suspicious?"

"It wasn't perfect. I mean we worried that the dealer would find out and get him.

"He said they'd protect him, but I didn't believe it. He

was a black drug addict. They were white cops and prosecutors."

"But he didn't die."

"No, he never went to jail. The charges were dropped. He got this loft when that building was renovated. After that he never asked for money. I mean, you can see he didn't have a lot of stuff, but he wasn't starving."

"You still brought him food?"

"I'd perfected my cooking on him. Drug addicts never seem to remember to eat."

"Did you try to get him clean?"

"In the beginning, maybe. But I got older, and by the eighties, there was tough love and letting addicts hit rock bottom."

"He never hit bottom, though."

"I think he did on that Saturday night, on October third."

"When he was murdered?"

"Drugs are not the only thing that kill addicts."

"Who do you think murdered Jabari Roach?"

"I'm not a psychic, so I don't for sure know who did it. But I'm one hundred percent sure Tyisha Cooley didn't pull the trigger."

"How can you be so sure?"

"Because Jabari knew his days were numbered long before he got involved with Cooley."

TWENTY-FIVE
BLAKE
DECEMBER 24, 2009

know I shouldn't have been blindsided by the fact that Nicole Long was black, biracial as it were, but I was. That meant her mom was a much lighter version of me. Then Logan's daughter too. His ex was a black woman like me? I'd have to process all my feelings about the intersection of white cops and black people later.

Much later.

While Logan and Long cleaned up, I got my notes from the bag I'd hung on the coat tree by the door. Everyone had scattered from the living room like roaches with the light turned on. I wandered over to the fireplace and tried to think of an excuse to go home.

Leave crime fighting and justice seeking to those who'd taken on the mantle. My window of opportunity closed when, after a bathroom break or maybe a mental health break, we were all in the room, me with pen and paper in hand.

If we hadn't all been middle aged, sitting on real furniture after eating real food, I could have imagined it was a college study group. But nothing I did in college had life-or-death consequences like this. For a long moment, I was jealous of Logan's daughter and her carefree youth.

Feet thumping on hollow wooden steps, Logan ran up to the loft above us, then came down with a huge Post-it note pad that he stood on the low, square coffee table. The blue and white lights from the tree left little bokeh spots on the paper. Logan cleared his throat before he got to the crazy part. The part where he was going to have to ask them to take the same leap of faith he and I had already made together.

"I've talked to you, or Blake has talked to you all individually to some degree about what I think is going on," Logan started. "Bottom line, I guess, is that I think Lori Pope is actively setting up the prosecution of people who are not only not guilty of the crime charged, but that have wronged her in some way."

Justin McPhee shook his head, regret etched in his features. Thumped his empty pad of paper on the coffee table. The Post-t pad jostled, but didn't quite fall.

"While I appreciate that none of you like what Lori Pope may be doing, the only people affected are my clients," McPhee said. His first real acknowledgment that he was in this as deep as the rest of us. "She's indicted Tyisha Cooley for the murder of Ja Roach. No offense, but why would someone who's been a lifelong upstanding citizen suddenly get a gun and take out the prosecutor's former CI."

"Are you representing Wetzel?" I asked. Vernon Dinwiddie had been there for her first appearance, but he was a civil rights guy.

"Uh—"

"I know you can't tell me if someone is your client. But if it looks like you're going to put in a notice of appearance, which will be public record, I think we can keep that to ourselves in service of this bigger goal."

"I'll be keeping Tia Wetzel's interests at the forefront of my mind," McPhee acknowledged.

I took that as a yes.

"That said, Loren," the lawyer continued. "What's the goal here? I have people to keep out of jail. But all of you know how much pressure there is to get people to plead to something. That's why Cooley and Wetzel are starting behind the eight ball as convicted felons. You all know that juries are allowed to discredit the testimony of witnesses who are felons. Wetzel and Cooley can't even testify and take up for themselves. And with these new charges. Unless some kind of directive comes down forcing you"-he pointed toward Long-"or someone else in the prosecutor's office to drop the charges altogether, they're facing another conviction and possible jail time. I get that you all feel used to some degree, but all of you get to go home every night, sleep in your own bed, and revel in your freedom."

"Why do people take the pleas?" I asked. "I always thought the justice system could actually work if every single defendant went to trial."

"But they don't," McPhee said. "They take the pleas to

stop the madness. I don't mean to be glib, but a trial is seriously expensive and seriously stressful. And no matter how many times the appellate courts slap the common pleas for the practice, the judges still give longer sentences to those who are *found* guilty by a jury than those who *plead* guilty to a judge."

"It's true." Long shrugged. "It's part of the pressure we use to get a plea."

The prosecutor's nonchalant lift and drop of her shoulder was what I really wanted to ask about. Now that I knew the truth about her, I was trying not to judge the part she played in putting people like me...like...us behind bars.

"And get a stat," McPhee said. "But I was saying that Wetzel, Cooley, and whomever else is in the crosshairs have a lot more to lose than anyone else here."

"You have a point," I admitted. "As much as I want to take down Pope, my motivations are different. First I do want to put out there that I'm passionate about justice. I've always believed, and have spent my whole career trying to shine the light on injustice. Despite evidence to the contrary, I still believe that if we shine light on corruption, police brutality, overzealous prosecution, and unfair sentencing, then I can bend that arc of the moral universe toward justice a little more quickly."

My little speech had probably been over the top, but I felt some kind of need to prove my cred, especially without an entire newspaper behind me. The threat of front-page exposure was great leverage. A featured post on a fairly anonymous blog, not so much.

"Do you think I work for peanuts because this is the only attorney job in the world?" Nicole Long's voice was unapologetically strident. "I work as a prosecutor because I believe that criminal justice is the only way to punish some wrongdoers. There are far too many people who get away with far too much. If I can convict even a handful of those people, I can sleep at night."

Logan held up his hands when my mouth opened to speak.

"Alright, we're not going to have a moral relativism debate." he boomed. "We swore to uphold and defend the Constitution. I think we all picked the jobs we did because we believe in justice even if we can't one hundred percent agree on what that means. IN THIS CASE, I think this means that we need to deal with Pope."

I'd never taken any kind of oath, but I was a hell of an investigator not limited by any institution. I grabbed the Sharpie from Logan, then wrote two things on his pad.

1. Find Malcom Pointer's murderer.
2. Find Ja Roach's murderer.

"If we can connect her with either one of these"—I thumped the marker on the pad for emphasis leaving black dots everywhere—"then I think the other dominoes can fall."

"Are you out of your gourds?" Webb asked. "I'll be the first to say that something's up, but murder?"

Everyone looked at each other. The Cleveland Heights

detective had a point. Murder *was* a big leap. Even I wasn't one hundred percent convinced, but in my experience, every investigation had to start somewhere.

"She murdered Sister Danica Lozano," Long said.

The prosecutor might as well have dropped a bomb. The silence was that deafening. Or our eardrums were busted. I had about a million questions, none of which I wanted to broach out loud.

"How do you know?" Webb asked the question we all had.

"I am not a witness. I did not *see* her do it, exactly. I do have evidence that she was there. Physical evidence."

"Does she know you have the evidence?"

"Why do you think I still have a job?" Long threw up her hands, exasperated. "Everyone here, everyone in the damn county knows I'm a huge fuckup. It's the world's worst-kept secret."

It was like we'd cut our fingers and shared blood. After Long's confessions, there weren't any more secrets. We each agreed on tasks for our nameless corruption investigation, which is how we talked about it. We certainly didn't veer over into using the word conspiracy to take down an elected official.

Once that was done, Logan sliced the panettone. Handed around fresh-brewed decaf coffee.

"This isn't gross," I said of the dried-fruit-laden treat. "It's really, really good, actually."

"It's not from a box that's been on the supermarket shelf since the dawn of time."

Long picked out the dried fruit. Probably because they were really rum heavy. Yesterday, I'd have judged the hell out of her. But if I knew that my boss was a murderer, I might want rum-soaked raisins as well.

A buzzer sounded somewhere. Logan unwound his long-legged self, put down his empty plate, and went to answer the door. He had some really friendly neighbors. I wondered what kind of gifts this one would give.

When I looked over my shoulder to satisfy my curiosity, I was surprised that it wasn't some unknown person. Instead Valerie Dodds stood at the threshold, shifting from one foot to another. Logan looked at us, taking in each one of us in turn, silently inquiring as to who'd invited her. Obviously no invitation had come from him.

"Can I come in?" she asked.

Logan didn't exactly say yes, but he stepped back from the door. Valerie's boots clicked on the wood floor, echoing off the super tall ceilings.

"You all need to watch your backs," she said while cold came off of her like an open freezer.

"Why?" Long asked. She looked the most shocked to see Dodds. Worried about reporting back, probably. Even to me the prosecutor's job seemed precarious.

"Pope knows that you're here." Dodds' voice was loud, clear. "She sent me to spy on you. Try to ingratiate myself, and report back."

"How did she find out?"

Dodds shrugged. "Is one of you a mole?"

Hard headshakes all around.

I threw up my hands.

"I'm the only person here who has never met Lori Pope. I don't have her on speed dial, or even her private cell number. One of you must be way less careful than you think." I couldn't help that my eyes went to Nicole Long.

She probably had the most to lose, but also the most to gain. It wasn't a big step from Pope stepping down to Long being promoted as interim leader with the next step being elected into the job she already had. Everyone loved to pat themselves on the back for having appointed a "first black" official.

"What are you going to do? Ingratiate yourself with the boss? Report back?" Logan asked Dodds.

The junior prosecutor shook her head. "Not that."

TWENTY-SIX
SEASON 2, EPISODE 6:
FIFTEEN TO LIFE

Things have gotten complicated. As I say that, I'm thinking it's the biggest understatement I've ever made out loud.

When I started this season, I thought it would be an investigation into garden variety corruption. The kind that Boston, and Detroit, and Chicago, and even Cleveland have mastered, made a fine art. Instead, I think I've opened Pandora's box.

This is *The Murders Began* with me, your host, Blake Hardin Tatum.

Tia Wetzel was indicted for the murder of her date, Malcolm Pointer. There was little surprise there. From my interview with her, and Vernon Dinwiddie, we know that Wetzel has gotten on the wrong side of a few people in law enforcement and in the prosecutor's office. She says she's been framed a second time. Even though it sounds like the plot of one of those police procedurals we all watch in reruns every night at ten, I'm inclined to believe her.

My investigation has turned me into a spider. Whenever I put one leg on one part of the web, another part vibrates.

In the same grand jury session where Wetzel was indicted, another woman was as well. This time it was a woman named Tyisha Cooley. Her charge was also murder. Like Wetzel, Cooley isn't new to the justice system.

I'm not saying that right. I do not want you to think she's a career criminal. Far from it. For the majority of her life, she lived like any upstanding citizen, working as a rule-following compliance officer for Society Bank.

Cooley is relatively new to the system. A couple of years ago, she was indicted for involuntary manslaughter. Her supposed crime: giving a fatal dose of heroin to Sarah Pope; yes, she was related to the county prosecutor. She was Lori Pope's half sister.

I know it sounds bad, Tyisha Cooley helping Pope shoot up, but there's a lot more to the story. Cooley had been her best friend since they met on a fateful night of the 1966 Hough riots. The younger Pope was a lifelong drug user. Cooley had gotten her friend of forty-plus years a spot in a residential rehab. Sarah begged for one las hit in order to stave off withdrawal. With many collapsed veins, Sarah Pope often needed help injecting. At the direction of a guy named Ja Roach, Cooley did the shot. Sarah Pope did not survive the night.

Who has Tyisha Cooley allegedly murdered this time around? Jabari Roach. He was an addict who had supplied Sarah Pope for years. Roach and Cooley only came in contact with each other because of Pope.

In a plot twist that's unlikely to be a coincidence, Roach was possibly an informant for Lori Pope, starting when she worked for the city of Lakewood. Roach was a twenty-year resident there. Despite Roach being involved in criminal activity for two long decades, he was never arrested, never charged, nor was he ever convicted of any crime.

One third of Americans are arrested by the age of twenty-three. Fifty percent of black men have been arrested by that age. Obviously the majority of Americans and half of black men manage not to run afoul of the police. But those are the more law abiding of us. Those who regularly engage in criminal activity, violent and non, are arrested at nearly a one hundred percent rate. Yet, Ja Roach has somehow managed to escape this increasingly common fate.

And now this former bank compliance officer is

standing accused of murdering a lifetime intravenous drug user she only met a single time.

A lot of things happen in the criminal justice system that make little sense. This Tyisha Cooley case is one of them.

TWENTY-SEVEN

LOGAN
JANUARY 3, 2010

"FYI. Sunday morning in Parma is not how I imagined my new year would start," I said to Blake Tatum. I didn't mention that I was over the moon that she called, even under these circumstances. I'd probably worn out my welcome with new neighbors and old friends who were no longer sorry for my bachelor state.

"After your Christmas Eve dinner where you proposed this grand scheme, this takedown if you will, where did you think you'd find yourself?" she asked.

"In Cleveland Heights with my ex, maybe? Even though I heard she has a new boyfriend, I think I imagined she'd have come to her senses and we'd be back together by now."

"Maybe it's you who needs to come to your senses." Despite the raised eyebrows, she seemed to close off to some degree. "Sounds like she's moved on."

"Maybe you're right." I regretted my words as soon as they left my mouth. My boundaries dulled by a week of indulging in too much food and wine, I changed the subject back to the matter at hand. Something far more urgent than my failed marriage—the dead body in the other room.

"What in the hell happened?" I asked Tatum. Her shrug wasn't really an answer.

"I didn't know who else to call."

"It's fine," I assured her. "Calling me was the right thing to do," I said though I doubted the truth of it. As any wrongly convicted prisoner could tell you, it wasn't a good idea to be at or near a crime scene no matter how innocent of that crime you were. Guilty by association was too often the name of the game in the justice system. I'd warned my own daughter to steer clear of any situation that looked dodgy or could go pear shaped. Glancing around the apartment at Tatum and forensic evidence invisible to the naked eye, I put my left hand behind my back and crossed my fingers. Whether for good luck or to ward off bad, I couldn't decide.

"She called me," Tatum said.

"Who?"

"Anna Moretti, of course." Tatum spread her arms wide to take in the main living area of Moretti's overly warm and pin-drop-quiet apartment. "Who else?"

"After the Wetzel setup, I just wanted to be clear." It wasn't that I didn't believe Tatum. I just needed her to say it. To be the one to put forth the fact that we were smack-dab in the midst of another frame-up.

"Anyway," Tatum continued, "she said that she had more information on Lori Pope. Something she had been afraid to share before. She said she'd gone to the library. Read some of my stories in the *Plain Dealer*, and knew for sure I was legit."

"Do you think that was genuine. That she had more to share? Or do you think someone was figuratively or literally holding a gun to her head."

"I don't know. I was kind of amazed that she'd done research. I was more intrigued than suspicious, I guess."

"Was it her?"

"Now that you ask, I wouldn't swear my life or my pension on it. It was familiar enough, I guess."

"What kind of information did she say she had?"

"She wasn't exactly specific." Tatum made a hand gesture cutting off my protest. "You have to know that civilians aren't always detail oriented around documents or information. That said, it sounded like medical records. I was thinking that there was more to those psychiatric visits than she'd said. Like maybe that Pope had been evaluated when she was young, but doctors hadn't shared the results. And that she'd come across it since my first interview with her."

I didn't say it, but she was losing some of her objectivity. It sounded like she'd gotten the tiniest sliver of information and had backfilled it with a whole story she'd made up on her way over from the east side. That forty-minute drive on surface streets could put ideas into the most rational of minds.

"Why would someone not share information with a mother?" I needed to poke some kind of hole into her story.

"She was institutionalized. Her husband was a cop. It was the nineteen fifties. That's a bunch of reasons right there. I could see a world where they hid information from a mother to preserve her sanity or some crap like that. My mother wanted to get her tubes tied and the doctor required her husband's permission."

My wife's doctor had asked the same, and that had been the nineties. Ex-wife, I corrected in my head. I zeroed in on Tatum.

"So you came over? On a Sunday after New Year's?"

"When people are ready to share, I have to strike while the iron is hot. Far too often people change their minds if you wait."

She was very right about that. It was the reason that murders were easier to solve in the immediate aftermath. Had to talk to people before they thought better of it.

"How did you get in here?" I turned toward the single entrance fitted with a turn lock, a deadbolt, and a chain.

"The door was open. She's older. I figured maybe she'd unlocked it, then had gone and done something else. It's the kind of thing my grandmother did when she was unable to walk from the back of the house to the door in a reasonable amount of time."

"Did she seem frail when you saw her before?"

"Not too. She was eighty. Spry, but acted her age. But... well...I didn't think of how she was before versus now."

I didn't ask any more questions. Had to wonder if I was getting bogged down in unnecessary details to avoid what was going to become the unpleasant part of my day...another murder victim.

"Where is she?" I looked where Tatum's eyes had shifted,

toward the back of the apartment.

"The bedroom."

"Are you sure she's dead?"

"I'm not a medical professional. But no pulse and no movement and being kind of cold were clues."

"I'm going to go back there. Don't go anywhere, but don't touch anything either."

Lori Pope was some kind of grim reaper. I hadn't seen anyone surrounded by so much death outside of a funeral home. I hitched up my jeans and strode to the back of the small apartment. The door on the left was ajar, and I went in. There she was. Lori Pope's mother. If she hadn't been on top of the floral bedspread, I would have guessed that she'd just lain down for a nap.

I snapped on a glove.

Touched her wrist.

Waited for a pulse to beat.

Nothing.

I took a look around the room. There was no obvious murder weapon or any immediately apparent signs of struggle. If anyone had come to this scene but Tatum and me, the body would have already been zipped up in a body bag and delivered to a funeral home, the cause of death assumed to be natural. Especially when Lori Pope reported a lifetime of drug abuse and institutionalization for mental health issues. The case would have been closed before it was ever opened.

Now I'd have to decide how to handle this.

"So what are you going to do?" Tatum was standing at the threshold.

"We can't leave her here." Though I wanted to do just that. I wanted to take Pope down. Make her pay. But it seemed like every action I took was met with swift retribution. I didn't need any more bodies on my watch.

"Do you know someone here in Parma?"

"Not that well." I was thinking about a woman I'd met at some FBI counterterrorism training, though I couldn't think of her name. From partnering with her on a couple of exercises, she'd seemed on the up-and-up. "I could put in a call to the special investigations unit. Her connections on the west side probably run deeper than mine."

"Are you from Cleveland?" Tatum asked. It was a question nearly everyone asked. Negative net migration numbers showed it wasn't a city most moved to voluntarily.

"No, Boston."

"Where's your accent?" It was the question everyone asked.

"You want me to park my car in Harvard Yard," I said with my heaviest Southie voice. I'd worked hard to drop the accent.

"Okay. Sorry. How long have you been here?"

"About ten years. Worked for the Boston police. Then came here as a trailing spouse."

I could tell she wanted to ask about a thousand questions. I knew that the night she first saw the picture of Clementine. I wasn't going to indulge her curiosity until she had the guts to ask.

"Special investigations?"

"Parma has about four or five guys who handle more

complicated cases."

"In a city of eighty thousand?"

"Lot of crime, I guess." I shrugged trying my damndest to remember the woman who'd had no partner when her colleagues had paired up.

"Or too much policing."

"Ericka Warwick." I snapped my fingers with the memory. Pulled my glove off and then my phone from my pocket. Thanked God that I'd somehow put her number in my contacts.

"Wait? What's the story? What in the heck are you going to tell her?"

I'd dialed before I thought of the answer to the question for myself. If I'd waited, I may not have—my thoughts cut off when a "hello" came through the receiver.

"Loren Logan here. Homicide detective Cleveland. I'm here in Parma. I came upon a witness who...turned up dead. I need your help."

I gave her details about where I was.

"She'll be here in ten."

"That's fast."

"Small town."

"Should I stay, or should I go."

"Go. You should very much go. If it comes up, I'll explain away any forensic evidence."

"What?"

"If you left a hair, fingerprint. Whatever. You're a reporter looking into something. Don't worry. Just go. I'll call you much later, if I have something."

TWENTY-EIGHT

SEASON 2, EPISODE 7:
A DATE GONE WRONG

"Give me the man and I will give you the case against him," is a translation of a phrase popularized by Stalin-era officials. Lori Pope's office is starting to look like they're taking lessons from the Soviet-era secret police and their operations behind the Iron Curtain."

The most unfortunate victim in this whole conspiracy is probably Malcolm Pointer. According to Wetzel, Pointer was just a regular guy who was looking to find love. You've already heard Wetzel's account of this meeting. She went to have tapas for her birthday. Malcolm bought her a glass of wine after her colleagues left. The rest, shall we say, was a very short history.

Soundscape of Euclid Avenue, Cleveland, is heard in the background which included honking cars and general city noise. Heels clicking on pavement.

In five minutes, I'm going to interview Malcolm Pointer's girlfriend.

Yes, you heard that right, girlfriend, and I don't mean Tia Wetzel. I was as surprised as you probably were to hear of her existence. According to her, Malcolm wasn't looking for love. His relationship wasn't open. This wasn't polyamory or ethical nonmonogamy. Pointer's reason for pursuing Wetzel may shock you.

This is *The Murders Began*, and I'm your host, Blake Hardin Tatum.

I'm on my way to the apartment Sunshine Whittington shared with Malcolm Pointer. Ms. Whittington lives in one of the newly renovated downtown buildings. I love the idea of making what's old new again. The last time I interviewed someone here it was still an office building full of attorneys and other professionals. A lawyer involved in the Sheila Harrison Grant case met with me when the now former federal judge allegedly left the county taking her daughter from foster care along for the ride.

Soundscape of an elevator pinging, shoes on carpet, a knock and answer.

"Thank you for having me in your home at a time like this. I'm sorry for your loss."

"I hope that you can bring Malcolm's killer to justice."

"Can you tell the listeners who you are."

"My name is Sunshine Whittington. I'm thirty-eight years old."

"Where do you work?"

"I'm a nurse anesthetist at MetroHealth."

"How long were you in a relationship with Malcolm Pointer?"

"Three years. It would have been our fourth anniversary this month."

"Were you aware he was...dating outside your relationship?"

"If you mean, his relationship, as it were, with Tia Wetzel, then yes, I knew about it...from the beginning."

"I know this may be a probing question, did you have an open relationship?"

"No."

"How did Malcolm come to date Tia Wetzel, then?"

"It's a deal he made with the prosecutor's office."

"What did he get in exchange for betraying you?"

"Betrayal is an interesting word. It felt like the lesser of two evils at the time. The prosecutors, they agreed to close an investigation they were making into some alleged noncompliance with state financial reporting laws."

"What was his job?"

"He was a senior compliance manager at Society Bank."

Let me pause for a moment. I want to connect the dots for you listeners. I mentioned in an earlier episode that Tyisha Cooley was a compliance officer for Society Bank. Occam's razor leads me to assume there's no coincidence that two people from one small bank department have caught the attention of the prosecutor's office. Let's get back to my interview with Sunshine Whittington.

"Did you know him to be dishonest?"

"Never. He was a type A rule follower and made for that job."

"What possessed him to assist the prosecutor's office?"

"Like every other free citizen, he didn't want to go to jail. He was ninety-nine percent sure that an investigation would turn up nothing. But he's human. His entire department is filled with humans. We all make mistakes which come to light under a microscope. I work in surgery and our malpractice insurance is sky high because we're not perfect, even though the law acts as if we're supposed to be."

"What was he asked to do?"

"Take Tia Wetzel on a few dates."

"Did they tell him why dating someone was necessary, or how long this would last? What was his guarantee that this would be the end of the so-called investigation or any future requests?"

"There was none. I thought he was naïve to think it

would be. Blackmail can't end without violence. Either the person blackmailing has to die or the person black-mailed has to die or some other stalemate has to come about. That's the only logic that works. I've thought about it a lot. In this case, Malcolm was the one to die."

"You don't think Tia Wetzel is the murderer?"

"She thought she was going to get a boyfriend. An employed, nice guy. Not a drug dealer."

"When you say not a drug dealer, what do you mean?"

"I heard your other podcast. That's why I contacted you. It made more sense once I put two and two together."

"What was your sum?"

"Tia Wetzel has been...unlucky in dating. That drug dealer landed her in all the hot water. If she was poking around, thinking about suing the police or the county or the prosecutor's office or whatever, then she had to be feeling better in some respects. My guess was that she, like the rest of the women in her age bracket, was pretty desperate for a relationship. What's that statistic? That a woman past forty has a better chance of being killed by a terrorist than finding a mate? I'm sure it was easy enough to pick her up."

"What do you think the endgame was, then. He was going to date her, and then what was going to happen?"

"If they were going to frame him, then I can only assume the plan all along was to kill him and frame her. It made zero difference what he did."

Sunshine Whittington starts crying, choking out a few more words. "Once the prosecutor's office had zeroed in on him, his time left was a ticking time bomb. Tick. Tick. Tick. Boom."

Neither one of us had to say out loud that the bomb had been detonated.

This has been *The Murders Began*, and I am your host, Blake Hardin Tatum.

TWENTY-NINE
NICOLE
JANUARY 4, 2010

I t wasn't yet noon, but the parking lot was nearly empty. People who actually checked the weather had stayed home. Folks like me who were surprised by the storm moving in were making our way out of downtown before the roads got bad. Dodds had said that a half a foot was predicted.

Determined to not let the cold, dark lot set me on edge, I zipped my parka to the top while I trudged to my car. My BMW stood alone in its usual corner. The dome light above my car was out. The glass on top of my car showed it was clearly vandalism. In the Justice Center of all places.

Damn it to hell.

Nothing went my way in this place. For once, though, it wasn't my fault.

I'd have to call someone or pick a different space. I'd chosen this one because it was well lit, even if a little bit isolated. Never again would I put myself in a position to be a victim. I swiveled my head. No one was around that I could see or sense.

Parking lot issues were next week's problem, though. After I unlocked the doors, I popped open the trunk and hefted in my briefcase. It was full of all my current case files. I'd work from home if the weather kept up like this.

I slammed the trunk, and came around to slip into the driver's bucket seat. Then I put the little key fob in the slot, put my foot on the brake, and was about to press start when someone all in black banged on the window.

Who in the hell?

I wasn't ready for carjacking to become a thing in Cleveland. I wasn't even sure we had laws against that in Ohio. I was prepared, though. In all the years since Baton Rouge, I'd come up with a long list of maneuvers to get out of trouble. In my car, I was safe. I started the car with a jab at the start button.

With my right hand in a death grip, I shoved the shifter into drive. Pressed the gas. The engine roared loud enough for me to hear it through the closed windows.

The car didn't move.

Then, two men appeared. Dark hoodies blocked their faces. In seconds, one was on each side of the car. It was my worst nightmare come to life. All the self-defense classes I'd signed up for but didn't attend, flashed before my eyes.

Daddy always had a gun on him. More than once he'd tried to get me to carry that Springfield Armory Hellcat he'd bought me after Seth Collins. It was in a lockbox in a closet in my condo, not here where I needed it.

I tried very hard to convince myself that I didn't need to be scared. Whoever these guys were had to know that there'd be enhanced penalties if anything happened to me. I touched the window button for a moment, allowing just enough space for them to hear me.

"I'm a prosecutor for Cuyahoga—"

Hot breath and an angry voice came through before I could finish.

"What are you doing?" one of the guys asked as he pressed his face right up to my window.

"Excuse me?" I made sure my voice was full of bravado and confidence I didn't have. "You must have me confused with someone else. I don't think I know you."

"I think you do. I hear that you're snooping around our turf."

"Again, you must have me confused with—"

"Who? Detective Darlene Webb. I promise you we have not confused you with *that* woman."

They glared and me long enough that I figured out who they were. Probably were. Nicola and O'Callaghan. The Cleveland Heights detectives Loren Logan thought may be on Lori Pope's payroll.

I should have expected this. Especially after Valerie Dodds had given us the heads-up. Despite the warning, I'd plowed ahead digging through old case files turning up one rock after another. Most had nothing substantial under them, but it was only a matter of time before my snooping alerting someone. Pope had to have crossed someone somewhere who wasn't afraid of her.

"What do you want from me?"

I regretted the question the moment it left my mouth. Since I wasn't willing to give them a single thing, I should have kept my mouth shut, and put my fingers on the phone in my pocket to dial Loren Logan. I needed a cop to go up against these cops. Fighting fire with fire.

"What Seth Collins got."

The bottom fell out of my stomach as I considered the implication and my exit routes. Someone had been messing around under the hood, so the car was out. Running in my stilettos was out. Running through the snow in tights was out. Ten years ago, I'd taken a single kickboxing class, but the nightmares had been so bad that night, I'd never gone back.

I rolled up the window and closed my eyes. I wasn't a year old, and knew that making them disappear from my view wasn't a solution. But I needed to do something to calm the fear, so I could think my way out of this.

They started pounding on my window. Their fists a cacophonous stereo. I didn't know enough about automotive glass to know how long I had before they could break it with their fists, or even if these cops had some kind of special tool to break car windows or if that was limited to firefighters. I put my hands up to my ears as I tried to drown out the voice in my head that was caught up in trivialities like lamination versus tempering.

The pounding stopped. My own heart nearly stopped as I realized I was only moments from living my worst night-mare...again. This time it would be worse, much worse. They wouldn't leave me in my own bed in my own apartment, an hour from my parents' house.

I'd be lucky if I got out alive. I started praying for my death then because I couldn't see how I'd want to live after they were done with me. Maybe I could get out of this car and attack them. Nixed that idea as quickly as it formed. One of them would shoot me out of training and instinct.

Suicide by cop.

All sound disappeared as the whoosh of blood took over and muffled the world. One more deep breath, then I put my hand on the door handle.

Before I could pull at the cool chrome, I heard one of the men cry out, then the other. The pounding stopped. Everything stopped. My eyes snapped open to see Valerie Dodds standing about five feet from my car. Her arm was outstretched, her hand had a canister in it. With my would-be assailants on the ground, I managed to get my door open far enough to get out. I only held my keys in my hand.

"Let's go!" Dodds shouted.

"What about—"

"Nicole Long. Let's go!"

What was obviously pepper spray started burning, so I started running as fast as I could in heels. I was three or four feet behind Dodds, but it was less than a minute before we were at her car. She blooped her fob, and I grabbed the handle and got in the passenger seat. She was in the driver's seat, and in a moment I heard her Honda's tires squeal as we sped from the parking lot.

Dodds barely slowed to swipe her card. The barrier lifted.

With an inch of clearance, we were out. She turned right. Sped down Lakeside, past the WPA-era courthouses and Federal Reserve building. We skid to a stop at a red light at East Ninth. When it turned green, Dodds swung a hard left. Came to a stop at a bus stop across the street from the city's iconic Free stamp.

"What in the hell was that?" Dodds asked, her eyes wild.

"An ambush from the Cleveland Heights cops that Wetzel was going to sue."

"The ones who framed her?"

"The ones who *raped* her."

"What in the hell are you talking about?"

There was no time to explain all that.

"We can't stay here. Not at this bus stop without drawing attention."

"Where in the hell do we go? Your place? My place? They know where each and every one of us lives."

"Does Pope know that you're a double agent?"

"I'm not in the CIA."

"Does she know that you're not reporting everything back to her. That you joined in on our meeting on Christmas Eve. Is that true? That you're not feeding her information. Or are you going to go back to her so that you can be the head of Major Crimes?"

I realized that questioning my rescuer in her car, when the alternative was being left outside barefoot in a snowstorm, was not the wisest move. But I needed to know where I stood—now.

"Even if that were my plan, I'm gonna go out on a limb

and say that dousing two police detectives with pepper spray will foil my scheme."

"Drive!" I pointed through the windshield. "There's a bus behind us."

"Where do we go? Where is safe from Pope?"

My personal phone contacts list was so slim, it didn't take more than a second to scroll to an answer.

"Justin McPhee said something about moving back home. I think we go there."

THIRTY

BLAKE

Justin McPhee's house looked like an old lady had shepherded his interior design. The front door opened directly into the living room. From the looks of things, I was the last person here.

Self-consciously, I stomped my boots on the rug, then left them on a rack by the door.

I took in the spindly dark wood furniture and Tiffany lamps, and I could envision his mom or grandmom writing birthday cards and thank-you notes.

You had to love generational wealth. If I had kids, I'm not sure I'd have anything to hand down besides a couple of mortgages that rental income was barely covering.

Nicole Long and Valerie Dodds were on the white leather living room couch in matching gray sweats, obviously hastily purchased from a discount store.

Logan had texted me last night filling me in on the attack by the Cleveland Heights detectives and the prosecutors' decision to seek out refuge with the defense attorney. That eliminated any question about whether they were bad cops. Didn't confirm that Pope was their puppet master, but it was pretty damning.

It had been a good idea, the two prosecutors holing up at McPhee's place. Going after the defense attorney would have been the act of a desperate woman. Attacking a member of the bar went beyond the pale. I didn't think Pope was there quite yet. What last night showed, though, was that she was getting too close.

"How are you?" I asked the women as I took a seat in the vintage chair, hoping it would hold my weight.

Long shrugged in response to my question. Dodds looked like she wanted to say something, then thought better of it. I was too scared to keep quiet.

"She knows who we are." I stated the obvious to let them know that I was starting to get scared. I wasn't in my twenties anymore, so I took my own mortality a lot more seriously. My sigh was deep. "I am not one to give up on anything, but maybe I'm ready to give up on this. I don't want to end up dead."

"Dead?" Justin McPhee looked over toward a pack-n-play I hadn't noticed. There was a toddler in there who looked like he was blinking awake. I'd have been quieter if I'd been warned. McPhee went to get the kid. I kept talking.

"Pope's own mother bit the dust," I said. Then I described what had happened with Anna Moretti. "I'm no spring chicken, but I'd like to live at least another forty years on this earth, even if it's in snowy Cleveland." Flakes piled outside on the sill of the window next to my chair bringing home the point.

"You have a gun?" Long asked.

"A gun?" She couldn't be serious. "No. Do you?"

Long nodded, but as I'd learned on Christmas Eve, she was from the South. I didn't need to ask Logan or Webb. They were armed right now.

"I don't," McPhee said. "Didn't grow up that way." He was bouncing a baby on his knee. Somehow I didn't expect that. The defense lawyer had covert fuck-boy vibes. After years with Woody, it's something I could spot a mile away. If I were a betting woman, I'd put what little money I had on the probability the gurgling kid wasn't planned.

"Maybe it's time to get one," Long said.

Logan looked away. He knew better than to say anything to me. I'd already shared my views on our founding fathers and the Second Amendment and gun violence. Crime reporting had changed during my tenure at the paper.

What started with looking at the causes of crime and the effects on victims had turned into learning the mechanics of various semi-automatic rifles and collecting mass-shooting statistics. Shootings in America were deliberate or random, scary, unpredictable, and becoming entirely too commonplace.

"So I can increase my risk of death by gunshot by one hundred percent," I retorted. "No, thank you."

"If we don't do something," Long fretted, "we're going to end up dead, or worse, on trial."

I was trying to find a way to frame the problem Lori

Pope had created. The issues we'd created for ourselves, and maybe a possible solution. A solution that would probably be unlawful, but would maybe keep us from a trial worse than death. I was coming up empty. Everyone else must have been as well because there wasn't much talking going on. The loudest person in the room was the gurgling baby.

"Have you ever heard of the concept of chaotic good?" Long asked into the nearly silent room.

"I dropped philosophy," Dodds said.

"Like the alignment in Dungeons and Dragons?" McPhee guessed. "My brother-in-law used to talk about this kind of stuff. I tuned out, ate more pierogi."

"It's the idea of doing what's right, but not necessarily what's lawful," Long answered. To Dodds, she said, "*I* didn't drop philosophy."

"What are you suggesting?" Dodds asked. I could see the younger prosecutor's mind turning. I imagined she was wondering how in the hell she'd wandered into this hell-mouth when all she'd been looking for when coming back to the city was a chance to advance her career. No lawyer imagined themselves on the other side of justice.

"We need to catch a killer. The only way I can think of doing that is to do the same thing Pope has done," Long said as she punctuated her statement with a fist on her palm.

"I'm not signing up to murder someone." Dodds' voice was strident.

"We need to frame the framer," Long said matter-of-factly.

"For what?" McPhee asked, his breath moving the curls on the toddler's towhead.

"Murder." Somewhere along the way, Long had gone somewhere very dark. We'd need to decide if we wanted to follow her.

"Of who?" That question came from Darlene Webb. They were the first words I'd heard her speak since I'd arrived.

"Except for the nun, do we know who she killed and who she didn't?" I asked.

To Nicole Long, Logan asked, "What's the biggest unsolved case in the county. Do you have something you took to the grand jury, but they declined to indict?"

"Taneka Parr."

"I don't know that one," Dodds said. The way Nicole Long cut her eyes toward her colleague, I knew there had to be more going on below the surface. Whether that was related to this or something else, I couldn't figure out. I made a mental note, though, because a weak link could get us all in trouble.

"It happened when Sledge Hammer was active," Long explained. "She was a pros— she was trafficked. There were some rumors that she was willing to testify against him, give evidence about how he locked her up and forced her to service johns. Our investigators tried to find her, but they were unsuccessful."

"What's your thought on this?" I asked the question this time as I tried to see how we could figure a way out of this mess without any more death.

"I think I can find her," Long said.

"Living?"

Nicole Long shook her head slowly, her usually smooth hair had faint waves and moved around her face. "Unfortunately, no."

"Then what?" McPhee asked.

"Is this the part where we're now bound in a conspiracy," Dodds chimed in. "Feels like a bad law school hypothetical."

I had the least legal training of anyone in this room, but even I knew that everyone who participated in a conspiracy could be found guilty of the worst crime. We weren't actually going to kill anyone, but we weren't exactly innocent either.

"Then I make it look like Pope did it," Long finished.

"What would be the motive?"

"That Taneka Parr was going to provide evidence that would have exonerated Hammer and his partner. That she was going to take the fall for moving the containers or procuring the girls or some such. That Pope wanted the actual perpetrator put in prison because he was going to skate again."

"He did skate...twice," McPhee said. "It was only the feds who finally got him."

"It could be argued that if Pope had successfully prosecuted the trafficker, it could have launched her to a higher office," Dodds argued.

"Who was the cop on that?" Logan asked. I had to wonder if he had favors to call in. Ways to get information that others didn't have. I hoped so.

"It was the FBI." That came from a new voice in the room. A woman walked in with a baby bag on her arm. She looked familiar. I was sure I'd seen her in the courtroom a handful of times. "Agent Lou Valdespino," she finished.

"Shit!" McPhee hissed the explicative through tight lips.

"Casey Cort," the woman introduced herself to us. It clicked then. I'd seen her before, in the courtroom during the Catholic sex abuse trial, and even before in some other high-profile case I couldn't bring to mind at the moment.

She continued, "I'm here to pick up my son. Now I'm thinking I'm going to have to keep you out of jail, Justin. Wasn't how I was planning to spend the new year."

"No worries on your baby daddy," Long said to Casey. "I'm the fall guy."

THIRTY-ONE
LOGAN
JANUARY 7, 2010

FBI agent Lou Valdespino and I were the only two people in the self-described tavern and grille that bordered the federal prison in Elkton. The ninety-five-mile drive from Cleveland had taken two hours in the snow which still fell outside of the restaurant's window. During that long drive, I'd worked hard to tamp down my guilt over what I was doing, roping in an innocent agent, conspiring to do the wrong thing for a greater good.

Finishing up my vanilla ice cream–topped apple dumpling and coffee, I wondered if I'd regret the treat. I couldn't eat like I had in my teens and twenties, but I was still surprised to have to keep a bottle of pink indigestion medicine in my glove compartment. Valdespino, wiser than me, had nursed a Diet Coke for a half hour.

"You're looking for Taneka Parr? Why?" The FBI agent had held his questions while I mowed through the home-made dessert. "Sledge Hammer and his closest associate, Dion Fortune, are in prison for a good long time."

"What did they get?" I deflected. I had no good reason to be here. Long had finessed this enough to get Valdespino down here, but she hadn't shared what she'd said to persuade the agent.

"Sledge Hammer, two hundred forty months, Fortune, one hundred twenty," he answered. I translated the federal sentencing into years in my head. So the mastermind had gotten twenty, the deputy ten. It was respectable for crimes against women. Those usually had the lightest punishment.

I wasn't unaware that I was engaging in borderline criminal behavior myself, and may soon join those two men, even if it was—to borrow a term from Nicole Long—chaotic good.

"And the second-in-command is going to talk to us? Why?" I asked shifting the subject a few degrees away from my true purpose.

"Guy doesn't want to be in prison. He turned on his boss to get half the time. If giving up information on Taneka Parr could lower his sentence, then he'll shout to the rooftops."

Before Valdespino could ask another question, I put out an inquiry of my own to keep him on the back foot. He seemed like a stand-up guy, so I almost felt bad for using him in this way...almost. I didn't quite get the chaotic good, but greater good, and the ends justifies the means worked well enough for me.

"Did anyone investigate the whereabouts of this Parr girl when you all got the case?"

"No one asked." Valdespino's shrug was almost imperceptible, but I saw that, and the minute change in his expression. He had some guilt around the handling of the case. "He'd let some girls go," the agent continued. "Grand...that was his street name, said Parr was one of the girls who got away."

"Did you look for her?"

"Assumed she didn't want to be found." He shook his head when the server took my plate and asked if we needed anything else. "When they get out of the life, some girls just want to put the whole thing behind them. Plus we didn't need her for prosecution. Lori Pope had already lost cases against this guy, twice. It was about putting this monster behind bars for what we could prove. That tape with Tom Brody put the final nail in the coffin."

"Tom Brody was something else. I wonder where he ended up."

"Landed on his feet in five-hundred-dollar shoes. Don't worry. So what's your interest in all this? I didn't get much information."

"My bosses are cleaning up old files. There was an anonymous tip that Parr may have been killed, and that there was a body."

"By these guys?"

"That's not the working theory, exactly. We're looking at a different crime that may have intersected with this one."

"Pope is still bitter, huh?"

"Maybe. It was a two-time loser for her office. But I'm just a worker bee here."

"Hmm." Valdespino's non-committal response kept me

from running my mouth any more. Calibrating deception was hard.

"What kind of leeway do you have?" I asked.

"If we get information that leads to finding the girl and successful prosecution, maybe time served. That depends on prison regs. Bottom line? Cutting one hundred twenty in half to sixty months."

"You have a prosecutor on call?"

"Miles Siegel. He found the girls in the containers years ago. Took a toll on him while the county had it, bungled it, but he was the one to finally get the conviction."

Long had judged this one right. The assistant United States attorney still had a dog in this fight.

"We have everything we need, then, I guess."

I paid the bill and got in his car for the short drive from the diner to the prison. We'd decided to drive past the barbed wire–topped gates together to shorten the vehicle inspection time. After the whole song and dance with the guards shining a mirror under his unmarked, and letting us badge our way through the body search, we were finally led to a room to wait for the prisoner.

Dion Fortune, or Grand, was not what I expected. Though I had to check myself, because what did one expect from a person who sold underage girls to the highest bidder? To keep from arousing suspicion, I hadn't pulled the Container case paper file from archives. There was zero chance the log wouldn't end up in the wrong hands, and alert Pope or her minions that we were up to something. Guilty people tended to be paranoid.

Instead I used my partner's username and password. Walsh kept his login credentials on a Post-it on his desk, not that it took a lot to remember his password, which was the word "password" with the "p" removed. My partner had joked about it over drinks at the Side Car one time too often.

Using his credentials, I'd logged in to the database and read up on the case and the defendants to the extent I could. Police were slow to move to electronic records. The ring-leader had only been arrested a few times. Never convicted by Pope. This "Grand" kid had evaded arrest until the ripe old age of thirty. So either he was a mastermind, or he got involved in crime later than his associates.

The slim man who came into the room looked almost boyish. His unfortunately colored greenish khaki uniform pants had a knife crease, his shirt was wrinkle-free, the undershirt underneath so white it looked like it had just come from the package. I wondered how he managed it without an iron and chlorine bleach. No way inmates had access to something that hot and heavy or toxic.

His hair had no stray curls. The close-cropped afro was wavy and flat. My ex would have called it fried and laid to the side. Life with my ex-wife and daughter clued me in on black hair care, which was a lot of work outside of prison. I couldn't imagine what he had to do to keep it that good looking inside. Even his thick-soled black shoes were polished.

"Loren Logan," I said as I stood and shook Fortune's hand. He took my hand, nodded, then sat down. He and

Valdespino shared a glance in greeting. I imagined they'd met before in a fairly adversarial situation.

"I don't want to blow smoke up your ass," I said without any preamble whatsoever. "I'm a homicide detective with the Cleveland Police Department investigating the disappearance or possible death of Taneka Parr. If you can in any way help with that, I would be grateful."

"How grateful?" His question was smooth, his words unhurried.

"This is why I brought FBI agent Valdespino. He has authority to get your sentence reduced if you give us information that leads to the arrest and conviction of the perpetrator of her kidnapping or murder."

"Reduce. How much?"

"Thirty-six months," Valdespino said. He laid his palms up as if that offer was the best he could do.

"Nothing less than time served, and arrest, not conviction. I've seen the Cuyahoga County prosecutor's work up close. I wouldn't bet my freedom on a conviction. They couldn't even convict me."

Touché.

"Parr's location and arrest of the suspect who disappeared her," I—who had no room or leverage to negotiate—interjected. What I couldn't say was that we already had a suspect in mind. Arrest was guaranteed.

I kept my eyes trained on Fortune. Despite that, I could feel Valdespino's eyes burning into the side of my head like hot laser beams were trying to melt my brain.

"I'll do that deal. Time served?"

"Cut your sentence in half," Valdespino said. "And that's really all I can offer. If that doesn't work, I'm up and out of here and slip sliding all the way home."

"Deal," Fortune said. Nodded in emphasis. "I'd take it."

"Is she missing or dead?" I flipped open a little notebook to record his answers.

"Dead."

I tried not to let his lack of emotion get to me. It was like Pope, nice and shiny on the outside, hollow and rotten to the core. He'd have made a great Wall Street bro.

"Where?"

"Sleepy Time Motel."

"East side. Warrensville Center Road," Valdespino filled in for me.

"There's a little strip of grass between Sunrise, Sleepy Time, and their parking lots," Fortune added. "She's there."

"Taneka Parr," I confirmed.

"That's the girl you're asking about."

I tried to imagine how we could place Lori Pope at a motel. I was used to unraveling crime puzzles, not creating them. I'd leave it to Long. That would be her job. Instead, I took some written, but more mental notes to share with the prosecutor later.

"How'd she die?"

"You've got to be kidding me. Just because I'm behind bars doesn't mean I've lost all of my constitutional rights. I'm going to exercise the one from the Fifth Amendment."

I'd gambled with that question. I had to ask though, otherwise Valdespino would have been suspicious. But an answer would have seriously boxed us all in to his narrative. I was happy that Fortune was smart enough to remain silent.

"We'll get back to you." Valdespino stood. Signaled the guard. Getting out was nearly as time consuming as getting in. No search, but we had to wait to get through a series of electronically controlled gates, each opening one at a time. Then picking up our weapons from the lockers before we could leave the building. Squalling snow dusted the parking lot's pavement as we made our way to his car.

"What's the hotel's jurisdiction?" I asked while we were making the short drive to the tavern parking lot.

"Warrensville Heights."

"Shit." When Valdespino turned to me at a stoplight, I realized I'd said it out loud.

"You're trying to figure out how to keep the case in Cleveland, aren't you?"

I didn't say anything. I couldn't figure out what would have been a good answer. Maybe this part was above my pay grade.

"They don't even have thirty officers in that department," was what finally came out of my mouth. Felt like a poorly written TV cop battling it out over jurisdiction.

"Any homicide would be handed over to the Valley Enforcement Group." Valdespino pulled next to my vehicle, shifted into park and left his car running.

"That sounds vaguely familiar. What in the hell is it?"

"Fifteen, maybe sixteen small towns in the Chagrin River Valley have combined resources for SWAT, and complex investigations. Too much economic upheaval. They had to cut budgets for everything. So they got together. Share resources."

"What you're saying is that it would be a box of chocolates." It was a reference to that Tom Hanks movie. With unknown officers, it could be an in-depth investigation, or they could put her in Potter's Field and dust off their hands.

"Of course, if your higher-ups push for it, they could tie it into the Cleveland police Container case. I'm pretty sure Warrensville Heights would hand it over in a heartbeat."

And there was my dilemma. I didn't have any higher-ups to go to bat for me. I'd lied my way through this thing and didn't have a backup plan or any kind of plan at all. Each one of the six of us was well aware of the problem with conspiracy, so we were operating as silos as much as we could.

"I can't see trying to convince my lieutenant to add this case to their budget. They'll definitely want me to turn it over and consider it closed and off our books, if that happens."

"What about Chief McCormick?"

"Good idea," I nodded, then curled my fingers around the door handle before I told too many more lies. "I'll have Nicole Long liaise with him." Pulled open the door handle and stepped into the snow before giving him a mock salute in farewell. "Good looking out."

THIRTY-TWO
NICOLE
JANUARY 9, 2010

"When do you need me out there?" Lori Pope asked. She was having a hell of a time keeping her unbridled ambition in check.

I wanted to be surprised that my boss was standing in my office on a Saturday afternoon, but it was exactly what I was hoping. Cuyahoga County prosecutor, Lori Pope, may be crazy, according to her mother, but I was starting to get an appreciation for what motivated her. Fame, or at least notoriety was bait she couldn't resist.

"Need you?" I played dumb. "Out where?"

Stuck a pencil through the middle of a short stack of vintage Bakelite bangles: orange, yellow, and black. I nudged them so they knocked together noisily.

Lori Pope picked up the bracelets. Fingered each one of them in turn.

"These seem a little cheap for you. Everything you wear reeks of nouveau riche."

Backhanded compliments were Pope's bread and butter these days. I chose to take her comment as a sign of admiration. She wanted to say I had great taste in accessories and that she envied my style.

"Picked them up at *Les Puces*." As I'd predicted, Pope hid her ignorance. This time I didn't pretend. I needed to sell it, hard. "*Les Puces de Saint-Ouen*. It's the best flea market. The one in the eighteenth arrondissement." I waited a beat. "In Paris."

My boss picked up the trio and slid them on her wrist, arranging them just so. Keeping an eye on her right arm, I said, "I was planning to go out with friends before this call came through. It's seventies night at the Velvet Cat." That last bit, at least was true. She didn't need to know I didn't have any friends, despite my newfound desire not to be alone all the time any longer.

I lowered my eyes to my orange-and-brown knit minidress I'd picked up along with the bracelets at a Cleveland westside vintage shop. I'd been to Paris many times, but never to pick up vintage goods. Nouveau riche luxury handbags were more my style. Pope shoved the bracelets from her arm. They hit my desk hard. It was the happiest noise I'd heard in a long time.

"You leaving soon?" Her voice had gone from casual to snappish. "It's already two o'clock. If I call Victoria Greenlee, she would probably be there by four. We'd have something to show then."

"You mean the dig site?" I mimicked slow comprehension.

"Of course. I want all of Ohio to see that we're serious about fighting crime. That we'll finally get a jury verdict against Sledge Hammer right here in a Cuyahoga County courtroom. The feds only got twenty years. I could get a judge to give him life."

I was a prosecutor and even *I* thought she sounded a little zealous.

"There's no guarantee." I kept my voice casual.

"Of what? You don't think we could get life or even *death* in Lucasville?"

"Not that." My headshake was suitably emphatic. If I lost my job, maybe I'd try writing. I was getting really good at spinning tales. "There's no guarantee that there's a body. Dion Fortune came to the police because he wanted to reduce his sentence. Not out of the goodness of his heart. According to the detectives, he thinks Sledge Hammer has put a hit out on him. This could be a Hail Mary. He's in isolation pending the outcome."

"There might not be a body?"

"Might not. Don't you think he'd have used this as leverage when we indicted them, or when the feds did? This late-day revelation doesn't make much sense."

Pope pulled her lips tight.

"Since when do we take the word of convicted felons?" I asked. "This dig *is* the verification." Pope didn't look convinced. I pulled the ace from my sleeve. "When I was like sixteen or seventeen, my dad roped me in to watching this stupid TV special. That talk show host Geraldo Rivera was going to open some mobster's vault that had been sealed for a million years or something.

"I swear we were in Daddy's den for like two hours while this guy was digging through dirt or drilling a door or something. Anyway, I don't know if you saw it or remember the press around it, but at the end of the day, he found nothing. He was the butt of late-night talk show hosts for a really long time."

After my little monologue, I kept silent. Let Pope wrap her mind around the idea of being embarrassed in front of TV cameras. It wasn't millions of viewers, but if the exhumation came up empty, her misstep would be seen by voters, and in today's growing social media age could even go viral.

"I'm not calling Greenlee until there's a body." Pope was firm with her one-eighty.

"I think that's the right move." I was making my glance at my Tank an exaggerated one, when my phone buzzed. There was a text from Logan that consisted entirely of one character, a question mark. "They're almost set. I've gotta get over there."

"Call me as soon as you know what's what."

"Gotcha." I pointed gun fingers at her. Pope stalked out. I lifted that same pencil from my desk, slipped it through the three bangles, and put them in an open Ziploc I had standing up between some stuff in my briefcase.

"What in the hell took you so long?" Logan asked a solid forty-five minutes later.

Detective Loren Logan was standing, shivering in the

parking lot between the two motels that had been ground zero for Sledge Hammer's sex trafficking operation several years ago.

I wanted to tell him that maybe he should put up the hood and close the zipper of his parka against the wind and snow. Instead I answered the question he'd asked.

"I was convincing Lori Pope that she didn't need to be here."

"Be here? Why would she want that?" His question wasn't misplaced. Pope wasn't one to get her hands dirty. She liked the popup when it was time to take credit.

"If we dug up a body, she'd be the hero for returning a girl to the bosom of her family. Even better that the girl is black. She wouldn't be portrayed as one of those law enforcement people who only chased missing blond girls."

Logan looked past the bulldozer and crime scene investigation van toward the road.

"Should we...expect her?"

"I told her if she called the press based on a prisoner's word and we came up empty, she'd be more infamous than Geraldo Rivera after Al Capone's vault opening."

"No infamy today. How in the hell are we going to do this? What exactly are we...well, *you*...going to do?"

"If I told you, I'd have to kill you." As his chin tucked into his chest, I reconsidered my humor. "It's snowing. It's a Saturday. Someone's going to have to pay time and a half. Let's get these guys working. At some point, I'm going to need you to pull the diggers and the CSI folks to the side. I'll need four minutes tops. Then we'll proceed as it would normally be done."

"You're relying on the CSI folks to connect the dots?" Logan looked a bit skeptical of his fellow officers.

"We have to believe that someone can do their jobs."

"Will it be enough?"

"It will have to be," I said. We'd all committed to this plan, and I had no desire to rethink any of it now. "I did the best I could to make it irrefutable."

"Fine." Logan stalked over to the uniformed officer standing next to the dozer. A succession of shouts and whistles went among the guys. One referred to some papers in hand, then spray-painted a fluorescent green "X" on a snowy spot that probably covered dormant grass, gravel, or dirt. He capped the paint, walked backwards toward caution tape, then raised a hand in the air.

The big yellow machine lumbered through the lot and over concrete separators until it was in place. The teeth of the metal bucket scraped the surface, taking away the green-colored snow. The soil underneath crumpled like paper. An investigator held up his hand like a stop sign. He lifted a shovel and probed at the dirt. We waved the dozer arm back over. The bucket scraped up more soil. This time, the investigator poked more delicately. He raised his hand again.

"We've got something here."

Logan and I walked to where the crime investigator stood. He wasn't wrong. Dion Fortune had been right, about this at least. A black trash bag was ripped. Pink fabric poked through. I squatted to take a closer look. From the little bit I could see, the girl looked...mummified.

I tried to dredge up what little I'd learned about body decomposition from hearing the medical examiner testify in various trials. I knew that plastic could speed it up because of a greenhouse effect. Also excluding insects could slow it down. I wondered how much each effect would cancel the other out.

For once the fact that the date and time of death couldn't be pinned down to anything specific would be in the favor of law enforcement. It would eliminate the possibility of Pope having or creating an alibi.

I stuck my hand in my coat pocket. In one I had the cheap bangle bracelets with Pope's fingerprints, and in the other the fingernail from Sister Danica Lozano's murder scene. With fairly careful evidence collection, the two should be enough to point the finger of suspicion toward my boss.

The body's hands weren't yet visible. I had to plant the evidence now before anything else happened. How in the hell would I get bracelets on her wrists? I wasn't that squeamish, but a nip of bourbon would have certainly eased the process of disturbing the dead.

Would I have to lift her arm? Would it turn to dust if I tried? I really wish I'd thought this out a bit more. No wonder the people I prosecuted were so easy to convict. There was a lot of work in committing a crime, then not getting caught. I had the advantage of education, and sobriety, and yet I was about two minutes from getting caught red-handed committing a felony.

"Are we going to need pictures *in situ?*" the head technician asked.

Pictures were permanent and immutable. It was now or never.

"Absolutely," I said.

"Don't want to leave any wiggle room for these guys to get off even if we have a solid witness and eventually a confession."

Fuck.

I had about a minute left to figure this out. Logan cut his eyes toward me before he put a beefy arm around the technician physically turning him around. Then he shouted out something that made the men come huddle around him like he was a quarterback.

I slipped the baggy from my right pocket, turned it upside down so the fingernail fragment fell into the girl's clothes. My other hand grabbed the bag with the bracelets. I definitely couldn't get them on her wrist. Or maybe I could. I dared to touch the flesh. It was frozen. As quickly as I could, I stuck a finger under her forearm, moved it enough that I could slide the bracelets on. I had to hope the technician wasn't particularly observant.

When a team came back. I did an exaggerated sign of the cross, then stood to get out of the way.

Loud enough for everyone to hear, I said, "Time to call Lori Pope. She wanted to be here if we found something worthwhile."

The technician shook his head. "The last thing we need is a media circus."

"My boss is a politician first and foremost." I didn't want her here either. But having the media around while the evidence was found would make it hard as hell to refute the findings.

"Give us a ten-minute head start," the investigator relented.

I nodded, then walked to the far side of the lot, disposed of the baggies in a dumpster there. Logan was hot on my heels.

"What did you put in the dumpster?"

"I had to bring the evidence in something. I didn't want to contaminate it with my own prints or DNA."

"Why didn't you find somewhere else to get rid of it."

"They won't search the dumpsters. It's not an active crime scene like that. There's no two-year-old evidence lurking in there. And if anyone asks, I'll just say it was a sandwich or something. I'm a drunk. They'll assume something else."

He shook his head, but had to accept my answer. Either one of us dumpster diving to get the storage bags back wouldn't do anything but bring more suspicion down on our heads.

"Were you serious back there, about calling her?" Logan said as he got to the real reason for following me over. "I thought you'd been successful at keeping her at bay."

"I did. But as I was...I was thinking. If the media is here and there are cameras, and Pope is prowling around like a tiger circling pray, then everyone will be extra careful to preserve evidence. Nothing will get lost."

"And it will increase the likelihood she goes down," he nodded obviously following my line of thinking.

I lifted my phone from the bag, and with his slight nod, made the call.

THIRTY-THREE
BLAKE
JANUARY 9, 2010

S *howtime.*

I zipped my parka, snugged my leather gloves, then crunched across the snow-and-ice-covered asphalt away from the murder victim and toward one of Cleveland's most popular TV reporters. When her perfectly coifed head turned her perfectly made-up face toward me, I stuck out my hand. She only hesitated a moment before her gloved hand shook mine.

"Victoria Greenlee, right?" I had a policy of confirming the names of well-known people. Plausible deniability made introductions smoother. I said, "I'm not sure if you remember me. I'm—"

"Blake Hardin Tatum. Used to be with the *Plain Dealer*." Was this how she did introductions? Claimed to know who ordinary citizens were? I'd use that tactic in my future. Her fawning continued, "I love your new blog and that...podcast on my iPhone, by the way."

"Oh...thanks," I stuttered. Posturing had slowed my response. In a moment, I gave my usual script. "I like the freedom to work on the projects that I think are the most interesting and can do the most good."

"Great spin," Greenlee said with a smile.

Pretense was exhausting, especially when I was cold and tense from furthering a serious criminal conspiracy.

I was candid. "Most people buy it without too many questions."

Greenlee's own guard visibly dropped. She leaned close.

"It's like when I moved here, I leaned heavily on the Rock and Roll museum and—"

"The Flats," I filled in.

We laughed in unison, catching the attention of the fairly somber technicians who were working in fits and starts because they had to warm their fingers and hands every few minutes to do the dexterous work of digging around the remains so as to not disturb the body *in situ* or any evidence.

"Lori Pope is going to be here in about twenty," Greenlee said after her cameraman and driver shot her a signal.

When Logan had called me, I'd gotten into my Jeep and started driving before I'd worked out how I'd do my part to further the conspiracy. As far as I could see, my role was to call attention to the bracelets and point out any sloppiness in evidence gathering. We needed to make sure these exurban techs with less experience were as meticulous as possible.

"Didn't you report on this case?" I asked Greenlee. "I didn't the first time around. What should I know?"

"This guy, this Sledge Hammer, he was an animal."

I tried not to cringe. I hated it when journalists referred to black people that way even when their crimes were truly reprehensible. Dehumanization was always the first step toward genocide.

"Why couldn't Pope convict him?"

Greenlee looked around, and satisfied no one was too close, lowered her voice. Leaned in close.

"That first time? I think Nicole Long over there was drunk most of the time. That said, I'm not sure if she lost the case or whether Casey Cort won it. The defense attorney did a really good job."

"The jury didn't think he was as bad, obviously."

"That first time, it was a small case. He was only on trial for possible prostitution at his strip clubs. He claimed he didn't know what the girls were doing. It was plausible. It's not unheard of, women doing some sex work on the side while the owners didn't know or turned a blind eye. Either way, the jury believed him."

"And the second time?"

"Tom Brody happened."

I did remember that controversy even if I hadn't covered it myself. Despite all my years at the paper, I hadn't been the first choice for big scandals involving the county's major players.

The prosecutor, Tom Brody, had been the head of Major Crimes before Long had stepped into the job. The world had been his oyster. His father was, and still is, the county's presiding judge. His uncle had been in Lori Pope's job before becoming Ohio attorney general. Another uncle had also been a judge of some kind before retiring. All Brody had to do was exist and he could have had a long and successful career with minimal effort.

"He couldn't keep his hands off the merchandise," Greenlee said. "He was in bed with Sledge Hammer, figuratively, of course. And literally with underage girls." I had to shake my head at the whole thing. Rich and powerful men had a huge sense of entitlement.

Thought they were invincible.

Most of the time, they were.

Greenlee and I shared a look. Ostensibly, while we continued shop talk, we slowly sidled over toward the exhumation site. The technicians were taking another break. We stopped about four feet away. Greenlee's cameraman was behind us. He had black electrical tape over what would be the red blinking recording light. I would have bet money that he was recording. I took a peek down into the shallow grave. She was wearing pink. The polyester fabric of the jersey dress looked brand new. The pile of hair near her head was weird until I realized that she'd probably had a synthetic weave that had survived where her natural hair had decayed.

Some huge plastic bracelets had survived intact as well. They were probably Bakelite. It was the perfect detail that would be great when recording. I took my own recorder from my pocket.

"This is *The Murders Began*, and I am your host, Blake Hardin Tatum. Tonight I'm standing in a parking lot in an inner-ring suburb of Cleveland. The sun has set, so what was a balmy twenty-nine degrees is getting colder and snowier by the second.

"What started with Tia Wetzel has taken many twists and turns. Every time I follow a lead, it takes me to another body. There's a bigger conspiracy going on here, but like those of you who are reading the blog and listening to this podcast, I'm figuring it out as I go along.

"Right now I'm standing next to the shallow grave of a girl who was killed, stuffed in a plastic bag, and buried between two motels. Allegedly she's the victim of Sledge Hammer, a man who trafficked girls in Cuyahoga County for several years before finally being caught. After his true identity was revealed, he was convicted in federal court."

A Cuyahoga County sheriff's SUV rolled up in the parking lot, and I stopped speaking, but didn't stop recording. As I tried to figure out whether there was going to be a law enforcement turf battle, Lori Pope stepped from the back of the car.

My stomach bottomed out. The rubber was about to meet the road. I'd erected a kind of virtual wall between Nicole Long and me. I didn't know what she did to rope Pope in coming to the scene of this crime, though I had to wonder.

The lawyers, McPhee, Dodd, and even Casey Cort, had explained that we were guilty of conspiracy if we got caught committing some kind of crime. Which would mean that we'd all be guilty of the worst thing any of us did. But we'd built in some plausible deniability by siloing some issues. I stopped ruminating about my chances of life in prison when a bright spotlight lit up the area. The TV reporter lifted her microphone to her lips.

"I'm Victoria Greenlee. More than four years ago a man known on the streets as Sledge Hammer became infamous in Cleveland for crimes he'd started in the late nineties. He was the worst kind of criminal, he bought and sold underage girls and women into sex work.

"Six years ago on July tenth, I stood exactly where I'm standing now. The FBI had found a container of women and girls."

As a journalist I knew the package that eventually aired would show a desaturated version of what had aired that July during that voice-over.

"Now it's come to light that at least one girl died," Greenlee continued. "The dozers came in during this snowstorm and, after digging through layers of frozen ground, found a mummified girl who was probably sweet sixteen when her life ended in a hot-pink dress and the kinds of plastic bangle bracelets that I stole from my mom's costume jewelry drawer."

Ever the professional, Greenlee paused and let that sink in. I knew every female viewer would have done what I just did, walk down memory lane remembering secretly digging through an older woman's box of baubles. Marrying that with the horrors of a girl being pimped out to depraved adult men adorned with pop beads or Bakelite painted a horrible picture.

"Her identity will be held until the immediate family is notified."

The reporter did a slashing motion across her neck as she wrapped a cord around the mic. The cameraman then swung toward Lori Pope. In high-heeled boots, it took the prosecutor more than a couple of minutes to cross the crime scene tape and get to the body.

In all the years she'd been in the public eye, I'd never seen her lose her composure. Whatever Nicole Long had done, it was obvious to the top prosecutor. I could practically see her mind working as she was trying to worm her way out of a possible murder rap.

Victoria Greenlee was on top of Pope the minute the prosecutor stepped back from the dig, microphone extended, cameraman's lights blazing.

"Lori Pope, are you going to bring up Sledge Hammer for murder?" Greenlee asked. "Are we finally going to get a conviction and justice in a Cuyahoga County court?" The reporter shoved the microphone toward Pope, leaving the prosecutor no time to walk away from the aggressive and likely unwanted questions.

"Of course, I can't comment on a pending investigation, but we're going to aggressively work to bring the perpetrator to justice."

Greenlee barely took a breath before she trained her microphone at Long.

"Nicole Long, you are head of Major Crimes. Are you looking for vindication with this case?"

"Like my boss said, it's all about finally bringing the right person to justice. For far too long certain criminals have gotten away with the worst behavior in our county. I've made my share of mistakes in that regard, but no longer will we be soft on crime. For the murder of this young girl, I'll be seeking the death penalty."

THIRTY-FOUR
SEASON 2, EPISODE 8:
TANEKA PARR

On January ninth, the body of a girl named Taneka Parr was exhumed from its resting place. Not a cemetery, but a parking lot. That little strip of grass between concrete stop blocks.

This is *The Murders Began* with me, your host, Blake Hardin Tatum.

The crimes of the trafficker known as Sledge Hammer became infamous in Cuyahoga County. Parr was a heretofore unknown victim. Sledge Hammer operated for years in and around Cleveland, and yet not all of his victims are known to us. Some of them went back home, did the best they could to resume their lives. Others, we'll never know what happened. There could be more women like Taneka Parr. Statistics say that even women who come to sex work involuntarily, have a hard time leaving.

Either way, Taneka Parr didn't live long enough to make that choice. Coroner estimates put her death at two to three years ago while the sex trafficking ring was still in operation. She would have been about twenty years old when she was put into the ground.

Taneka Parr came of age before social media, so rooting out her origins has been less than easy. The county usually keeps a victim's identity secret until the next of kin is notified. Despite diligent efforts, her family could not be found.

I was able to locate a birth certificate that matches her details, putting her birth at Huron Hospital in East Cleveland. Her mother, Renee Parr, would have been fifteen at the time she was born. Her father was marked as unknown on her birth certificate and was never identified in any later documents.

Renee, the mother who was listed at birth, subsequently died, cause of death accidental—Renee was killed as a pedestrian, hit by a car while crossing East Fifty-fifth. She'd been going to a gas station mini mart for a pop.

Whether the inability to locate next of kin was because Taneka Parr has no living family or they don't

wish to be found, remains unknown. If anyone listening
to this podcast knows of Taneka's relatives, please have
them contact the Cleveland police or they can contact
me. My information is on the blog and in the show notes.
I'll put them in touch with the right people.

Back to figuring out who Taneka Parr was when she
was alive. Have you heard of the term "throwaway
child"? I hope the answer is no, because it's a horrible
way to refer to one of the most vulnerable among us. But
if you haven't, let me define it for you.

The term originated in the nineteen eighties as a way
to describe children...no one wanted. Often they were
kicked out of their parents' homes, had flunked out or
been expelled from schools. Didn't have real family or
community ties.

The bottom line is these kids have no safe place to
rest their heads. Many, if not most of these youngsters
end up homeless, selling drugs to support themselves, or
become victims of sex trafficking.

While Taneka Parr was of legal age when her life
ended, it's likely she was not when she fell prey to Sledge
Hammer. From what we know of his operation, she was
likely forced to have sex with multiple partners every day
for money that she couldn't keep. There are a lot of
unknowns and suppositions, but let me tell you what we
do know.

From her autopsy, we know she didn't have regular
dental care. That her arm was broken at some point, but
not set properly, leaving her crippled and likely in

constant pain. Her jaw had been dislocated on more than one occasion.

We know that her growth was stunted and that she showed signs of malnutrition.

We know that her uterus was scarred from multiple abortions, and that had she gotten out of sex work alive, she would likely have been infertile.

We know that her death was probably slow and painful due to the gradual hemorrhaging of blood.

Taneka Parr can't speak for herself. Even the detailed autopsy can't speak for her. Three years ago, however, reporter Victoria Greenlee interviewed one of Sledge Hammer's longtime victims only known as Stephanie. Let me play you a portion of that interview."

Victoria Greenlee speaking.

"Today in this special report segment, I'm speaking with Stephanie," Greenlee started. "We're withholding your last name per your request. Thanks for joining me today."

"Thanks for having me, I guess."

"How do you feel about federal charges being brought against this so-called Sledge Hammer?" Greenlee asked.

"It's good I guess," Stephanie said, her altered voice young, hesitating. "He probably needs to go to jail for what he did."

"You're not sure?" Greenlee asked.

"It's hard I guess," Stephanie answered after a beat. "I feel like it's as much my fault as his, but no one has come to arrest me even though I committed crimes as much as he did."

The debate on the criminalization of prostitution for the unwitting victims of trafficking is not up for debate on this podcast. Suffice it to say, everyone involved could have been arrested, charged, jailed.

With me tonight, I have Stephanie.

"Thank you for talking to me in the wake of the discovery of Taneka Parr's body. Listening to that interview you did almost three years ago, do you still think it's your fault?"

"No. Never. I know now that a kid can't consent to that. What I did wasn't a crime before the age of consent, or turning eighteen. Probably shouldn't be a crime even after that, when we weren't there of our free will."

"You were held prisoner by Sledge Hammer for quite a few years."

"Five."

"During those five years, did you meet the deceased, Taneka Parr?"

"Didn't know her last name back then, but yeah, I met her."

"How? From the information that's come out since then, the men holding you kept you separated."

"For the most part, but when the police started to catch on, they moved us to an attic room in a house. She came with us. There were seven or eight of us up there."

"What do you remember about her?"

"We weren't allowed to talk much. She took a long

bath that first day. She was more popular than me because she was more light skinned." Stephanie pronounced the last word with an extra "-ed" on the end. "Guys treated her better. She didn't get as many burns or bruises, like I did."

"She was alive when you last saw her?"

"I don't know. When Grand let me go, I didn't look back. But that was two thousand four."

"Do you think it's likely one of your captors killed her?"

"Captors?"

"One of the men who kept you locked in that motel or that house."

"Probably not. Probably was one of the johns that did her in. Sometimes they got real mean. Sledge or Grand, they'd get us patched up the best they could. Didn't take us to a doctor, but there was a girl who sometimes gave us bandages or medicine. If it was bad, though, then she could have died. I'd heard it had happened to one other girl before I started."

"Do you want to talk about that? The other girl."

"No, I don't."

"Do you still fear for your life?"

"Sometimes. That prosecutor, Tom Brody, wasn't the only rich guy who came by. There were others who had important jobs and some were even cops. Those men... they already ruined my life. I'm sure they'd kill me if I ruined theirs."

THIRTY-FIVE
LOGAN
JANUARY 18, 2010

"Why is Marty Todd asking me about some girl named Taneka Parr?" My partner had come up to my desk in the bullpen, his eyes ablaze. I knew that Neil Walsh was planning to cruise straight to retirement, and was all about avoiding any bumps in the road between today and his gold watch.

"What did the captain ask?" I kept my voice neutral despite my unease. It was only a matter of time before there was a clash between my actual job duties and my use of official resources for unassigned investigations.

"Your answer wasn't 'who in the hell is Taneka Parr?' because that's what I said. So, who in the hell is Taneka Parr?"

My usual methods of distracting Walsh didn't look like they were going to work. I sighed, thought long and hard about what information I could give him while maintaining the integrity of our little conspiracy.

"Remember the Sledge Hammer trafficking cases?" I offered the tastiest bait.

"Who could forget? The department is still mad at being embarrassed by the prosecutors letting these cases go down in flames when we all did our jobs."

I'd bet all my pension money and free healthcare that there had been no Walsh in "we."

"Taneka Parr wasn't only a trafficking victim," I said. "She was a murder victim."

"But not in the city of Cleveland, apparently. So what were you, an officer who wasn't even a detective back then, doing at a dig site on a Saturday afternoon in Warrensville Heights?"

"The prosecutor...Nicole Long asked me to stop by." I hoped my voice was all innocence and light.

"Why?" I think my partner was actually curious.

"The cities over there, they don't have dedicated police. She just wanted my opinion on what they were doing."

"She wanted the opinion of a cop who's been homicide police for all of ten minutes."

"It's actually been more than twelve months. Anyway, we became friendly during the Catholic priest abuse case."

"That's all there is to it?" Walsh may not be the sharpest tool in the drawer or the most dedicated cop, but he hadn't survived this long without a certain sixth sense for bullshit.

I decided to lean heavily into his paternalism and likely misogyny. "You know she has a drinking problem. I don't think she was wasted on Saturday, but I wouldn't want that guy to get away with even more than he has because she can't hold her liquor."

"You're doing stuff off the books?" Walsh asked. I couldn't tell if it was pride or condemnation.

"I didn't put in for overtime."

"You need to keep me in the loop on what's going on. I know that you're talking to witnesses without me around. I was fine with you going out on your own. You're not some rookie. But if you're flagging the captain, then I need to be involved. I know how to keep him out of detective bureau business that's not his."

"Good looking out." I gave him a salute, got my jacket off the back of my chair, and started to make my way out of the bullpen.

"Where are you going?"

"My shift is over. I'm going home. I don't need you to escort me to my car. I'm pretty sure I can make it."

I got my stuff from my locker, then walked to my car. For once it wasn't snowing, or raining. At forty degrees, it was nearly like a spring night. I unzipped my coat a little, then unlocked my truck with the key fob. I was already considering whether I had some kinds of leftovers or whether I should get the eggplant parmesan from my favorite place around the corner. I already had my phone in hand to place my take-out order to be ready in thirty minutes, when I felt a hand on my shoulder.

I turned to see Walsh behind me. Food forgotten, I put the phone in my pocket.

"Did I forget something?" I swatted at all my pockets.

"You forgot to tell me why you're targeting Lori Pope."

My stomach fell. He hadn't missed a thing. He'd probably figured I was being cagey because we were in the precinct. Maybe thought I'd be more honest away from prying eyes.

"Targeting?" My wide-spaced hands made me feel like an overacting sitcom kid with a stupid catchphrase. "What do you mean?"

"Captain Todd said that he'd gotten a call from the OBI with some very bizarre information."

"Are you going to share, or do I have to guess?" The Ohio Bureau of Investigation was the state's answer to the FBI. I had to think Todd's call was on the down-low, some kind of back-channel communication otherwise Nicole Long would have had a heads-up.

"He said that there was evidence of Lori Pope's fingerprints and DNA on the dead girl."

Well, whatever Long had done had worked. Whether that evidence would ever see the light of day was another story. I let the bait dangle.

"Is this a different Lori Pope than the one I'm thinking of?"

"No, it's exactly the Pope that comes to mind."

"Sweet Jesus," I said in my best aw-shucks, rookie voice. "What is the captain going to do with that?"

"Why don't you tell me?"

"What do you mean?"

"Look, I know that I'm not the brightest bulb. I know that I'm not at the top of anyone's list when it comes to being the first choice for big cases. Everyone is waiting for me to pull the pin. And I will, when my North Royalton house is done. Until then, I'm not interested in being on the wrong side of Marty Todd."

The man had succeeded by being the grayest rock in the world. If Walsh were a skipping stone, he wouldn't make a single ripple in Lake Erie.

"Well, look. I'm pretty hungry." I looked at my watch. "I was planning on getting some food, and Mia Bella's doesn't stay open too late."

Walsh made himself comfortable on the roof of my SUV.

"It's not that easy. You need to tell me what's going on. The one thing I've relied on is the belief that there are no coincidences. That's ninety percent of detective work. If I haven't told you that, consider this my gift to you."

I shrugged when he ran out of air as I debated what he could have figured out, and how I could get out of this conversation I didn't want to have.

"What do you have on Lori Pope?" he asked when I was quiet far too long.

"*I* don't have anything. You're the one saying that she's connected to the murder. That's one hell of an allegation. The political elite in this city are practically immune."

"I'll let you go get your dinner, then," Walsh said. He patted my hood.

"Thanks. I'll let you know if I hear anything."

The minute I was out of sight, I pressed a button on my phone to call Blake.

"Lori Pope is circling the wagons. What now?"

THIRTY-SIX
NICOLE
JANUARY 20, 2010

When my assistant had asked where I was this morning, I'd begged off, saying I was taking a working day at home because of the weather. Of course it was the one time this month there wasn't snow falling from the sky. She didn't have the guts to push back against her boss, though.

I was *really* home because the last thing I wanted to do was encounter my boss. Looking over my shoulder every day since the meeting in Logan's loft and being accosted in the parking lot had me on edge. I was home because I needed to figure out *something* in relative safety. Something that would keep me out of hot water, out of Pope's crosshairs, out of jail. Something that would put her in.

From Tia Wetzel to Sunshine Whittington, everyone was pointing fingers at Pope. Not a single person had proof. They had conjecture, innuendo, theories, but not a goddamn thing I could put in front of the police or Ohio

Bureau of Investigations or a special prosecutor or even a damned jury. I had a lot of bodies. What I needed was a smoking gun.

Twenty minutes later, Loren Logan was pacing my living room like a caged panther. I'd called him over so we could make a plan. I just hadn't told him that.

"What day was Taneka Parr's body exhumed?" he asked, uncharacteristically impatient.

"January ninth."

"So why hasn't someone arrested Lori Pope?" There was practically a finger snap in his question.

"It's not that simple."

"When you said you'd plant evidence, it *was* that simple. I've heard through the grapevine that Pope's fingerprints and DNA are all over that scene."

"Wait, what?" I was being frozen out. I had no one to go to, to get me the information, though. Putting my feelings aside, I looked Logan in the eye. "Oh, there's a but there. Must be because I've heard no such thing."

"My captain"—he used air quotes around the next word —"heard that she's tied to the body."

"But no charges? They didn't want you to arrest her?"

"No one said it directly, but I think they're not going to initiate anything. Not without prompting from some other agency. I got the distinct impression that I'm not to be that other agency."

"We have to be the ones—"

"—willing to go out on a limb. Speaking of, Ms. Long, I still haven't seen any autopsy results, even though I've asked...more than once. If Captain Todd knows what's what, then there must be some kind of report."

I got up from my perch on the couch where I'd been far too many hours since I'd taken on these cases, since I'd started white-knuckling sobriety, then pulled a file from my briefcase, and handed it to him. He didn't do more than skim the report, and skip to the end.

"Cause of death: hemorrhagic shock due to exsanguination," he read.

Having read hundreds of these, I knew where Logan's eyes were. There were five check boxes below cause of death labeled natural, accident, suicide, homicide, undetermined, and pending. The last was ticked.

"Pending?" His eyes lifted from the page, met mine. "Who's dead from natural causes, wrapped in a trash bag, and buried under a berm between motel parking lots?" he asked while thumping his hand on the pages.

"They don't think it's natural, obviously. The coroner's assistant said they're waiting for toxicology. There wasn't any remaining blood given the amount of decomposition, so they're testing tissues. With someone who's been dead a while, that's much more complicated. When the results eventually come in, they can make a determination of accident or homicide."

"Eventually? Accident? Did she accidentally fall into a hole in the ground?" Logan's question was a protest.

"Sometimes when people are witness to an accidental death, they think they're responsible and try to cover it up." I'd seen that more than I'd ever thought possible when I started the job. The combination of guilt and fear of punishment made people do strange things.

"What about Dion Fortune's testimony?"

"His statement confirmed that Taneka Parr died, not that they killed her."

"Goddamn distinction without a difference," Logan said, his voice raised. "Look, I'm not mad at you, but at myself," he said in a softer tone. "Because you were right. I'd been so concerned about finding a body to put on Lori Pope, that I hadn't thought about Grand's self-serving statements he'd made when giving up the body of Taneka Parr."

"At least he stays in jail," I offered, gratified with the sex trafficker's punishment even if my office hadn't been the one to get the conviction." My shrug was all I could offer. "Even if Pope isn't joining him immediately. After all, we're all doing this on the fly."

"What's the play here?" Logan rattled the file in my general direction. "What does this say about the bracelets? The fingernail?"

I took in a deep breath. He wasn't going to like the answer.

"They matched the fingerprints on the bracelets with Pope. The lab techs assume it's some kind of contamination with her being there at the time the body was exhumed."

"Is there any tape of her touching the body?" I could see him trying to search through his memories. We'd both been so focused on not getting caught that we hadn't been paying attention to what Pope was doing.

"Not that I know of." My voice was a shrug.

"Well, that refutes it, then," Logan said.

"They're not looking to prove a negative."

"And the nail?" he asked about the second piece of evidence I'd planted.

"It doesn't match DNA on record."

"How is that? How did the OBI...how did my captain know?"

I shrugged. "My guess would be a Brody connection, or Pope has her fingers in deep. I wouldn't put it past her to somehow have given a DNA sample under the guise of contamination, and to have it flagged. According to this report, though, it matches no one on *record*."

"The records include only some defendants who consented before trial and only some of the people who've been convicted, more in the last few years. Not comprehensive by any means."

"I thought the fingerprints might trigger testing," I said sounding naïve to my own ears. "Official testing. Now we'll just have to push a little harder to get that match on the record."

"Do you have the juice for that?"

"Working on it. I don't think I ever said this would be an instantaneous slam dunk."

"So what's your move?" He was still prowling the living room—frustrated. We'd agreed not to meet if it wasn't necessary, so my summons had been a little out of the blue. He probably wanted to get back out there, dig around, make sure the Taneka Parr evidence or something else would stick to my Teflon-coated boss.

And suddenly I thought I knew where I could find one.

"Do you need anything beyond this brainstorming session, Ms. Long? Meeting here—"

"Isn't such a good idea. I know. But we're running out of time. Either we're going to end up dead or in jail if we don't stop spinning our wheels. We need to get evidence, get it to the right authorities, and get out from under this. I don't want to end up in prison with all the people I've prosecuted over the years. And I certainly don't want to end up dead."

"Can I keep this?" He waved the stapled pages of the autopsy. I nodded. It was a printout of an electronic file.

"I've been going through the files," I said having finally worked up the courage to get to where I wanted this meeting to go from the start. I didn't have the bravado sober that I did with a little lubrication. "I think I've found the smoking gun."

Logan shrugged. Lasered in on my eyes as if sussing out whether I was sober.

I sighed long and hard, then finally said, "It's the gun."

"Excuse me?"

"Malcolm Pointer, Ja Roach, and the Fernández-Saldaño family were all killed with a three fifty-seven Magnum."

"That's one of the most popular calibers."

"But it isn't the most popular," I said. I strongly resisted the urge to pile my research onto his lap. A woman in charge did not do that. "Not even in the top three." I pulled out the research, and read from it. "According to the FBI, the most popular are thirty-eight, forty, forty-five, then nine millimeter. The three fifty-seven *used* to be far more popular."

"When?"

"In the 1950s."

"It's still not obscure. It may be sixty years ago, but guns tend to hang around."

I pulled out another sheet. Gave in to the urge to back up what I was saying, handed a copy to Logan.

"Here's a list of all the department-issued sidearms from the inception of the Cleveland Police Department until now."

He patted the firearm nestled in his shoulder holster. "I have the—"

"Glock semi-automatic Model 17 or 19 with a New York 1 trigger," I finished for him. "You're allowed to carry that as well as a personal firearm."

"I don't...carry a second."

So many did. It was often the subject of or bane of investigation in officer-involved shootings.

"No matter. The standard firearm in the nineteen fifties was the Smith and Wesson Military and Police service revolver. According to Blake, Lori Pope's dad was a Cleveland patrolman. My guess is if we do ballistic tests, the bullets from Roach, Saldaño, Fernández, and Pointer will match. We'll have the connection."

"Not Moretti. She wasn't killed by gun. It looked like natural causes, but may have been suffocation."

"You know the answer to that. She didn't shoot her mother because that one was personal."

THIRTY-SEVEN
LOGAN
JANUARY 23, 2010

"You won't regret this," I said to my partner Neil Walsh as I rubbed my ungloved hands together.

During the day it had been a pleasant fifty degrees, feeling all the warmer because it was a Saturday in January. I hadn't worn gloves. Something I was regretting as the winter afternoon sun was long gone, and the arctic winds were blowing in now at nine o'clock at night. We were standing outside the Cuyahoga County medical examiner's office. In addition to autopsies, the office did much of the lab and tech work for crimes throughout the county.

"If I couldn't pull the pin any minute, I wouldn't be doing this," Walsh said, his voice gruff.

"You don't want to be on the wrong side of history, when the shit comes down," I said. I'd been surprised when Walsh had offered to help with our Pope corruption investigation. Asked me what one thing I needed. During his thirty-plus years on the force, he'd made enough friends, or bought enough rounds, to get this tech to come in and do us an off-the-books favor.

"I don't give a crap where I am in history," Walsh scoffed. "I did my time. I want to fish and eat cake with my bourbon. The earth has all kinds of people. Famous people. Rich people. People like Ghandi or Martin Luther King Junior. Shit is important to them, being known, making money, changing the world.

"I'm not that guy. I chose this job because it was the easiest to get when I got out of the service. I could run a fast mile, shoot a straight shot. I didn't try to move up the rank past detective. I just did my beat, did my patrol, collected my years and that's it."

"Long speech." It was the most I'd heard him say off a barstool.

"You're one of the other kinds of people," Walsh observed. I didn't know if I liked my partner sober and philosophical.

"I'm just doing my job—"

Walsh coughed "bullshit" into his fist.

"If you were doing your job, the minute the captain came down on this extracurricular shit, you'd have closed up shop and moved on to the next easy case that could add to your close stats."

"Fine," I acknowledged. "Who is this guy we're waiting for?"

"Randy Chambers. Ballistics. He's the guy you want to reach out to when you need to get real answers—fast."

"You told him what we need?" I didn't want to walk into

a situation where Chambers shied away from doing something a little out of bounds.

"He has the bullets from"—Walsh pulled a small blue-lined and folded paper from his pocket—"Ja Roach, Malcolm Pointer, and that murder-suicide family."

"How did you—" Know who we suspected was what I'd wanted to ask. Cold fear trickled down my spine. We weren't as secretive as we thought. Someone was up to speed on everything we were doing. We didn't have much time to call checkmate, make a move that forced Pope's hand.

"Don't ask questions you don't need the answers to."

The sound of boots on gravel stopped me from pressing Walsh for his information source.

"Sorry. My girlfriend made risotto," said a harried guy. His curly hair looked as if he'd raked his hand through it. Chambers' jacket was half off, his heavy messenger bag pulling the sleeve off. Walsh flicked his hand and we followed the man into the back door of the medical examiner's building and up dimly lit stairs.

As soon as we came into the room, the guy turned on all the lights. Lifted his beat-up bag from off his shoulder and over his head. Shrugged the rest of the way out of his brown corduroy jacket.

Walsh shifted in his brogues. Looked around. "We all good?"

"Fine. Let me get everything turned on." The technician finally acknowledged me. "Randy Chambers." He didn't offer his hand, so I didn't extend mine. "You know how this works?" he asked as he walked to a slate-topped desk filled with equipment.

Was he asking for money? Secrecy? Something else? I shook my head slowly. Kept my mouth shut.

"This is a split-screen microscope," he said pointing to the large bulky black object in front of him. He lifted various evidence bags, marked with Roach's name and case number, Pointer's name and case number, then four more linked to the alleged murder-suicide. "I'm going to compare the striations on each of these spent rounds."

"What will you be able to tell me?" I asked. I thought I knew, but wanted to confirm I was going to get evidence that would move the case forward.

"If they came from the same gun, and the type of gun."

"Okay."

All that fit neatly within his job description. The reason we were all here, late on a Saturday night was that probable cause did not exist to make these exams. These links. Which means Long and I couldn't have done these legitimately.

The second problem was chain of custody. In order to prove that evidence wasn't tampered with, police and labs had strict controls over who, when, and where evidence that could be used for trial, was handled.

Things were put in bags, paper or plastic. Signed, sealed, and delivered. If they needed to be examined, then strict protocols existed to sign things out, open them, close them. Not contaminate them, spoil them, or in the case of biological samples, exhaust them needlessly or carelessly. Crime scene blood, DNA, fluids couldn't be collected a second time.

The last wouldn't be an issue. But explaining how and why one or all of our names were on the receipts would call a lot into question. There were official ways to address these kinds of things, and this wasn't it.

Chambers put on sterile-looking white gloves, took long thin tweezers from a drawer and committed the first offense, taking a bullet from a zipper-sealed bag.

He put it on a tray. Looked into the viewer. Pressed a button that looked like he was taking a picture. He did the same with one bullet after another. Walsh left the room at some point. I didn't have the guts to do so. It was like waiting to find out who the murderer was in a movie, but not being able to fast-forward the DVD to the reveal.

A loud rumbling sounded, and the tech went to a printer in the back of the room. Removed some sheets of what looked like photo paper.

"Get Walsh," Chambers barked.

I wandered the hall to the door until I found my partner. He was leaning on the brick wall of the building, looking up into the night sky. Two cigarette butts that weren't there before lay near his feet. My partner had given up smoking several years ago. I didn't comment on his relapse. Pope could drive anyone to sin.

"The guy is ready," I said. Threw a thumb back towards the door. "Wants you in there."

"Let's go see what's what, then."

I followed Walsh back into the lab.

Chambers took a deep breath, looked like he was going to launch into a lecture. Walsh did a cutting motion in the air.

"Bottom line," Walsh said. "You can save the details for him after."

"Fortunately, there were sufficient intact bullets for examination. If you look here at these marks." Chambers pointed to what looked like etched metal on blown-up pictures of the bullets. "They're the same across bullets."

"Like a fingerprint?" I asked.

"Exactly like a fingerprint."

"It's a three fifty-seven Magnum. If I had to guess, it's a Smith and Wesson Military and Police service revolver."

I tried not to let out my gasp of surprise. Nicole Long had been right on the money.

"From the fifties?" Walsh asked. At Chambers' nod, he continued. "My first partner had one of those. It was his other piece. Talk about a throwback."

"So what do we need to tie all these together?" I directed my question at the ballistics expert.

"The gun."

THIRTY-EIGHT
BLAKE
JANUARY 24, 2010

"Who do you think has the gun?" Loren Logan was at my dining room table, again. This time he was stuffing monkey bread into his mouth, so I wasn't sure I heard the question. "This is really, really good, by the way," he said around a bigger than average bite.

"It's flour with copious amounts of butter and sugar," I said as I refilled my favorite oversized turquoise mugs from a fresh carafe of coffee. "What's not to like?"

"I have really good timing," he said, wiping cinnamon and sugar from his hands on a paper napkin.

"Or a really good appetite."

Then my brain processed what he'd asked earlier. I'd thought a lot about this after he'd called earlier this morning announcing...maybe even asking if he could come over. I'd promptly pulled some biscuit canisters out of the fridge and prepared a treat. It was probably inappropriate and sexist in a lot of ways, but something made me want to cook and bake for him. I hated that "seek approval from men" part of myself. After all those years of being one kind of woman, I wasn't sure I could be another.

I stood, put my plate in the sink, and laid a clean kitchen towel over the Bundt pan as I tried to shake myself out of that thought pattern. I wasn't going to fix who I was at this moment.

"I think there are only three people who could possibly have it," I said when I was done fiddling with the food and turned around to face him.

"Three?"

"Maybe a million, but let's start with the three people who have been open about their hostility toward our little conspiracy. Tommy O'Callaghan, Rocco Nicola, and Lori Pope. After all it's her dad's gun, right? That's what you said. It was some kind of police-issue gun. Probably her dad's."

"You don't think there's some other person doing the dirty work?" he asked. I couldn't tell if he was playing devil's advocate or really thought there was more to it. Either way, I wasn't ready to let go of logic.

"Who? An addict like Ja Roach? Lori Pope needed someone who was a sure shot. Someone who could lure Wetzel away or get into that family's house somehow. Are you saying you think she hired a...fourth person. Like a hitman. Or she has some other CI?"

"Darlene Webb had asked Long for a list," Logan said. He finished his drink. Put his mug in the sink, rinsed it out. I put the cooled dessert into the fridge.

Logan turned to me, lips pursed. For a long second, I thought this morning was about to go in an entirely different direction. While I was trying to decide what I thought of that, he pulled keys out, jingled them. "I think we need to take a ride."

"Where?"

"Cleveland Heights."

I didn't know his exact plans, but I made sure the oven was off, put on my waterproof boots, and followed him down the stairs and out my front door.

The rain had melted away the snow, so it was a quick ten-minute drive over wet pavement to the Cleveland Heights municipal building. Logan had badged us right past the duty officer. Honestly I thought there'd be better security.

"Geez, Logan. You never call," Darlene Webb said as the two of us came into the bullpen.

I had to agree with her, but I didn't want to sidetrack the conversation, so I did so silently with a nod in her direction.

"There wasn't time." He flicked a hand. "Somewhere we can go in private?"

"Interrogation room. Crime is down these days..."

Webb put us in the room, left for a few minutes.

"Cameras and mics are off," Webb said when she came back. She pushed the door closed, creating a vacuum of silence. "Things won't ramp up, if at all, until tonight. Though if the rain turns to snow, it'll stay quiet. What do you guys need?"

"To find the gun," I said. Then we explained both what the ballistics expert had concluded, and our best guesses.

"So what?" Webb threw up her hands. "You want me to find O'Callaghan and Nicola and what, pat them down. Get a wand and wait until it beeps?"

"Do you have a second gun?" I asked Webb.

She'd been looking me in the eye, unnervingly so, up until that question. Webb stepped back, kept moving until her back hit the interrogation room wall. Finally gave a small shrug.

"After Troy Duncan, after Baldwin, I started carrying one." Webb's voice was full of contrition. I'm not sure she had anything to apologize for.

"Where do you keep it?" I asked not letting her get sidetracked.

"Ankle holster or glove box when I'm out of the station, but on duty."

"When you're here?"

"Locked bottom desk drawer. With my purse."

"Do you take it home with you?"

"Never. Only my department-issued weapon per regulations."

"Where do the other officers keep their second weapons?"

"Same as me. Car or desk. Sometimes their locker." Webb crossed her arms tightly across her chest. Her headshake was emphatic. "Don't think I don't see where this is going."

"I'll do the searching," Logan offered, as if conspiracy weren't a crime. "If there's one thing I know, it's that there are no cameras in the bullpen. Patrolman's Association wouldn't stand for the surveillance. Same is true for the back of the lot out there. I only need two things."

"What's that?" Webb asked through tight lips and closed teeth.

"Video camera and the keys to the right unmarked."

"Are you serious? How in the heck are you going to go to any state or federal court with this evidence?"

Logan pulled a palm-sized FlipShare from his pocket.

"That's what the video camera is for."

"Fine," Webb conceded. "Let's go."

I tried not to look suspicious. But a black woman breaking the law in a police station was at the bottom of a list of things I thought I should be doing. Webb came back with the keys.

"Keep me out of the pictures," I said. "I don't have the protection of a union." Or their skin color. But I didn't say that part out loud.

Webb nodded in understanding. Then she took the camera and started rolling. Logan introduced himself. Stated the purpose of his investigation. He used the key Webb had given him to open a desk Webb said belonged to Nicola.

Nothing.

He opened another locked drawer assigned to O'Callaghan.

Empty.

I tried not to let dejection wash over me. Without a gun, we were almost back where we started except in far more danger.

Webb and Logan walked out of the back door and back toward the parking lot, but not before she was filmed taking a key from a small wall locker, and recording a sign-out sheet where the detectives' names showed they'd been the last to access the car.

Into the icy-cold rain we all walked. Webb unlocked the door of the best-looking unmarked in the lot. Logan started with the trunk. It had a lock box for a shotgun that was, per regulations, empty. Under that was a spare tire. Logan slammed the trunk, then went right to the passenger door. He opened the glove box. There were flares, and a replacement Taser cartridge, and behind that, in a black leather holster older than all of us was...a gun. I'd done enough research and looked at enough pictures to recognize the revolver on the spot.

It was a Smith and Wesson Military and Police service revolver.

"The smoking gun," came from me as a whisper only I heard because I didn't need to be caught on tape.

THIRTY-NINE
SEASON 2, EPISODE 9:
FEDERAL MURDER

nless you live under a rock, I'm sure you've seen the articles in not only the ongoing corruption matters that go straight to the top of Cuyahoga County. For years, lawyers, judges, and contractors have operated under a pay-to-play system.

It's been whispered about in the hallways. It's been spoken about during parties. No one, though, has ever had the temerity to stand up against the system, until now.

This is *The Murders Began,* with me, your host, Blake Hardin Tatum.

Speaking with the promise of anonymity, is an attorney working in Cuyahoga County.

"Welcome to *The Murders Began,* can you tell me how long you've been working as an attorney in Cleveland?"

"I've been practicing as a generalist for about fifteen years. Before that I worked in the county clerk's office."

"Did you go to law school at night?"

"I did. Juggled a full-time job and part-time school. Took four years."

"What's been the worst thing about practicing law in the county?"

"It's a pay-to-play system. Always has been. Always will be."

"What do you mean, pay to play. Surely most people aren't having to fork over money just to do business in the county."

"Yes, and no. I had to work alongside people who didn't have to interview, work, or even show up for their jobs. Whenever work got dumped on me, I'd say something to my manager. They'd push back. Say the guy or girl was connected, and that was the way the cookie crumbled. It's what spurred me to go to law school. I wanted a job where I'd have more autonomy."

"Did it work out that way?"

"No. After four years of working forty hours, then another twenty or thirty besides, and taking on a small mountain of debt, I found myself in the same damn place."

"How so?"

"I went out on my own. First thing I learned was that it was the same shit, different day. Can I swear on here?"

"You can speak plainly."

"To get criminal case assignments, I had to give to campaign funds. For my clients to have motions decided in their favor, some judges took more...donations. I hated it when my clients asked me what it took to win. I knew what was required, but I wasn't willing to lose my law license to get it for them. I don't know if that made me a bad lawyer or a noble man."

Fortunately, federal investigators have finally broken through that noise. Fingers crossed it looks like maybe some justice is finally coming to one corner of Cuyahoga County government.

The question remains, what should someone like Cynthia Wetzel do? She believes the prosecutor has it out for her. What if the judge on a lawsuit she brings is corrupt. What if a cop she goes to is corrupt? What if the system can't work for her even if she deserves it?

The answer in the Jimmy Dimora corruption scandal was the United States attorney. Have you noticed when police can't be indicted or convicted, the first move is for the federal government to step in?

That's the play here. To accuse Pope of murder, the accusers have to go straight to the top.

Murder is almost exclusively a state crime. There are

very few statutes that allow a federal judge and jury to hang someone for murder. As with any law, there are always exceptions, and in this case, the United States frowns on witness tampering.

There's strong evidence that the Cuyahoga County prosecutor, Lorraine Pope, has single-handedly murdered, or has conspired to murder one or more people who can point to her guilt or another's innocence.

Whether anyone has enough power to bring her down...remains to be seen.

FORTY
NICOLE
JANUARY 26, 2010

"This feels like an ambush, but I'm not sure why," Casey Cort said. We were all again assembled in Justin McPhee's living room. All of us, except Valerie Dodds, that is. We needed to maintain our illusion of rivalry was the excuse. I'd have never said it to anyone else, but I wasn't sure that I trusted her. I couldn't tell if my tentative hold on sobriety was bringing clarity or confusion.

Everyone had gotten very quiet when Cort had used her own key to come in the front door along with a gust of arctic air. Despite the silence of five adults staring at her, she'd nonchalantly unwound her scarf, hung her coat, then did the same to her son before she sat with the toddler in the one empty chair.

Before anyone could speak, Cort's little boy wiggled out of her lap and started to crawl across the floor. Little Simon picked up some small colorful geometric blocks and thought long and hard before pushing one, then the next through the corresponding slots of a plywood cube.

"I need a favor from you," I said. Cort's eyebrows couldn't have risen higher. I knew my words were unexpected, but I didn't have any time to waste on niceties or social lubrication.

Cort's eyes met with McPhee's. Something unspoken passed between them before he gave the slightest nod. Cort turned back to me.

"What could I possibly do for you?" Her question bordered on incredulous.

"For justice," I countered trying to play to her strong sense of right and wrong.

"Oh, that's even better." Her sarcasm was thinly veiled. "Go ahead."

I took a beat. Tried not to match her energy. Every time we'd gone head-to-head, she'd won. As far as I was concerned, I was on the back foot. Especially needing to come to her like this, hat in hand. Resolved to push forward, I said, "We found evidence that links the chief prosecutor Lori Pope with at least six murders."

"I think you have our jobs confused," Cort retorted. "You have the power to put people away who commit crimes. I'm the one who defends them."

"I'm accusing Lori Pope, *the* county prosecutor, my boss. That seriously curtails my so-called power." A power I'd only used for good went unsaid because I knew my observation would likely be unwelcome. But I mean I wasn't the one who'd defended a sex trafficker.

Casey Cort raised a single eyebrow.

"Did you go to the OBI?" she asked. It was a different question than I'd expected. Somehow I assumed she'd want to know more about the favor I was seeking. One so big I'd gathered together all these people to back the need for her particular brand of help.

"The Ohio Bureau of Investigations is not my first choice here. I'm not sure who Lori Pope has in her pocket."

I didn't get into the details of how Captain Marty Todd was the messenger equivalent of a warning shot across the bow.

"But I am?" Cort gave a small, awkward laugh. "Your first choice?"

"I need to get to someone who can't be bought by her."

"Again—"

I cut her off because I didn't have the energy for this tit for tat. "I want you to call your former fiancé."

"Tom Brody?"

Awkward silence from me. No one else chimed in to clear up her misunderstanding. Finally, I said, "Um, no. Not that one."

"Ronald Pinheiro?"

I didn't know who he was or that she'd had...another... ex-fiancé.

"None of the above," I finally answered before the list grew any longer. Obviously I hadn't been keeping up with the Celebrations section of the *Plain Dealer*. "I meant Miles Siegel."

"Miles?" Cort wasn't giving an inch.

"He's a federal prosecutor," I started with the obvious. "I know that he's in no way beholden to Lori Pope or Tom Brody or any of the city, state, or county power brokers."

"I haven't talked to him in three years. What makes you think he'll take my call?"

I looked at her, woman to woman, until we locked eyes.

"He'll take your call. Even better, I think he'd let you up for an impromptu visit."

"Visit?" Cort's brows knitted.

"He doesn't have court today." I'd made sure of it before getting McPhee to call Casey Cort over. "He's in the office. So I imagine that he'd be happy to see a face from the past."

Casey sat back, crossed her arms against her still ample chest. Resigned.

"What do you want me to say to him?"

"You don't have to say anything. I can speak for myself."

"You want me to bring you, like a Trojan horse?"

"He and I are both prosecutors. For the most part, we're on the same side. Our...history leads me to believe he won't take my calls, and I need to see him sooner, rather than later."

That history being Siegel's successful prosecution of Sledge Hammer, the sex trafficker we couldn't prosecute because my co-counsel had thrown the case—on purpose.

"When do you want to go?" Cort said, vaguely gesturing toward her son whose pudgy, dimpled fingers grasped a toy that was nearing his mouth.

"I'm ready now." I stood up to my full height. I was wearing a suit, boots, and my briefcase was leaning against my chair.

"Do you...have the literal gun in there?" Cort's voice was incredulous. I didn't have the time or luxury to explain what had led all of us to where we were today.

"Logan handed it to me this morning in front of all these witnesses. I don't want to break chain of custody now."

Cort looked from me in my best charcoal suit and down at her own clothes, which could best be described as...casual. At worst, well, whatever one would call a lemon-yellow sweatsuit with tie-dyed drawstrings that clashed most unfortunately with her hair.

Cort gestured between Simon and Justin. "Can you watch—"

"Go," McPhee said as he picked up the little boy who'd toddled over to him. "Do the right thing."

Casey Cort had the sway I thought she would. Five minutes after we arrived in the new federal building, Cort, Logan, and I had visitor badges and were escorted to the U.S. attorney's office on the fourth floor. Men seemed endlessly dedicated to Cort, no matter how their romantic relationships had ended.

If Tom Brody hadn't been disgraced, I'm sure he would have seen her in a heartbeat. McPhee clearly loved her. There was even another ex in the picture. I'd never inspired a lot of male attention, but never that much devotion.

When we got to Miles Siegel's office, he looked at her like

she was the one who got away. I had to wonder what she did to inspire such dedication. After he embraced her, he finally took in the other two people in reception, Logan and myself.

"Come on back to my office," Siegel said before turning on his heel.

All three of us followed, crowded into the small office, with its ugly modern furniture and jail-cell-sized sliver of window overlooking nothing.

"Casey? Nicole? Honestly I never thought I'd see you in the same room together or on the same side of anything. So you must need something the U.S. government can give you that the state of Ohio can't."

"We need your help taking down Lori Pope," I announced. Bald and bold was the only way to go.

"Corruption? Because we're working on a huge case I really can't discuss. But it has tentacles that spread far and wide from the top down county government."

"If you're talking about Jimmy Dimora and Frank Russo, Lori Pope isn't part of that," I declared. There'd been a lot of water cooler talk in the prosecutor's office about who was and who wasn't part of the corruption case that was taking down half of county government. Lori Pope was a lot of things, but one who bribed judges, wasn't one of them. She'd fixed her cases long before they got before a tribunal.

"Maybe not." Siegel obviously didn't believe that, but I wasn't going to get into a pissing match over it. He was going to have to take me at my word.

"We're not here about bribes or kickbacks," Logan interrupted in that way that men had. He made himself broad, tall, stepped forward. He reached into my bag, slapped the .357 Magnum down on Siegel's desk with a loud knock. "We're here about murder."

FORTY-ONE
LOGAN
JANUARY 26, 2010

"Murder is a state crime," Siegel said. He hadn't flinched as if cops regularly dropped guns on his desk. I had to admire the steel in him. He wasn't as soft as most of the prosecutors I was used to, weak men who "fought" crime from behind a desk.

"Except when it's federal," Long said.

"There are seven very narrow exceptions," Siegel said as if he knew chapter and verse without reference to a single law book. "Like the victim being killed on a ship at sea or on federal property. During a bank robbery, or they're a federal judge, official, or in law enforcement. Nothing like that has come up on our radar," Siegel said.

"The other exception is section fifteen twelve of the criminal code," Long said. She'd done a ton of research before our morning meeting at McPhee's house. Sober and prepared, I could see why she'd been hired and was once a rising star.

"Witness tampering? You can't keep me in the dark. Is

this part of the Dimora case?" Siegel seemed like he was blinded by the biggest federal corruption probe the county had seen.

That was bad.

This was worse.

"Look, everyone and their brother is being indicted in the Dimora case. There's no crossover here. This isn't about bribes, or kickbacks, or no-bid contracts. No Vegas trips or strippers or prostitutes," I said.

"I have to ask," Siegel said. He was finally listening. "All that you mentioned. It's keeping this office busy. Everyone's working overtime on those. If new information comes in, we have to act on it right away."

"Fair enough. This is different. In many ways," I started, not above appealing to the man's ego. "There's a woman named Tia Wetzel. More than ten years ago, she was a defendant in a run-of-the mill drug case. She's claiming she didn't get due process and that her civil rights were violated. Vernon Dinwiddie had taken on her case."

"What's the witness-tampering part?"

"Lori Pope and two Cleveland Heights police officers conspired to kill an acquaintance of hers so that she couldn't testify against the police department or...the prosecutor's office."

Miles Siegel's eyes went wide.

"Did you handle her case?" he asked of Long.

"The first time." She shrugged. "And now."

"The proper channels for this would be to get a special

prosecutor appointed, work with the Ohio Bureau of Investigation—"

Nicole Long didn't wait to be fobbed off.

"I know the standard protocol. If I thought that was possible, I wouldn't be here. There are two reasons that will not work. You've been here long enough to understand why, but I'll lay it out for you.

"First the Brodys have state prosecution all sewn up. You know that. Pope and Liam Brody are as thick as thieves. She worked directly under him when he was the county prosecutor, then he anointed her his successor. I'm not willing to risk this on theoretical impartiality of the attorney general's office. Second, Lori Pope is on a murder spree. I'm not willing to stake my life following proper protocol."

"What evidence do you have of murder?" Siegel asked.

"That's why Logan's here. What he just put on your desk. That's the murder weapon. The gun used on almost all of the murders."

"How did you get it?" Siegel had been at it long enough to know that there was something hinky in the way we'd come in, even with my explanation about Liam Brody.

"That's where it gets complicated," Long said. She turned to me. "Logan?"

I was not a lawyer. I'm not even sure I was that great when prosecutors put me on the stand in court. Now I needed to make my case. I tried to organize everything that had happened over the last few months in my head. After taking a deep breath, I spoke.

"That Tia Wetzel. That was a federal case. Probably your

foot in the door. The rest is another matter altogether, but tightly bound to that," I tried to explain, but I could hear how twisted it all sounded.

I tried again.

"Pope had henchmen all over the place to do her dirty work. The main two were…are Cleveland Heights detectives. She or they used her father's gun—from when he was a beat cop in the fifties—to murder innocent people. Then she pinned those crimes on people she held a grudge against or people she couldn't prosecute any other way, like Monsignor Gregory Quinn."

Miles Siegel's gasp of surprise echoed what I'd felt so long ago. It was horrible I'd become so desensitized to this level of malevolence so quickly.

I continued, "One was a confidential informant she's used for years. The other, the one for which we have the least evidence, was her mother."

"Let me get a conference room." Siegel was suddenly in motion. "It's going to be a late night, but I think you need to lay this out for me."

"As I said before." I pointed to the gun on his desk. It was in an evidence bag. "Here's the gun."

Siegel stood, led us to an empty conference room. Before we could even get seated, he picked up a phone in the middle of the table. "Let me get Lou Valdespino up here."

FORTY-TWO
SEASON 2, EPISODE 10:
THE TARGET LETTER

This is *The Murders Began*, with me, your host, Blake Hardin Tatum.

If you've ever seen a mafia movie, then you've probably heard of a target letter. About three quarters of the way through the movie, when it's clear that the mobsters can no longer kill with impunity, the federal investigators move in. On screen, the main guy gets a target letter. Cue grand jury montage before everyone's in a courtroom.

For once, real life and fiction hew pretty close

together. If you remember Episode 4 focused on grand juries. There I talked about state grand juries. The biggest difference between the state and federal systems is that the U.S. attorneys will sometimes warn a potential defendant to the fact that they are under investigation.

Given wire taps, and undercover work, it would seem odd that the FBI and prosecutors would alert someone that they're under suspicion, but the more complex the crime, the harder it is to get evidence. It's especially hard when coconspirators refuse to testify.

The target letter usually has three distinct parts. First, it details what kind of crime the target is under investigation for. Two, it advises that person of their constitutional rights. Lastly, and this is optional, it can invite that person to testify before the grand jury.

Why, I'm sure you wonder would someone testify when they could be indicted. Targets often do. They could provide exculpatory evidence that would shield them from prosecution. For example, they could provide a reasonable explanation for hinky-looking behavior, or they could provide exculpatory evidence—something that shows they're not guilty—all but eliminating the prospect of prosecution.

Two weeks ago the U.S. attorney for the Northern District of Ohio served Cuyahoga County prosecutor, Lorraine Pope, with a target letter. Though these matters are usually secret, Pope publicized her letter. She released a statement which read in part, "I am not guilty of any wrongdoing. I'm sure I received this letter in light of the ongoing investigations of many of the county's top players. While the revelation of widespread corruption has been unfortunate, I'm one hundred percent sure that no one in my office has been or will be found liable for inappropriate or illegal behavior."

Whether she'll be indicted or whether this is specifically targeted at her actions or part of the wider corruption probe remains to be seen.

What I can say is that the Cuyahoga County prosecutor may one day be held accountable for the things of which she's accused. Hopefully justice can be equal for everyone.

FORTY-THREE
NICOLE
FEBRUARY 9, 2010

Loren Logan and I were waiting in a little Lebanese restaurant that was oddly situated between the Justice Center and the new federal building.

I was downing hummus like I hadn't eaten in the last ten years. As I dipped more pita into the chickpea blend, I wondered whether I could get away with unbuttoning my skirt. I knew the answer was no. After I unfastened it, the side zip would inevitably ease down. My silk blouse would poke out of the side. Sartorial disaster could ensue. I wish there was some middle ground between white-knuckle sobriety and getting fat.

"Are you going to eat something?" I asked Logan. I'd had more than my share.

"Too nervous. Siegel has to come back with good news."

"How would that look?" I asked. I wouldn't say it out loud, but I was resigning myself to Pope never going to jail. My sense was that she'd get hers, but maybe not in this lifetime. Wish I had a greater belief in the afterlife, but New Day church had killed my faith. Seth Collins had put a nail into the coffin.

"An indictment, of course," he answered. "Pope, and whomever else she's roped into helping her."

"He said the hearing would probably be over by four." I pointed to a clock on the wall that read half past the hour.

"I'll get those za'atar fries, then," Logan said. Signaled for the waiter.

By the time Miles Siegel came to our booth in the back of the restaurant, I'd eaten most of the salty, spiced fried potatoes Logan had ordered for himself.

"What's the verdict?" Logan asked, no preamble.

"You know it's an indictment, not a verdict," Siegel said as he pulled up a chair to the top of the U-shaped booth.

"He wasn't being literal." I defended the cop. He was a smart guy who I didn't want lumped in with the euphemistic, dumb-jock-cop stereotype.

"Sorry. After a day in front of a grand jury, I lose all ability to deal with nuance." Siegel's face and body visibly relaxed. He took a stick of seasoned potato.

"Don't keep us waiting," I begged. "I need to know that Lori Pope is going down."

"The grand jury did vote to indict," Siegel started. Took water proffered by a passing busser. Drank deeply, then looked at each of us in the eye. "Just not Pope."

"What?" Logan and I exclaimed nearly simultaneously. Lowered our voices when the other patrons turned out way.

"They are going after the two Cleveland Heights cops," Siegel added.

"On what charges?" I asked. I wanted the bandage pulled, the bottom line.

"Twelve six oh one, of course."

I nodded, taking in the information. Trying to decide if I felt vindicated or angry. Logan squinted and looked between the two of us. Waved his hands looking for more information.

"In English."

"Federal civil rights violations."

I swallow my feelings of defeat. The federal government had so much power, but rarely used it for good. The shaky politics that permeated my upbringing in the so-called New South were evidence of that.

"The kind that come with consent decrees that never really change anything," I concluded.

"That obstruction of justice addresses the physical harm," Siegel said. He was placating me. Regret crept through my bones. Despite the risks everyone was taking, my second big idea was coming to nothing. Slaps on proverbial police wrists. The law was failing us.

"But nothing for Lori Pope?" My clenched fist pounded the table loud enough to get the attention of those around us, again. I immediately put my hands in my lap. Lowered my voice. The small city had big ears. "What in the heck happened? You need to go as hard at her as you're going against Dimora."

Siegel's voice lowered as well. All three of us leaned in a little closer.

"The U.S. attorney sent her a target letter."

Talk about giving her a massive heads-up. My involuntary shiver had nothing to do with the freezing sleet and snow blanketing the pavement outside the restaurant window. It had to do with my actual fear of my possible premature death.

"Why?" I whispered.

"We have to do it if we want them to testify."

This. This was why I hated the feds. They were always about trying to make these picture-perfect cases as if they were being graded by law professors or pundits on Court TV. Those in my office did what was necessary for a conviction. Getting the bad guys off the streets was far more important than faultless procedure. I worked to keep my hands in my lap and from around his throat.

"Jesus Christ." I leaned in even further, letting my fear propel me. "The woman's own mother called her a psychopath. Lori Pope talked her way out of it and walked herself out of court, right?"

With a single, petrified eye open, I'd skimmed a book on the personality disordered over the weekend. Smart, crafty, with no care for right and wrong, sociopaths had an uncanny ability to outsmart those around them and talk themselves out of anything. The book had described Lori Pope to a "T." Explained so much about why my boss appeared to be Teflon coated even with evidence of wrongdoing raining down like the sleet outside.

Siegel's only concession was raised eyebrows. He said, "She wove a story that suggested O'Callaghan and Nicola were sole actors, or in concert, but not with her."

"How'd she explain them having her gun?"

"She did admit to them having special access to her. She said that she just liked to have eyes and ears on the ground, especially when confirming the information from confidential informants. She invited them to her house, because talking at her office or the police station was a problem. She'd mentioned the gun at some point. They'd wanted to see something that antique. She claims to not have noticed it had gone missing."

"So there's no connection," Logan concluded while shaking his bowed head. I could feel that his sense of defeat was as heavy as my own.

"Not for her, but for the other cops. If your theory is correct, they pulled the trigger, and are still responsible. After all, you say they assaulted Wetzel. They're hardly innocent."

"But Lori Pope is hardly innocent either," I said. I could hear the whine in my voice, but it couldn't be helped.

"We tried." Siegel pushed himself back from the table. Stood. "If something else comes up, you can let me know. But for now, we're just going forward on the Cleveland Heights detectives. I'd love to join you for dinner, but I have to get back to work. It's all hands on deck right now."

Without so much as a good-bye, Siegel was up and out of the door. I looked at Logan. Shook my head.

"We still have a problem," he said.

"I have no idea how to solve it, but in no way do I want it to end with our deaths."

"Maybe without her trigger men, it won't come to that."

FORTY-FOUR
BLAKE
FEBRUARY 12, 2010

The most exciting part of my job at the *Plain Dealer* was when I received a tip from an unknown source.

It was when I knew that an investigation that I'd been working on was about to take a turn, usually in such a way that it would crack wide open.

The scariest part of my job as a journalist is having a clandestine meeting with an unknown source offering a tip.

This morning I'd received a message through my blog that someone had information about my investigation into Tia Wetzel. They want to share it with me, but only in person. I'm pretty gutsy, but fear of assault and death was real. Not everyone who claims to be helpful is. On top of all that, it could well be a ploy by Pope to get me in a dark corner of Cleveland to:

Warn me.

Scare me.

Intimidate me.

Eliminate me.

I shook my hands, trying to get rid of the tremors of fear. I needed to let down my guard and pull out the big guns— literally. I picked up my phone from the dining room table where I'd been trying, unsuccessfully, to trace the anonymous email on my laptop.

"I know I probably shouldn't call you," I said when Loren Logan answered, "but I need your help."

"You've never called me before." I couldn't tell if he was happy or annoyed.

"I'm sorry," rushed out.

"No need to apologize." Logan was brusque. I had to wonder if he was surrounded by other cops in the bullpen. "What do you need?" he asked, finally.

"I got a call from an anonymous source," I started, then paused realizing how crazy it probably appeared.

"Like Watergate?" he asked confirming how cloak and dagger I sounded.

"Hopefully not like Watergate. They asked me to meet."

"Where? When?"

"The Flats. In forty-five minutes."

"You want me there?"

"Can you? Be there, I mean? I'm supposed to go alone. But you're a cop. Surely you can somehow find a place to lie low. Just to keep an eye out. I'm about ninety percent sure it's legit. But if it's ten percent craziness, or even a Pope setup. I don't want to die. Not for a story."

"Tell me where and when. You won't see me, but I'll be there."

During my career, I'd once reported a statistic on American mortality. The likelihood of living to tomorrow is ninety-nine point nine percent for all of us. Somewhat reassured about the likelihood of me seeing the morning, I increased the chances that I could die by nine hundred percent once I got in my car and drove from the east side of Cleveland to the corner of Elm Street and Washington in the center of the Flats, a warehouse district restored.

As I walked on Elm toward the underside of the bridge called the Superior Viaduct, I tried not to think of the horror movie that shared the same street name. I didn't want this to me a nightmare.

I zipped my moto shearling up to my neck, trying to keep the snowflakes from melting on the back of my neck. I should have worn the parka, but I wanted to be both warm but have my legs free to run if it came to that. I had no plans to go down like a horror movie victim, my legs pinned down by stuffed nylon. Everyone knew black women died first.

"Blake Tatum?" The voice was male, gruff, older, startling me from thoughts of my demise. I turned to see the source. But he was hiding in the shadows. Probably couldn't have picked him out of a lineup, if Logan asked later.

"That's me."

"I read your blog."

Was I supposed to say "thanks"? I couldn't decide, so did what I did best, remained silent.

"You're never going to get Lori Pope. She's like a house mouse. She gets in and out, only leaving damage behind," he said.

"So why are you here? Did you build a better mouse-trap?" I waited a beat, couldn't resist asking what I really wanted to know. "Why do you think we're targeting the county prosecutor?"

"In the future, you're going to want to firewall your blog. TypePad is easy to hack."

"Hack?"

"I'm the kind of person who reads the back of the book first. So I made a way in to read the blogs before you publish them."

I had no way of knowing whether this guy was telling the truth of whether my site was vulnerable, that my TypePad host didn't have proper protections in place.

Didn't make much of a difference because there was nothing I could do while wind blew off the Cuyahoga River, and snow continued to dust my hair, shoulders. I'd left my hat in the car.

"Either you have something or you don't." I called his hand.

The man held out a large yellow envelope, the generic kind every stationary shop sold, untraceable. I stepped forward, grateful I'd at least had the presence of mind to put on boots with some kind of traction, and took the envelope.

"Is there some way to contact you?" I asked flipping the envelope, blank on both sides.

"No need. It'll be everything that you need."

"So justice is your reward?"

He laughed. "Something like that. You better be getting home before the weather turns bad."

"I hope my thanks are in order."

He gave a two-finger salute, spun on his heel like a soldier, and disappeared right into the shadows. If I hadn't been holding that envelope in my hand, I'd almost have thought I dreamt the whole thing.

FORTY-FIVE
LOGON
FEBRUARY 12, 2010

"What do you think it is?" I asked, my leg bouncing in the passenger seat. I'd taken my unmarked car back to the station, and hopped into Tatum's Jeep for the ride to the east side.

"I'm going to wait until I get home," she said as she turned the corner from MLK Drive to Larchmere.

"You do well with delayed gratification. I don't, so it's good that we're already here."

She pulled up to the curb, crunching through the snow that had accumulated in the last few hours.

Though there was no overt invitation, I followed Tatum up the stairs. By the time she unlocked the door to her apartment, the hands on the clock in her living room had eased past midnight. Despite the time, I was anything other than tired.

Without hurry, Tatum took off her coat, brushed off the water that spotted the coat. She picked up the small package from the skinny entrance hutch and walked it to the dining room table. Dropped it.

"Do you have gloves?" Tatum asked.

I held up the leather gloves I was about to store in the pocket of the coat I'd hung up on her rack.

She shook her head. "No, the other kind."

"Good idea." I reached into the inside pocket and pulled out four latex gloves. Handed over a pair. They were generic, the right and left the same. Large sized.

Mine fit...like a glove. Hers looked like she was wearing her father's.

"You want to do the honors?" she said. I silently cheered. More than anything I wanted to go first. Carefully, I looked around until I found what I was looking for. Picked up a heavy brass letter opener. Pinched the top of the envelope to make sure it was empty, then slipped the metal through the thick paper. Inserted my left thumb and forefinger, widened the opening. Peeked in.

"Are you going to keep me in suspense?" Tatum asked.

I pulled out a tiny wad of tissue paper. Slowly, I unwrapped until I found what was inside. A tiny flash drive, less than an inch and a half in diameter each way. 32GB SD was printed in stylized font prominently on the label.

"You have a reader?"

"Of course." She opened a drawer in the brown wood credenza I'd seen her take napkins from. Only this one was a certified junk drawer. In a few seconds, she took out a reader. The blue plastic gadget had a female slot on one end, and a USB on the other. She lifted the lid of her laptop, plugged in the USB cable on the side. With her gloved hand, she picked up the tiny disk, pushed it into the reader. She sat. Tapped at the trackpad. I stood over her shoulder and waited. A window opened, there was a single mp4 file.

She glanced over her shoulder. Our eyes met. My slight nod was answered by hers. She double-clicked. The computer's media player opened, the video buffered, loaded a single frame. The time of the entire clip was about 10 minutes. It was a grainy image of what looked like—

"Hallway? In an apartment building, maybe?" Tatum's voice was a question.

"Play it."

Tatum swiped her middle finger down until the cursor arrow hovered over the triangular play button. She pressed, tapped, clicked. The hallway was empty. Then a figure comes from the stairs, female shaped. She slows down as she looks at the door numbers. I had a guess as to who it was, but was waiting, hoping for her eyes to glance up toward the camera's lens. For a moment she did. It was Lori Pope. Tatum's gasp reflected exactly how I felt.

"Why did she look at the camera?" I asked, surprised to hear my thoughts out loud.

"It was in a light fixture. Saw that when I visited. I figured they were saving money. Didn't want to install more electrical. It was like a camera surrounded by LED lights."

"Did your source say he worked for the complex?"

"He didn't say much of anything, really. Definitely not that."

Pope slipped a key into the lock. Opened the door of

number 206, then pushed her way in. The door closed. The hallway remained empty from 1:06 on the video until 10:23. Nine minutes, seventeen seconds. That was how long Pope had been inside her mother's apartment. When the prosecutor emerged, she was carrying something.

Tatum paused the video. We both leaned closer to the screen. She maxed out the brightness. It was flowered fabric. She started playback again. On the laptop, we watched Pope fold what was probably a pillowcase into smaller and smaller squares until it was small enough to shove into her coat pocket.

The prosecutor looked right, then left, her face captured again. Then she walked to the steps and disappeared from screen. Playback came to a stop. The opening screen appeared again as the thumbnail.

"We got her," I shouted. Pounded my right fist into my left palm.

Tatum shrugged because she knew what I wasn't saying. Evidence like this would just be the first step.

"Now what?"

FORTY-SIX

SEASON 2, EPISODE 11:
THE DEATH PENALTY

This is *The Murders Began* with me, your host, Blake Hardin Tatum.

I'm not here to debate the death penalty. Twenty-seven states still have executions including Ohio. Yes, the United States joins China and North Korea and Saudi Arabia in executing adults and minors alike.

It's been a long road from Tia Wetzel to here, but Cuyahoga County prosecutor, Lorraine Pope, has been charged with the aggravated murder of her mother, Anna Moretti.

In Ohio, when a person plans and executes the death of another, and they're found guilty, there are two punishments available, life in prison or death.

Because of the person indicted here, the attorney general has stepped in as special counsel. Life in prison is not what Pope deserves, according to Liam Brody. He is seeking the death penalty.

In a criminal case, where the defendant can be deprived of his or her life, the stakes are high and the resulting procedure more complicated. There are two phases to a death penalty case.

First, a jury would have to find Lorraine Pope guilty of aggravated murder, that proof, of course, would have to be beyond a reasonable doubt.

If, and only if, that happens, then a jury moves on to a death phase. Just because a prosecutor seeks death does not make the sentence automatic. A jury has to listen to and weigh evidence of aggravating and mitigating factors when determining whether a defendant can be sentenced to death.

Usually, at this phase, prosecutors focus on the heinous nature of the crime or crimes committed. Defense attorneys call the defendant's friends, family, and others to demonstrate a defendant's better qualities. There are only two possible outcomes. Death or life in prison without parole.

Either would likely end Lorraine Pope's alleged life of crime. Only time will tell what a jury decides.

FORTY-SEVEN
NICOLE
APRIL 1, 2010

"Are you ready to go forward?" Judge Kathy Maldonado asked.

She was talking to my...boss, soon-to-be former, I hoped, Lori Pope. It had nearly taken an act of congress to get here. The last two months had been a circus.

Pope's arrest had come among all the others for corruption. There'd been a lot of ink spilled on whether this arrest had come at the end of a corruption probe, or whether it was a personal vendetta from the powers that be.

Then there was more attention when Pope had been bonded out because the charge of murdering a family member didn't touch witness intimidation in terms of seriousness. Most aggravated murder charges would have had her in jail until trial. Then there was Pope's insistence of a speedy trial, when any other defendant would have taken all nine months to prepare. She knew enough about our office to be aware that moving quickly was not our forte.

"Yes, Your Honor," Gerald Popovic said. "We're ready." Popovic was the most revered defense attorney in the county. Pope had obviously spared no expense on her legal team.

"You know, Mr. Popovic," Judge Maldonado started, "your client can have more time. Just because the special prosecutor is pushing for a speedy, and very public, trial, doesn't mean that your client is not allowed to avail herself of all the constitutional protections to which any defendant is entitled."

"I think we can all agree that my client is well aware of her rights," Popovic retorted. "She'd like to put Ms. Long and Mr. Brody to their proof."

"And you...Ms. Pope, are you sure you waive any conflict with Ms. Long acting on behalf of the Cuyahoga County prosecutor's office?"

The moment I'd gotten the indictment against my boss, I had to turn over the case to the attorney general appointed special prosecutor. I'd been only somewhat surprised when Liam Brody had professed interest in the case. Usually, someone far lower in the food chain would have had to move temporarily from Columbus to Cleveland to try a case like this.

The AG's office would have displaced us, swooped in, and taken over, all in the name of fairness. But Brody had insisted I stay involved with the case, for which I *think* I was grateful. It was possible I was being set up as a fall guy...again, by a Brody. I planned to worry about all of that much, much later.

"My client so waives, Your Honor," Popovic answered for Pope.

"Then let's get the jury in here. Opening arguments."

The convention for a criminal trial was that the prosecutor, who had the burden of proof, had the first word and last. Once the jury was seated, and the journalist-full gallery quiet, Judge Maldonado looked at our table.

"Ms. Long, Mr. Brody? Would you like to give an opening statement?"

I stood. Buttoned the jacket of my gray suit, took a deep breath, and prepared to give what I hoped to be the best argument of my life.

"Do you know who Sir Arthur Conan Doyle is?"

A couple of jurors nodded. The rest clearly had no idea, but a rhetorical question so early piqued their interest.

"He's a Scottish author who created the famous detective Sherlock Holmes."

I prized the looks of recognition that dotted some faces.

"What I loved about his books were his character's powers of deduction and his most famous phrase, 'It's elementary, my dear Watson.' I'm going to ask you, the jurors, to solve what was for law enforcement, a murder mystery."

They looked both intrigued and intimidated. I waved my hand.

"Don't worry, this isn't going to be hard. I'm going to give you all the clues so that you'll reach the inevitable conclusion, that Lori Pope, the Cuyahoga County prosecutor, a woman elected by you and your fellow citizens to uphold the law, broke it. Not once, but many times. This woman is a killer. She committed one of the most depraved crimes anyone ever could. She killed her own mother."

Their widened eyes told me that I was on the right path. If jurors loathed child molesters, they hated matricide nearly as much. The ire against the Menendez brothers proved that. I moved a little closer, pitched my body forward a little, lowered my voice. They all leaned just an imperceptible amount closer as well.

I continued, "I'll show you a tape of Lori Pope walking into her mother's apartment, as cool as a cucumber, nine minutes and seventeen seconds later, and she will come out. She will pause and fold up the fabric case that covered the pillow she used to suffocate her mother to death, then walk away as if it were a normal Sunday visit without a dead woman on the other side of the door.

"I will lay out all the evidence for you, the reason Lori Pope killed her mother. How Lori Pope killed her mother. What she did to cover up the murder of her mother. And lastly, what evidence she left behind that allowed us to tie Lori Pope to the murder of her mother."

Though I was facing the jury, I kept an eye on Popovic gauging whether he was going to object to my repetitive use of his client's name. Lawyers had more leeway with opening statements, but that didn't mean it would be above her counsel to object to interrupt me, distract the jury, throw me off my game. He wasn't looking at me at all, instead he was whispering frantically. So I wrapped it up while I still held the jury's attention.

"After you hear all of that," I concluded, "like Sherlock Holmes, you will put all of the clues together and come to the inevitable conclusion that Lori Pope should be found guilty of aggravated murder."

FORTY-EIGHT
BLAKE
APRIL 2, 2010

'd thought the Catholic church abuse case against Monsignor Gregory Quinn had been the trial of the century, but Lori Pope's trial was an order of magnitude greater. Presiding judge Patrick Brody had to institute a lottery system among the press for gallery seats. There was another entire courtroom, across the hall, filled with reporters watching the trial on close-circuit TV.

Fortunately, Nicole Long had excepted me from the seating sweepstakes, and had somehow wangled a permanent place for me right behind the prosecution table. My name and affiliation were taped to my space on the bench. Valerie Dodds sat to my right. Logan had a space to my left, though he'd yet to occupy it. The rules prohibited potential witnesses from watching and subsequently being influenced by other testimony.

The noise of everyone shuffling pulled my attention from seating arrangements.

"All rise!" cried the bailiff. I stood as the judge, then jury entered the courtroom from different doors behind the bench.

"Prosecution, please call your next witness," Judge Maldonado said after everyone had taken their seats. Long had spent the first days of the trial with the necessary, but boring witnesses establishing who had died and how. I leaned forward because now, she was getting to the good stuff.

"Your Honor." Long stood, straightened her clothes. "We call Detective Rocco Nicola to the stand."

Witness lists, like other documents, were filed with the court, and available to the public. Therefore I'd known at least one of the Cleveland Heights detectives would take the stand. As the burly middle-aged detective made his way through the gallery to the witness box, I had to wonder if he were going to plead the Fifth. I couldn't see a way his testimony wouldn't end up incriminating him and his partner as well as making the federal case indefensible.

Court TV was broadcasting Lori Pope's trial. I'd set up my DVR at home, and for once could pay attention to everything going on without having to simultaneously take notes using the complex system of shorthand I'd learned at the beginning of my career.

After Long got Nicola's name on the record, she asked her first question.

"Can you please tell the court where you work, your years of service, and any commendations you've received."

"I'm a police sergeant for the city of Cleveland Heights."

"What does it mean to be a sergeant?"

"It's a pay classification, not an indication of duty. I work as a detective for the department. I investigate murders and other serious crimes."

"How long have you worked with the department?"

"About twenty-five years. I came straight from a six-year stint in the Marines."

I took in his hair, high and tight, square jaw. Probably should have guessed that. I hadn't done a deep dive on the cops who'd assaulted Tia Wetzel, choosing instead to focus on the victim. Enough ink had been spilled on the idolization of so-called peace officers, and using the phrase "one bad apple," without the logical follow of that aphorism was weak logic and even weaker reporting.

"Do you have an assigned partner?" Long asked Nicola.

"Thomas O'Callaghan."

"How long have you two worked together as partners?"

"Twenty years, plus a little more. He had a partner when he was a rookie. I was assigned to work with him... to..."

I filled in his unsaid words in my head. To indoctrinate him. To rope someone into the off-the-books assignments. He couldn't say any of that. Fortunately, he'd thought better of it. Didn't leave the door open for Pope's counsel to poke all the fingers at him.

"When did you first meet Lori Pope?" Long gestured to the defendant. She wasn't going to let anyone forget who was on trial here.

"Nineteen eighty-eight or thereabouts," Nicola

answered. "Routine case. She was the prosecutor on duty. I think she was new then."

"Do you remember investigating the death of Wayne Cooley?"

There was a long silence. I could practically see the gears turning in his head. His eyes darted to the defendant, shifted away. Long gave him all the time in the world.

Nicola's "Yes" was somewhat underwhelming. Nicole Long handed him a piece of paper. She gave the exhibit number for the court reporter. Handed copies to Pope's counsel and the judge.

"When did he die?"

Nicola took reading glasses from his breast pocket.

"December twenty of eighty-eight," he read after perching his glasses on his nose.

"Was the Cooley wrongful death investigation ever closed by the Cleveland Heights police?"

"No."

"Sergeant Nicola, how did Wayne Cooley die?"

"Gunshot from a forty-five-caliber gun."

There was a lot of murmuring behind me. I knew the other reporters were thinking what I was. Was this a case they'd covered? How had a point-blank murder fallen off the radar? What did it mean that Detective Nicola knew what happened if it was unsolved?

"How do you know that?"

"Because I saw him pull the trigger."

My pen fell into my lap as the gallery erupted. Watching legal shows made court look exciting. It wasn't. Ninety-nine percent of the time, it was a snooze fest. There was a reason a coffee cart had nearly permanent placement outside.

When the room quieted, Long asked, "I want to be clear, Detective Nicola, you're saying that you know who murdered Wayne Cooley."

"Yes." Nicola's answer was quick this time, sure.

"Your Honor," Popovic protested before Long could draw enough breath for another question. "How is any of this relevant? My client is only charged with the murder of Anna Moretti."

"Under four oh four 'b,' prior bad acts can be admitted to show motive, Your Honor. Our theory of the case is that Moretti's murder was ultimately done to silence someone who had first-hand evidence of the defendant's crimes."

"Your objection is overruled." Maldonado waved a dismissive hand toward the defense table.

"Do you know the identity of the person who shot Wayne Cooley?" Long asked.

"Yes."

"Who was it?"

"Thomas O'Callaghan."

Popovic was up and out of his chair at the same time the gallery erupted.

"Objection!" Pope's counsel yelled while Judge Maldonado's gavel hit its block.

"On what grounds?" Long asked.

"Relevance," Popovic answered.

"We'll show relevance with the next question," Long said.

"Overruled, Mr. Popovic. Ms. Long, ask your question."

"Why did O'Callaghan fire at Wayne Cooley?"

"Lori Pope ordered him to."

"OBJECTION!" Popovic was on his feet, hands held up in outrage. It took longer this time for Judge Maldonado to gavel the audience into silence. I'm not sure it mattered what came after this.

A video clip of a police detective in full uniform pointing the finger at the prosecutor would be at the top of every nightly newscast and full color on the front of tomorrow morning's *Plain Dealer*.

"Your Honor, that's the very definition of hearsay!" Popovic added when his voice could be heard again.

"Ms. Long?"

"Sergeant Nicola"—Long turned back to the witness— "how did you know that Lorraine Pope ordered the murder of Wayne Cooley?"

"Because I was there when she gave the order."

Long closed her pad. Stepped away from the podium and went to her spot next to Brody. "No further questions of this witness, Your Honor."

Popovic was up and out of the chair in less time than it took me to take a breath.

"Sergeant Nicola," Popovic boomed. "I have a single question for you?"

Nicola nodded.

"Did the Cuyahoga County prosecutor's office give you immunity for all crimes you committed during your twenty-five-year tenure as a Cleveland Heights police officer?"

"Yeah, I got complete immunity."

"That's all, Your Honor," Popovic said before stomping back to his chair bringing his point home that Detective Nicola had all the reasons to lie. Despite the fact that there were no questions, Nicola kept on talking.

"Immunity doesn't mean that every word I have said wasn't one hundred percent true," the detective insisted.

"Your Honor, please strike the witness' last remark."

"It's stricken from the record. The jury is to disregard that last statement."

While, officially, Nicola hadn't said a thing, everyone knew the jury would never forget it.

FORTY-NINE
NICOLE
APRIL 2, 2010

"Call your next witness," Judge Maldonado demanded.

"I call Thomas O'Callaghan to the stand." It was a bold move that Popovic would probably push back the moment the detective was sworn in. Relevance was thin. But I wanted to keep the momentum going. The jury knew that Pope would order murder. Now I wanted them to hear what it was like to be at her mercy. I surely knew what that was like, but as the prosecuting attorney, I couldn't testify.

The judge held up a hand after Popovic rose to his feet again.

"I assume, Mr. Popovic, that you have the same objection of relevance?"

"Yes, Your Honor."

"Then I have the same ruling. I will give the jury an instruction before deliberation about the proper use of the evidence presented. I'm sure you'll include the same in your proposed jury instructions." Only when Popovic sat down, did she turn to me. "Ms. Long?"

A minute later, O'Callaghan was in the witness box being sworn in.

"What murders did you commit or did you cause to happen at the request of the defendant in her role as county prosecutor?" I didn't need to mince words or give anyone time to reconsider who they were discovering Lori Pope to be.

"Sarah Rose Pope," O'Callaghan answered, his tone flat.

"Who was that?"

"The defendant's half sister."

The jury shifted in their hard-backed chairs. Fratricide was nearing matricide as a taboo.

"Who else?" I asked.

"Ja Roach." This time it was the gallery moving on the benches. O'Callaghan was talking about murder as if he were picking up groceries. He had the effect of a career soldier, someone who didn't really fit into polite society. I wanted the jury to see who he was and by extension who Lori Pope was.

"Who was Roach?"

"A confidential informant we've used off and on for years."

I kept my eyebrows down. After this went on the air, the cops would be lucky to have anyone serve as a CI for a long, long time. Policing wasn't my problem, though. Putting the bad folks in jail was the only thing before me, and I needed to focus on it like a horse with blinders.

"Anyone else?"

"Liberdad Saldaño, Placido and Quirita Fernández-Saldaño. Also, Ermano Fernández. Basically, the four members of the Saldaño-Fernández family."

The jurors were looking at each other at this juncture. Their faces said that this was the most unbelievable thing they'd ever heard, a bald-faced admission of a stone-cold killing.

"What was the reason Pope gave you that justified these murders?" I asked, ready to expose the thin layer of excuses they used to execute innocent people.

"They all knew about the other crimes. Roach knew about Pope. Had helped get Tyisha Cooley to give Sarah Pope the hot shot."

"The kids?"

"Collateral damage." O'Callaghan was a cold one. Pope had chosen well when she'd brought the police officer into the fold.

"Anyone else?"

"Malcolm Pointer?"

"Wasn't Pointer working with you guys?"

"We'd orchestrated Pointer and Wetzel's relationship."

"Did you know when you threatened him with prosecution if he didn't go along with your plan that he'd end up dead...at your hand?"

O'Callaghan was silent. I let it go because at least he hadn't refuted anything I'd asked.

"Why was Malcolm Pointer killed in Tia Wetzel's home?"

"To make sure Tia Wetzel was indicted for a felony, and

to make it so she couldn't win her lawsuit against the cops and the county."

I wanted to lunge at the cop's throat. The reason he'd gone along with the others, was for Pope. But Malcolm Pointer. That was strictly to get him and his partner off the hook for abusing their authority to enter Wetzel's house and raping her. The same crime against me was what had propelled me to take this job. The fact that I was standing here having given complete and total immunity to a rapist turned my stomach.

The lesser of the two evils, was still...evil.

I stalked back to my table. Took a drink from my to-go coffee cup. I nearly spit it out. It was just...coffee. The urge to walk right out of that courtroom and into a bar was almost greater than my need to put my murderous boss behind bars.

"Ms. Long?" the judge prompted.

As the shock of facing a rapist sober wore off, I avoided the cop's eyes. This cold, bitter coffee was going to have to be enough.

"No further questions." If I never heard another word from this cold-blooded Thomas O'Callaghan, I'd die a happy woman.

FIFTY
LOGAN
APRIL 5, 2010

"Aren't you a detective in the city of Cleveland?" was Nicole Long's first question after establishing my bona fides. It was a slightly oppositional tack, and probably the right move. A way to normalize an off-the-books investigation. I hadn't gotten my captain's permission, so I needed to ask the jury for forgiveness.

"Yes."

"Then how did you find yourself at the murder scene of Anna Moretti in her Parma apartment?"

"Blake Hardin Tatum called me there." During the hours of prepping Logan, we'd debated on whether to include Tatum in my testimony. Our white hats weren't exactly clean, and we didn't want to get caught out. If there was video of Pope, then there was video of Tatum.

"Who is Blake Tatum?" Long asked.

It was an effort not to make eye contact with Tatum. During prep, Long said we needed to limit suspicion of a conspiracy. Instead I was more a bumbling Colombo-style detective with a need for truth.

I answered exactly like we'd practiced, "She's a journalist who was investigating Pope's corruption starting with Tia Wetzel."

"Do police normally work with journalists?"

"While we do have somewhat of a relationship with them, obviously we don't work with them per se," I hedged. It was the truth. Reporters sometimes had information we didn't have. The tradeoff was that they got exclusives. It was a well-known, if never talked about symbiotic dynamic.

"What was your relationship with Tatum during this case?"

"We became friends during the Quinn matter."

"Friends?" Long asked. If I hadn't spent hours with her responding to this question, I might think this was the first time we were talking about this. Characterizing Tatum's and my relationship as a friendship took the heat off our investigation. Made it look like we stumbled on a conspiracy rather than trying to dig up one.

"Like we've had brunch and dinner a couple of times. Anyway, journalists can sometimes make investigative strides that cops don't. They don't have limitations in who they can talk to. People are more willing to be open with them, and so on."

"How did Blake come upon the body of Anna Moretti Pope?"

"Objection, hearsay!" Popovic was up and out of his chair.

"Sustained."

"What happened when you arrived at the apartment in Parma?" Long asked instead.

"I was careful to put on gloves and booties. Then I told Blake to wait outside. I walked to the back of the apartment. The woman, Lori Pope's mother, Anna Moretti, was lying there on top of her bedcovers kind of like she was asleep... with her eyes open. I put my two fingers on her neck. No pulse."

"Then what did you do?"

"I called Ericka Warwick. Parma special investigations."

"Why did you call her and not nine one one?"

"Ms. Moretti, she was...had...obviously...expired. Lights and sirens or an ambulance weren't needed. As for Warwick, I'd done some counterterrorism training with her. Figured she'd be sensitive."

"What do you mean by her being sensitive?"

"That I could tell her who the victim is. That she'd call in the right people so the investigation was handled with the care it needed."

"So you thought it needed special handling?"

"I didn't handle the investigation into the death of Sarah Pope, but the gossip around the station suggested that Lori Pope was keeping an eye on everything. I didn't want to start the investigation of the death of her mother on the wrong foot. I wanted to be meticulous, to make sure everything was documented, so there wouldn't be any mistakes."

"Despite all that attention to detail, and gathering every

bit of evidence you, Warwick, and technicians could vacuum or tweeze up, did you have a suspect?"

"We didn't. No one had any leads."

"When did you begin to suspect Lori Pope had murdered her mother?"

"When Warwick and I reviewed the video from the apartment complex."

"Your Honor." Long lifted a burned DVD from her table. "I'd like to enter the video into evidence."

"Objection! A proper foundation hasn't been laid. Plus it's more prejudicial than probative."

Popovic was practically foaming at the mouth. He'd been suspiciously quiet. Now it was clear what the defense strategy was. Testimony about Pope had probably been largely improbably unbelievable to the jury.

It had all been shocking, grabbed everyone's attention, but I could see twelve jurors in a room talking each other out of a guilty verdict. Who wanted to believe that someone who'd been elected to enforce the law had been breaking it all along?

A video could cement her guilt in their minds. Popovic was going to do anything to avoid that possibility. I had to wonder if he'd be successful.

"Approach," Judge Maldonado beckoned the attorneys to the bench. With a motion of her hand, the judge had the courtroom deputy cut the microphone so neither the gallery nor the Court TV reporters could hear. I still could, though.

"Your Honor." Popovic's chest was big with bluster. "If

the jury sees this, my client will be all but convicted. It's way too prejudicial."

"Give me the disk," the judge asked. Long handed it over. "I'm going to have a look in my chambers, and I'll be back. Excuse the jury for a short break."

Ten minutes later, the judge was back without the jury, slapping the DVD in its case on the bench. The moment she slid into her high-backed chair, the attorneys came forward. No one had dismissed me, so I hadn't budged from my seat in the witness chair.

"What about that will prejudice the jury, Mr. Popovic?" Judge Maldonado tapped the DVD's plastic case with a fingernail.

"My client is coming out of an apartment, that we know is a death scene. They'll think she did it. All the video shows is that she folded some fabric."

"Ms. Long?" Judge Maldonado called for a rebuttal. Tatum had gone through so much to get that video. I hoped Long was up to the argument. I didn't want to say that she was a better attorney when she was drinking...but....

"The video is probative," Long started cutting off my speculation. "I think it shows irrefutably that Pope was there. That she was trying to hide evidence. In the police's exhaustive searches, Your Honor, we have not found the pillowcase she has there. If the evidence is gone, I believe it shows that she planned the crime and the execution, which are the elements of the crime aggravated murder."

"Mr. Popovic, do you stipulate to the authenticity of the tape?"

"Yes, Your Honor."

"Let's hear Detective Logan's testimony. If, after that, I decide this is the best evidence"—the judge held up the DVD, waved it—"I'll allow it. For now, I'm deferring my ruling. Step back."

With the jury back in, Long stood before me again, legal pad in hand.

"Detective Logan, before the break, we were discussing your receipt of a video from the night that the victim, Anna Moretti, died."

She led me through a series of questions where I described the nine minutes and seventeen seconds. The moment Long sat down, Popovic was up, eyes blazing.

"Detective Logan. Is my client, Lori Pope, seen murdering her mother on this video?"

"No."

"Is she seen talking or interacting with her mother?"

"No."

"What you see is a loving daughter entering her drug-addicted, mentally-ill mother's apartment. Then her coming out again folding something. Isn't that true?"

"Well..." I didn't want to walk into the obvious trap, but I couldn't see a way out that wouldn't turn the jury against me.

"Is what you see on the video Lori Pope walking in and then out, yes or no?"

"Yes."

"No further questions of this witness, Your Honor. I renew my objection to introduction of this video."

"Your objection is sustained. In this instance, the detective's testimony is the best evidence. The introduction would be more prejudicial than probative."

I could see Tatum's eyes go wide, possibly mirroring my own. All that work, and now the jury was going to have to take it on faith.

FIFTY-ONE
BLAKE
APRIL 13, 2010

"Mr. Popovic, call your next witness," Judge Maldonado said.

It had been a long trial. This was day nine. Neither side had wanted to leave a sliver of room for mistake. The prosecution had a parade of officers, crime scene technicians, and the coroner himself. The defense had rebutted with a separate parade of officers, and forensic experts. I couldn't imagine who else was left.

"I call Cuyahoga County prosecutor, Lorraine Pope, to the stand."

There was a collective gasp in the gallery. It was rare for a defendant to testify. Even more rare for a well-heeled, well-represented defendant to get on the stand, much less one who was a lawyer. These kinds of people mostly knew better.

With every question Pope answered, she would open herself to the scrutiny of Nicole Long and Liam Brody. It would take nerves of steel for Pope to manage that. I knew this was real life-and-death stuff, but I couldn't help but lean forward, putting my elbows on my knees, ready for a show.

I'd never heard Pope speak outside of a press conference, and I wanted to know if what her mother had said was true. That she'd be able to spin murder, death, and destruction as brown sugar and roses. I was here for it.

After she was sworn in, Pope remained standing and turned to the jury.

"I want to thank each and every one of you for your service, and possibly your vote for me when I ran for this office. I've relied on juries to seek justice for years and your sacrifice is appreciated."

Liam Brody's and Nicole Long's heads were together as they whispered fiercely. They broke apart, saying nothing. Probably didn't want to alienate the jury when Pope had said something nice and, at least on the surface, neutral.

Popovic continued after his client sat ramrod straight in the seat. Her tailored, fitted suit, wide-wale brown corduroy, somehow made her appear warm without being drab. The white mock turtleneck was spotless and smooth.

"Ms. Pope, can you please tell us where you currently work, and how long you've been there?"

"I'm the Cuyahoga County prosecutor. I was elected in two thousand four in a special election to complete the term of the attorney general, over there, Liam Brody, when he stepped down from office."

Politics in Ohio was practically incestuous. All the power brokers were inextricably entwined.

"Are you married? Have a family with children?"

"No." Pope composed her face into the very picture of remorse. "If I have a single regret, it's putting my career above my personal life. Losing my sister three years ago brought that home, but my biological clock had run out."

"How would you describe your job?" Popovic asked. It was a classic prosecutor's question. They loved to ask it of cops, making them out to be the bulwark between peace and chaos. Pope's counsel had taken a page out of that playbook. I had to wonder if she'd orchestrated her entire testimony.

"I run the largest legal department in the county," she said with confidence. "We have three hundred fifty employees in five divisions. Two hundred-plus attorneys, and over one hundred support staff."

"Criminal prosecution isn't your only job?" Popovic asked. His question implied his client was far too busy to be ordering hits.

"It's one job. Our civil division is the county's in-house law firm. Family law handles abuse and neglect complaints, and enforces child support. Juvenile law manages criminal matters of minors. Criminal and special investigation focus on felony prosecution of active cases as well as cold cases. The divisions are further divided into fifteen different units."

"That's a big job."

"Yes, it is. I set policy and rely on each division's head to manage the day-to-day operations."

Most politicians portrayed themselves as in touch, one of the people. Pope was doing her best to show that she was not in the trenches where life-and-death decisions were made.

"Are you involved in deciding on whom to prosecute and for what?"

"For the most part, no. I don't have any more hours in a day than other people. We had sixteen thousand seven hundred cases last year, and the numbers were down. In our busiest year, two thousand six, we had nearly twenty thousand criminal filings."

"By my back-of-the-envelope math." Popovic's voice was folksy. "That's about sixty cases a day."

"On a slow day," Pope quipped.

I looked from her to the jury. They were nodding. Maybe they didn't see that as glib as I had. Nearly one and one half percent of the county's population was being indicted every year.

"Let's turn our attention to some of the wild accusations that have come from the prosecution during this trial." Popovic tossed a glance at the prosecution table. "How did you know Ja Roach?"

"Before I was elected as the Cuyahoga County prosecutor, I'd worked for fifteen years in the prosecutor's office. Before that I was in the city of Lakewood law department."

I could feel my eyebrows going up. She'd completely and masterfully deflected the question with a résumé-like list of her career achievements. It was suddenly dawning on me how slippery she could be.

"Who was your boss in Lakewood and when you first got to the county?"

"It's always been Liam Brody."

My mind tried to figure out the strategy. Was she

blaming the attorney general or making some other deflection. In the pause, it quickly dawned on me that it didn't matter. All that mattered was that the blame on responsibility wasn't staying with her. Fucking brilliant. Fucking sociopathic. Anna Moretti had been dead on…which had made her just…dead. I didn't quite know if crazy people knew they were crazy, but Pope had swiftly shut down any talk of subjecting herself to psychiatric examination, even when being declared crazy could keep her out of prison and away from death row.

"Now, back to Roach. How did you know him?"

"Jabari Roach, called Ja, was stopped by a Lakewood officer some years ago. His car had drug paraphernalia, but no drugs as he'd consumed them. Since he was a user, not a dealer, bringing him into our confidence seemed like a good idea to get a handle on the growing drug problem in Lakewood. I met and interviewed him then."

"Did he provide good intel?"

"He gave us the names of several of the small-time sellers. We were able to buy-bust our way up the chain and nearly eliminate Lakewood's dealer problem. It became known that if users wanted to score drugs, Lakewood wasn't the place to come for that."

The one juror from Lakewood nodded in a self-satisfied manner as if he'd single-handedly removed the scourge from the small city. It was like Pope was magic. The jurors knew, had to know deep down that she was a murderer, but some of them were still being swayed by what she was saying.

"What did Roach get in exchange?" Popovic asked.

"A bullet in the head," Nicole Long said under her breath just loud enough for those of us in the first row to hear.

"We did what we usually did in those cases," Pope answered Popovic, "dismissed the charges against him."

"He got preferential treatment?"

"I wouldn't say that. Users, addicts need drug rehabilitation more than they deserve prosecution. I've been an advocate of the drug courts and deferred disposition in cases like his. It was just on an individual basis. He was never arrested for anything after he became a confidential informant. He wasn't a danger to the community."

"You heard the testimony of the Cleveland Heights police detectives. Did you, as they say, order the murder of Ja Roach?"

"No. I would never do that," Pope said. *I* almost believed her, so convincing she was.

"What about Wayne Cooley?"

"Wayne Cooley was one of my closest childhood friends. My younger sister, Sarah Rose, was best friends with his younger sister, Tyisha Cooley, so he was often around." A small tear escaped from the corner of her eye which Pope smoothed away with her thumb. "He was a great guy. Graduated college. Lived out in Brooklyn. I was devastated by the random act of gun violence that caused his death. It's the exact thing I've worked against my entire career."

"What about Sarah Rose Pope?"

Lori Pope closed her eyes, put her hand across them, hung her head. Was quiet for a solid minute. No one in the courtroom dared to breathe.

"When I was six years old, my little sister, Sarah Rose, was born." Pope's voice was quiet before her volume came back to normal. "It was such a big deal for my dad because my little brother had died of crib death. She was a huge bright spot in his life. She was the first baby for my stepmom too."

"Did you get along with your sister?"

"There was a big age difference, so we didn't play together or anything. But I loved her. Loved doing things like make special treats for her. She loved when I made french fries from scratch."

"Did your sister have any problems?"

"She was an addict, heroin mostly."

"How did that affect you and your family?"

"She never made it to college, so she was back and forth with Dad and Dot until they moved to Arizona. After that, my sister was always on the move."

"Was she sometimes homeless?"

Pope closed her eyes as if she were saying a silent prayer. When she opened them, she looked directly at the jury and nodded, then said "yes" out loud for the court reporter.

"She never lived with you?" Popovic asked.

"I learned early on with my mom and working in criminal law that tough love is needed for addicts, otherwise we enable them."

"Earlier the detectives testified that you had a hand in your little sister's death. Is that true?"

Pope shook her head slowly and looked around the

courtroom as if she were the most misunderstood person on the planet.

"Not at all," she said so softly that everyone leaned in. "Like so many addicts in Ohio and the rest of the Midwest, she died of an overdose. The detectives weren't even there. Sarah OD'd at the house of her best friend, Tyisha Cooley. It was particularly tragic because my sister was all set to go to rehab the next day. Unfortunately that 'one last binge' phenomenon is one that sometimes has tragic consequences."

"But you prosecuted Cooley for the crime?"

"While we have sympathy for addicts, we don't condone other people injecting them with drugs. That's what happened there."

"Let's turn our attention to a man named Malcolm Pointer. Do you know who he is?"

"There was earlier testimony that he was the boyfriend of someone who'd once been prosecuted by my office, is that right?"

I watched, almost with a sense of wonder, as the county prosecutor gaslit the jury, the room, probably an entire nation watching on Court TV. She'd gone from protesting testimony about other murders committed in her name or at her direction to garnering sympathy for being the unintended victim of addicts and police overreach.

"Did you have Malcolm Pointer murdered?" Popovic asked as he methodically addressed all of the earlier accusations.

"How could I? I don't even know who he is. I've never

met him. I'm pretty sure I've never been in the same room with anyone by that name."

I'd have bet what was left of my pension that no evidence existed of any contact between the prosecutor and Pointer. She'd perfected the art of distancing herself from years of dirty deeds.

"Lastly," Popovic started, "there were some pretty egregious allegations that you had an entire family murdered. Father, Ermano Fernández; mother, Liberdad Saldaño; and their children, Placido and Quirita. Did you order Thomas O'Callaghan to kill them?"

"No. Never." Her headshake was so emphatic that I almost believed her bull. Pope straightened up, slipped off her blazer and hung it on the back of her chair. If it was possible, she looked even more vulnerable with a delicate gold watch, and tiny gold studs more visible. Pope crossed her legs, furrowed her brow, sat forward. "I was told that this was a murder-suicide. The father shot the two children, their mom, then himself. My office wouldn't get involved with a case like that once the coroner makes a determination. It's a tragedy for sure, but not a mystery that needs solved, nor is there anyone to prosecute. The perpetrator gave himself a death sentence."

"Can I ask you about your mother?" Popovic's voice was soft, carefully modulated to elicit sympathy.

Pope put her hand over her nose and mouth. Her face started turning red, and she waved her other hand in the air.

"What do you need, Ms. Pope?" Judge Maldonado asked

as taken in as anyone in the room, except me and Logan and Nicole Long.

"Water. Tissue, please. I'm so sorry." She covered her face, wiped at her eyes. I couldn't see things close up so well without cheaters, but I didn't need glasses to see that her eyes were as dry as the Sahara. It was an act, albeit a very convincing one. When Pope had "composed" herself, Popovic resumed his direct examination of his client.

"Tell us about your mother, Anna Moretti."

"She was born in nineteen twenty-nine. She came from a big family. She always said she wanted a big family of her own."

"Did she?"

"Just me and my brother." Long pause. "He died as an infant, probably SIDS, though no one called it that back then. She never had any more kids. Unfortunately, she was afflicted like my sister and Jabari."

"Afflicted as in addiction?"

"Yes." Tough love Lori Pope came back as she interlaced her fingers and put her hands on the wood ledge before her. "For my mother, it was prescription drugs at first, then heroin later. Even after my father divorced her and remarried, I tried to help her. I paid for her to go to rehab maybe six or seven times over the years."

"You loved your mother?"

"Yes." Heavy sigh. "Of course. Despite all of her flaws, she was my mother."

"On the night of January second of this year, did you murder your mother?"

Pope sat back so quickly, she hit the witness chair with a smack.

"No. Never." Vehement headshake. "Of course not." She was like an actor aspiring to win an Academy Award.

"Why were you at her apartment?"

"This is so embarrassing. I'm one of the top law enforcers in the state, and my own mother breaks the law." Pope paused. Everyone held their breath. "Almost every year that I can remember, my mother...overindulges...on New Year's. I always call her on the first to make sure she's okay. She didn't answer that day or on Saturday, so I drove over.

"To keep her off the street, I pay for the apartment and have a key for emergencies. I opened the door, called her name, didn't hear anything. I ran to her room to check on her. She wasn't breathing."

"Detective Logan said you had fabric in your hand. Can you explain that to the jury?"

"When I was a kid, Momma always used handkerchiefs. Like the frilly ones. I...this is so stupid in retrospect...I wiped her face, there were flecks of something on there." Pope shook her head as if reliving this moment was pure torture. "I didn't want her to be found like some addicts I've seen. I didn't have anything really from my childhood. My mom didn't save anything with so many moves. My dad got rid of stuff when he married Dot. I just wanted a single nice thing to remember her by."

FIFTY-TWO
NICOLE
APRIL 14, 2010

For once, I put my ego aside and let Liam Brody handle the cross-examination of Lori Pope. Despite all his years of trial work, Pope stuck to her story like she was crazy glued to her lie.

Even the one question that I thought would undermine her, why she didn't call the authorities, she slithered around like she was a python, saying that there was no way to bring her mother back to life. That she was mortified about the reason her mother died and wanted to avoid the spotlight it could bring.

The thing is, it was convincing. Pope was the only defense witness, so the ball was back in our court. To bring this whole thing home.

Now I was sitting here waiting for the jury to come in, so I could make that final push, the most important closing argument of my career. I'd be lying if I didn't say that I hadn't fingered the red wax seals on the tiny Maker's Mark bottles in my drawer before I'd come up to court this morning.

I didn't have any alcohol at home, thanks to Valerie Dodds. But my desk was still stocked, in case of emergency.

This morning had felt like a real emergency. How in the hell was I going to deliver this sober? How was I going to convince twelve solid citizens that someone with thirty-two years in law enforcement was a criminal mastermind? With the Sledge Hammer sex trafficking case, I hadn't even been able to sway that jury. And that had been with a container full of girls.

The twelve sat in the box. All eyes turned toward me because I'd remained standing when everyone else had taken their seats.

"Ms. Long, am I to assume that you're closing?" Judge Maldonado asked me.

"Yes, Your Honor."

I used to prepare for court like my life depended on it. For the first time in my life, I was going to wing it. Hope that my fourteen years in the job would be enough. I took a deep, sober breath, stepped forward, and began.

"I promised you that I'd give you the clues to help solve a crime, so let's recap. Two detectives have testified, at a great cost to their careers, that Cuyahoga County prosecutor, Lorraine Pope, had them kill several people including a family with young innocent children.

"In this case before you, she's charged with the ultimate act of betrayal, killing her own mother. You heard quite the sob story, a lot of information about Pope's background. It's sad, maybe tragic. I'm sure many of us have something similar, family on drugs, or people in our family with mental illness. That doesn't make us murderers.

"Once Anna Moretti started talking to journalist Blake Tatum, sharing information about her daughter's possible involvement in various crimes is when Pope decided to visit her mother, and nine minutes, seventeen seconds later her mother ended up dead.

"I talked to you about Sherlock Holmes at the beginning of all this. The most famous quote from Sir Arthur Conan Doyle, the author who created the most legendary detective of our time, goes like this: 'When you have eliminated all which is impossible, then whatever remains, however improbable, must be the truth.'

"The simple truth is that Lorraine Pope killed her mother to keep the police off her trail, to keep them from figuring out she was on a decades-long crime spree that was unraveling. It's no more complicated than that. She planned a murder and she executed it. Given what you've learned during this trial, you have to return a verdict of guilty of aggravated murder."

Brody and I watched the great Gerald Popovic try to save his client. It was bog standard. If I had to guess, I'd say my boss had written it because it was a near carbon copy of her fabricated testimony.

With arguments complete, the judge was ready to get to deliberation.

"Thank you, counsel, for conducting this trial with such civility. I have your requests for jury instructions." Judge

Maldonado turned to face the jury. "Regarding a clarification of a point of law, I want the twelve of you to understand what weight you are to give the testimony you heard about other crimes Lori Pope may have committed.

"She is not on trial for anything other than the murder of Anna Moretti. What you heard is called 'other acts' evidence and you are to consider it ONLY for the purpose of deciding whether it proves the defendant's motive, opportunity, intent or purpose, preparation, and/or plan to commit the offense charged in THIS trial."

Judge Maldonado schooled the jury on the aggravated murder statutes and the lesser included offenses. Lastly, gave the jury the usual spiel about impartiality, not talking about the case outside of the deliberation room, and being kind to each other. With that we all rose and went our respective ways.

Now, it was a waiting game.

FIFTY-THREE
LOGAN
APRIL 15, 2010

'd never thought the jury would come back in less than twenty-four hours. Especially after ten days of trial. Then again, maybe they wanted to run home and make sure they made their tax deadlines. Juries had ended deliberation for more frivolous reasons.

Quick verdicts meant twelve strangers had come to a unanimous agreement with little friction. As they strode in, I grabbed Blake Tatum's hand. She gripped mine back.

Once the dozen sat down, the bailiff took the verdict form directly from the woman who'd been elected foreperson.

"On the charge of aggravated murder, how do you vote?"

Tatum gripped my hand harder.

"Not guilty," the foreperson said. I turned to Tatum. Her eyes were wide with shock and disbelief.

"Hold on," I whispered in her ear, "we weren't at the end of the road yet."

Judge Maldonado, who already knew the final result, asked the foreperson about the other possible charges.

"On the lesser included offense of murder, how do you find?"

"Not guilty."

At this point Tatum let go. She'd gone from shock to scribbling something on her journalist notepad.

"On the lesser included offense of voluntary manslaughter, how do you find?" Maldonado asked of the only possible charge remaining.

"Guilty."

The crowd erupted. Whether it was in vindication or surprise I couldn't tell. Maldonado banged the gavel until there was silence. Almost brusque, the judge continued.

First to the jury, she said, "Thank you for your service. You are dismissed. Lorraine Pope, you have been found guilty of voluntary manslaughter, a felony of the first degree, punishable by a definite prison term of three to eleven years. You will be immediately remanded to the custody of the Cuyahoga County sheriff."

Judge Maldonado held up a hand to stop Popovic from speaking. "For her own safety, the defendant will be segregated. Sentencing will be thirty days from today."

FIFTY-FOUR

SEASON 2, EPISODE 12:
EXONERATE

Whenever I've interviewed anyone who feels as if they've been wrongfully arrested, accused, charged, or indicted, they usually want a single thing.

To be proclaimed innocent.

To be exonerated.

Being found not guilty isn't the same.

While it's the one thing the accused want, it's the one thing they can't have.

Innocent until proven guilty is not in the U.S. Constitution. Rather it derives from the thirteenth-century Magna Carta. While it's a pithy phrase thrown around quite a bit, is it really true?

It has long been the policy of newspapers here in Ohio and nationally to publish mugshots for crimes major and petty. Alongside Saturday lists of men who solicit prostitutes are a popular feature. I, as I'm sure many of you, have scanned the lists to see if anyone I know is there. I've found names of husbands or public officials and tsked.

Yet, these people are presumed innocent. The moment that picture or list is published, though, the presumption of guilt weighs heavily. As I'm sure you have, I've said to myself, well, then why were they on Detroit Avenue on a late Saturday night? How did they get arrested if they weren't doing something to get the attention of the police?

When they come into a courtroom with their arms and legs shackled in full orange jumpsuit and jail slippers, innocence isn't the first thing on any of our minds.

This is *The Murders Began* with me, your host, Blake Hardin Tatum.

There is no doubt that former Cuyahoga County prosecutor, Lorraine Pope, has left a path of destruction in her wake.

Her mother and sister are dead. They were both addicts whose time was going to come sooner or later, but Pope has been accused of hastening their demise.

Libby Saldana may not have been convicted of

murder, but she still pled guilty to a misdemeanor. Liberdad Saldaño lost her life. Her husband and children as well.

Jabari Roach and Wayne Cooley found themselves at the wrong end of a .357. Tyisha Cooley was luckier. She too pled to a lesser crime, tampering with evidence. Though she received probation, she lost her job in compliance. A career field where a criminal conviction is functionally equal to a firing.

Lorraine Pope's fingerprints were found on the body of Taneka Parr. Whether she was the victim of traffickers or the prosecutor remains unknown. The OBI and attorney general are still investigating.

On April fifteenth of this year, Lorraine Pope was found guilty of voluntary manslaughter. She escaped both the death penalty and life imprisonment. Her guilty verdict and three-year sentence feel more like exoneration than condemnation.

FIFTY-FIVE

NICOLE

"We've gotta go." Valerie Dodds slammed my door open until it hit the rubber stop. When I didn't budge an inch, she waved her hands. "*Now!*"

I looked at the pile of files. Stacks on each chair. A heap on my floor next to the desk. On the one hand, I was gratified that the jury had seen through Lori Pope's carefully crafted mirage. On the other hand, every defense attorney worth their salt was looking for some way to get their client's plea or conviction overturned. They were all happy to suggest that somehow the hand of corruption had visited their case.

"Where? I have a crapload of cases to go through. Everybody and their brother are appealing their conviction. The head of the Appeals unit has me reviewing every felony case I've handled in the last thirteen years. I may never come out of this office again."

"Press conference," Dodds added.

I looked around my office as if Lori Pope was going to materialize. My ex-boss had loved the press. It's what I believed made it so hard for the jury to think bad of her. Even if they didn't have specific memories, I'm sure each and every one of them had seen her one time or another behind that podium in the press room, authoritatively speaking about wrongdoings she was going to tackle or a major conviction that had made the county safer.

"Who? What?" Without Lori Pope, there was no one to puff out their chest. Not that there was any shortage of men vying to replace her.

"It's in five minutes," Dodds insisted.

"Fine," I said. I slipped my feet into my stilettos, buttoned my suit jacket across my growing middle, then followed Dodds down to the press room. It had been a ghost town there in the weeks since the conviction of Pope. No one wanted to be anywhere near the fallout, especially not on camera or in front of microphones.

Once downstairs, I shouldn't have been surprised to see the room packed to the gills. But I was. I followed Dodds to the front of the room where there were reserved seats for department heads. Dodds patted my shoulder, then went to stand behind the podium. I was confused, but didn't have a moment to get clarification because the men in charge started to pile in. The new county executive and eleven-member council stood in a long line, the four women somehow sidelined at the two ends.

After the Jimmy Dimora corruption scandal, the county commissioner system had been dismantled to be replaced by these twelve folks who were somehow supposed to be incorruptible.

Executive Ted Fitzsimmons stepped front and center, introduced himself. Once the room got quiet, he spoke.

"I'm here with Executive Order twenty ten dash zero one one." No preamble. These new politicians weren't yet media trained. Awkwardly, he held up a couple of sheets of paper that were the executive order in question.

Fitzsimmons continued, "On April sixteen of this year, Lorraine Pope resigned as Cuyahoga County prosecutor. Ohio Revised Code section three oh five requires this board to act in case of such a vacancy. I, Theodore Fitzsimmons, by virtue of the powers vested in me by the Charter of Cuyahoga County and the laws of the state of Ohio, do hereby appoint Valerie Elizabeth Dodds as acting Cuyahoga County prosecutor effective immediately."

I looked right and left as if some clarity were going to come from the people seated in my row. Instead, reporters were nodding. The other department heads, Appeals, Civil, Family, Child Support, were as calm as the eye of a hurricane. Did everyone know except me?

I hadn't even had a minute to lobby for the position. I didn't know it was even up for consideration, yet. I'd been assigning new cases, and reviewing the old ones. For sure, I thought there'd be a meeting about succession planning. Or maybe there had been and I hadn't been invited. Dodds may have tried to sober me up, but between this and her relationship with my ex, I didn't think I could trust her as far as I could throw her.

I'd been on Team Justice.

She'd been on Team Dodds.

I tuned back in to Fitzsimmons, he said, "Ms. Dodds comes to this office after an exemplary career. During her tenure at the prosecutor's office, she's had a nearly perfect conviction record."

I wanted to jump up, point out that every prosecutor had a near perfect conviction rate. We rarely took on cases we couldn't win. The big ones with high-profile defendants with equally high-profile defense attorneys were few and far between.

"She was born and raised in Shaker Heights. She's a graduate of Spelman College and Case Western right here in the city. Additionally," Fitzsimmons continued, "Valerie Dodds has been on the other side, working at the prestigious District of Columbia Public Defender Service, so she understands fairness. Here's Ms. Dodds, to make a few remarks."

Valerie Dodds came to the podium and didn't even blink at the flash from the cameras.

"I thank all of you for your trust in me. I assure you that corruption will no longer be a problem in this office. My first action as prosecutor will be to open an independent investigation into every case where there may have been wrongdoing.

"I want there to be public trust in this office. Everyone in this county is deserving to be free from crime, and every defendant needs to be treated fairly, have their constitutional rights respected.

"I'm proud to be the first black woman to hold this office,

and will make sure to include all voices, have everyone come to the table when it comes to doing my part in making this county a wonderful place to live and raise a family."

Fitzsimmons shook her hand as did all of the members of the council. He came back to the podium.

"I understand that all of you have questions about accountability, and we will answer them in a future press conference. For now, we need to let Ms. Dodds get to work."

FIFTY-SIX
NICOLE
MAY 30, 2010

"What do you want?" Justin McPhee was standing by a huge grill in his large fenced-in backyard. His dog, Morro, looked at his owner as if he'd been asked the question. The dog's silent answer was, *gimme the meat.*

"What are my options?" I asked in a much more civilized fashion as I took my place by the grill. Everyone else had already had their turn. I'd been last in line because standing up made it easier to ignore the beer-filled ice bucket, and open bottles of chilled wine on the table. Ohio wasn't the kind of place that catered to those trying to avoid legal temptation.

"Polish sausage, barbecue chicken," he answered as he moved the kielbasa and grill-marked breasts off of the high-heat center.

My head said chicken, my mouth, "sausage."

Two halves were gently placed on my plate as the dog watched the transfer with rapt contemplation.

"Vegetables?"

I nodded, and McPhee piled some grilled vegetables and potatoes onto my paper plate.

"There's mustard on the table, along with potato salad and everything you need."

"Thanks."

I walked to the table, looked really longingly at the beer before I poured myself some fizzy limeade from the same cooler.

McPhee came right after me and sat at the glass-top patio table, umbrella shading us from the hot Memorial Day weekend sunshine. There were the six of us who'd worked together to get my boss convicted, seven if you included McPhee's dog, Morro, who was sniffing the meat smell out of the chair. Eight if you included two-year-old Simon who had fallen asleep on Casey's lap after he'd eaten a tiny cut-up version of our barbecue meal.

"Have we figured out how Lori Pope knew about us?" Blake Tatum asked. She was used to flying under the radar and Valerie Dodds' announcement and the subsequent attack on Dodds and me sat uneasily. "For a while, I thought I'd been hacked," Tatum mused. "But I hired an IT expert, and there's no evidence of breach."

"I think it may have been Valerie." It was the first time I'd spoken my suspicions out loud. In my mind there was no coincidence that she got the top job. I was convinced that she'd played both sides against the middle.

"Where *is* Valerie?" Casey whispered her question into her little boy's curly hair.

"It's a holiday weekend," Tatum said not acknowledging my own conspiracy theory. "Hopefully she's out celebrating somewhere."

"Probably doing her very big job at her very big desk in her very big office," I added. My voice held bitterness. Without the social lubricant that alcohol brought, it was hard keeping my emotions in check.

"You aren't happy with her appointment?" Logan asked.

"I think a broader net should have been cast for candidates," I said working hard to keep my voice neutral. "Liam Brody handpicking Lori Pope is exactly the kind of thing that landed us in this mess."

"How do you mean?" Webb asked. I always forgot that she was a good decade younger than any of us. Her political naivete is exactly what had lost the cop her first job with the Cleveland police.

"Once someone had a job, even if they're 'acting,' them being elected into the job is nearly guaranteed," I explained.

"*Oh*, so she will be the next prosecutor, officially, I mean," Webb concluded.

"Unless someone runs against her. And that person would have to be a big name. She'll campaign and say, I already have the job, and have these accomplishments. The other candidate will only have rhetoric on their side."

"So kind of like running against a sitting congressman," Logan interjected.

"Exactly. The win rates of incumbents is ninety-eight

percent," I added. Something I knew because Daddy had speculated about going from pulpit to podium until he realized how hard it would have been. "Those aren't winning odds."

"Would you have thrown your hat into the ring?" Cort asked as she shifted her kid until he was lying across her lap. It was a little hot outside to be covered by another tiny human. I was looking for the dagger behind her words, but she seemed genuinely curious.

"Maybe? I'm not sure," I admitted. It's a question I'd asked myself a hundred times in the last few weeks. "But I didn't get a chance to be considered."

"I'm excited to see the first black woman in that job," Tatum said. "That's a huge first for the county."

"I would have made exactly the same history," I lobbed, tired of being discounted.

You'd have thought I dropped a bomb in the middle of the table. I was sure they'd heard me the first time, didn't want to talk about race and color. Suddenly I was far less interesting than kielbasa. Even the dog sat down hard on his haunches and twitched his stick-up ears toward the neighbor's yard.

To this day, my birth mother, Aubrey Theriot, and her husband worked for my parents. When I'd asked her about still being there, she pointed out that she was well past fifty with no more than a high school education. Her own family, intertwined with my adoptive mother's, had been on that land for generations, first as slaves, and later as servants. The guilt that she'd given up her life to secretly keep an eye on mine ate at me some nights while I drank.

After that conversation turned away from politics, and Dodds' possible treachery, we talked about the hot weather and what the county was like following the slew of indictments and prosecutions of top officials. Eventually, I excused myself to go into the powder room. When I was done splashing water on my face and washing my hands, I turned to find Casey Cort behind me.

"I transferred Simon to his crib," she explained.

"Are you and Justin...together?" I asked because my curiosity got the better of my manners.

"We're talking about it." She fingered a large engagement ring on her left hand as I thought talking wasn't quite the solution to her dilemma. But who was I to dish out relationship advice given my paltry experience. "Can I talk to you about something?" she asked. Cort shifted on her feet and I realized she'd probably been waiting to talk to me alone.

"Sure." I shrugged. "I guess..."

"Do you remember my friend Lulu Mueller?"

"Did I meet her?" I asked when I couldn't match the name to a face.

"Once, maybe. Probably. I guess it doesn't matter. She graduated in my year at law school. Works at Dalton Lacey."

"Okay?" I did some quick math in my head. "Did she not make partner? Does she want to work at the prosecutor's office? We do have a couple of openings, but it's a huge pay cut."

"No, she doesn't need a job. I mean maybe she does or will, but that's...that's a different issue," Cort stammered.

"Okay." I was done guessing. "What do you want to say about Lulu."

"I need to know how hard it would be to get a felony abuse indictment. Her...fiancé hits her."

That hit *me* like a ton of bricks. I knew better from personal experience, but I was still surprised when a strong, smart woman made herself a victim.

"How long have they been together?" I asked not because it was relevant, but because I couldn't think of anything else to say.

"Maybe four years? He was married in the beginning. They got engaged two and a half years ago. His wife eventually divorced him. A while back, I got her to change the locks, leave, but it didn't take."

I'm sure she knew that with abuse victims, on average, it took seven times for leaving to stick. My stint in the county's family law unit had burned me out quicker than child abuse. The children had nowhere to go. The same couldn't be said of their mothers.

"Does she want to leave?" I asked. That rotation had taught me right quick that what victims said and what they did were often at a mismatch.

"He needs to be behind bars," Cort insisted.

"That's where I come in, I guess. Who is he?" I hated to ask the question, but perpetrator's position mattered.

"Richard Sinclair."

"Wait." My mind's Rolodex whirred. "Isn't he a professor at Cleveland State?"

"Not anymore. He left and became a partner at Dalton Lacey."

"So, is he her boss?" Large law firms had an odd hierarchical structure. The partners were owners. The associates were employees. But there wasn't the same boss-subordinate relationship like in my county government job.

"Technically, yes, I guess."

"Why do you think there needs to be court intervention?" As far as I was figuring. The victim had resources. Her alleged abuser didn't need to go to jail for her to leave and get back on her feet. "Does she have family here?"

"A big family. Supportive parents. None of that will make a difference because, as I see it, if something doesn't change, I think he'll kill her."

A look passed between us. I wanted to say that we'd definitely indict if there was a murder. Neither of us needed to say the names Juliana Clarke or Kendrick Walker out loud. We'd been on opposite sides of a domestic violence case that had led to murder. It never needed to get that far.

"Say we got Logan to arrest him," I speculated, "and I was able to persuade a grand jury to indict, would she be willing to testify? That's the biggest problem, you know. We do the heavy lifting, then come trial, the victim disappears, reconciles, whatever."

"If you think you could indict, I'd promise to get her to the courthouse." Cort's tone was solemn, firm.

She squinted. Looked me up and down, her mental assessment somehow falling short.

"Since we're getting personal, can I ask *you* a question?"

I rarely experienced dread, but it was descending upon me now for sure. Under no circumstances did I want to talk about what involvement I may have had in Lori Pope's misdeeds. Despite that, I found myself nodding as I spoke. "You can ask."

"Are you sober?"

Her words felt like a smack in the face.

"This is day one hundred ninety-nine." I'd had to give up drinking to grit my way through this whole Pope ordeal.

"Do you go to meetings?" she probed.

"My father was a preacher, the last thing I need is more God."

"White-knuckling it?"

"As best I can."

"Look." Cort's face softened. Something like empathy was in her hazel eyes. "We've been on opposite sides for so many years. We may be again, I don't know. In the meanwhile, here." Cort pulled a card from her jeans shorts pocket. "This has my cell and home number. If you ever need to talk, you can call me. I'll be the first to say after all these years that Cuyahoga County and its justice system have a lot of problems. Let's not be two of them."

It was the most awkward thing I'd ever done, but I leaned forward and let her envelop me in a big hug. I was starting to see why a string of guys wanted her in their lives permanently. She was the voice of reason all of us needed.

FIFTY-SEVEN
SEASON 2, EPISODE 13:
TIA WETZEL

You may remember when I started this season of *The Murders Began*, I wanted to explore how Tia Wetzel had become a magnet for injustice.

I'm your host, Blake Hardin Tatum.

Ultimately everything that happened to Ms. Wetzel started at the top with Lori Pope. While Rocco Nicola and Thomas O'Callaghan were responsible for much of the wrongs visited upon her, they were not held legally responsible. Through a series of legal maneuvers and immunity agreements, the only person who will be held responsible is the disgraced and now imprisoned former Cuyahoga County prosecutor, Lorraine Pope.

"Ms. Wetzel, I've asked a lot of you this year. I asked you to have faith as I started down the winding road of unraveling all the threads that pulled you, an innocent victim, into the justice system. Selflessly, you delivered. Why was that?"

Tia sighed. "I don't want to downplay how hard this was. Having faith in a system that had failed me miserably not once, but twice. But, truth be told, I didn't want what happened to me to happen to other women, other vulnerable people on probation or parole."

"Are you satisfied with Pope's conviction. Is that vindication for what happened?"

"I sincerely wish these bad cops. Cops who were doing everyone dirty for over twenty years had gone to prison with her. They act like they're not responsible. That they didn't have a choice but to take orders from the top. I can't believe that. Nothing good for civilization ever came from people following orders."

"Thank you, Tia Wetzel."

Thank you, listeners, for your thoughts, your help, and your kind words. Your downloads have made this one of the top-five podcasts in the nation. This experiment proves to me that journalism will always matter, and that justice can sometimes be served.

I hope you'll join me next season. In the meanwhile, this has been *The Murders Began* with Blake Hardin Tatum.

READERS NOTE

On July 28, 2008, more than one hundred federal agents blanketed Cuyahoga County, Ohio, with search warrants as they raided homes, businesses, and government offices. The targets of the investigation were county commissioner, Jimmy Dimora, and county auditor, Frank Russo.

When I lived and worked in Cleveland and Cuyahoga County, both men were mythical figures. Russo's name was on my real estate tax notices. Dimora was one of the county commissioners and the defacto head of the county's Democratic party.

It was virtually a single-party county, so everyone who aspired to or held elective office had to interact with him. That includes all forty-nine trial judges, twelve appellate judges, the prosecutor, and many other offices for various government functions.

Over the next several years more than seventy people were indicted in the corruption scandal. In many ways I felt vindicated because I'd moved to Cleveland, noticed so many issues, when everyone else acted like it was normal, or this was just the way things were done. It was like the emperor had no clothes, but I was alone in noticing he was naked.

When I conceived of this story, it fit in exactly with what was going on at the time. I knew that Lori Pope could get away with a lot, and in the face of everything else that was going on, would go unnoticed.

By 2016, all of the matters were concluded. Before that, though, the county went through huge changes. As mentioned in the book, the county commissioner structure was abandoned when a new charter was adopted.

Lord John Emerich Edward Dalberg-Acton is famous for the quote, "Power tends to corrupt; absolute power corrupts absolutely."

While many different safeguards were put into place to avoid something of this magnitude happening again, only time will tell if the county can remain corruption-free.

ABOUT THE AUTHOR

Aime Austin was born in Brooklyn, New York, and graduated from Smith College and Cornell Law School. She is the author of the Casey Cort and Nicole Long Series of legal thrillers. She is also the host of the podcast, *A Time to Thrill*.

When Aime's not writing crime fiction or interviewing brilliant creators for her podcast, she's in a yoga pose, knitting, or reading. Aime splits her time between Los Angeles and Budapest. Before turning to writing,  Aime practiced family and criminal law in Cleveland, Ohio.

To hear about Aime's latest books first, and to be eligible

for member only giveaways, sign up for the exclusive New Release Mailing List here: http://ebooks.buzz/aimenews.

Reviews are gold to authors! If you've enjoyed this book, please consider rating it and reviewing it at your favorite retailer or bookish site.

To connect with Aime Austin
www.aimeaustin.com
aime@aimeaustin.com